THE ACCIDENT THAT CHANGED EVERYTHING

I didn't do it on purpose, obviously. Kill Jared Richards, I mean. Miss Eveline said I shouldn't say that, that I killed Jared, because it was an accident, what happened, and that wasn't the same thing at all. But accident or not, Jared Richards died, and I was the reason, so what was the difference? Either way, I killed him.

I hit the hockey puck at a bad angle, that was what happened. We were out playing on Cedar Lake last February (February 12, if you're counting, but who is?). I'd heard that some of the guys needed another player to make it even, so I'd asked if I could join them. I wasn't the best skater, but everyone knew I was a pretty good athlete all around, so they said sure.

Funny thing was, when it started, I thought it was going to be a really good day.

Anyway, I hit the hockey puck at a bad angle, and Jared was standing where he shouldn't have been standing, and it got him—*whack!*—right in the chest. Which probably wouldn't have been so bad—I mean, I got him hard, so it would've hurt anybody, but it shouldn't've *killed* him—but it turned out Jared had a bad heart. A "defect," that's what they said. No one knew about it before. Only found out when it was too late.

One bad shot, that's all it took. One bad shot and one bad heart.

OTHER BOOKS YOU MAY ENJOY

Absolutely Almost	Lisa Graff
Al Capone Does My Shirts	Gennifer Choldenko
Almost Home	Joan Bauer
A Clatter of Jars	Lisa Graff
Close to Famous	Joan Bauer
Counting by 7s	Holly Goldberg Sloan
Double Dog Dare	Lisa Graff
Fish in a Tree	Lynda Mullaly Hunt
Hope Was Here	Joan Bauer
The Life and Crimes of Bernetta Wallflower	Lisa Graff
Mockingbird	Kathryn Erskine
One for the Murphys	Lynda Mullaly Hunt
Remarkable	Lizzie K. Foley
A Tangle of Knots	Lisa Graff
Three Times Lucky	Sheila Turnage

LOST IN THE SUN

LISA GRAFF

PUFFIN BOOKS

PUFFIN BOOKS
An imprint of Penguin Random House LLC
375 Hudson Street
New York, New York 10014

First published in the United States of America by Philomel Books, 2015
Published by Puffin Books, an imprint of Penguin Random House LLC, 2016

THE LIBRARY OF CONGRESS HAS CATALOGED THE PHILOMEL BOOKS EDITION AS FOLLOWS:
Graff, Lisa (Lisa Colleen), 1981–
Lost in the sun / Lisa Graff. pages cm
Summary: "As Trent Zimmerman struggles to move past a traumatic event that took place several months earlier, he befriends class outcast Fallon Little, who helps him understand that he can move on"
—Provided by publisher.
ISBN 978-0-399-16406-4 (hardcover)
[1. Friendship—Fiction. 2. Guilt—Fiction. 3. Brothers—Fiction. 4. Disfigured persons—Fiction.
5. Remarriage—Fiction. 6. Tricks—Fiction.] I. Title.
PZ7.G751577Los 2015 [Fic]—dc23 2014027868

Puffin Books ISBN 978-0-14-750858-4

Edited by Jill Santopolo.
Design by Siobhán Gallagher.

Printed in the United States of America

3 5 7 9 10 8 6 4 2

To Daphne

LOST
IN THE
SUN

PROLOGUE

WHEN WE WERE REAL LITTLE KIDS, MOM USED to take Aaron and Doug and me to Sal's Pizzeria for dinner almost every Tuesday, which is when they had their Family Night Special. I think she liked it because she didn't have to worry about dinner for three growing boys for one night, but we liked it because there was a claw machine there—one of those giant contraptions with toys inside, all sorts, and a metal claw that you moved around with a joystick to try to grab at the toys. As soon as we got into the restaurant, Mom would hand us two dollars, which is how much it cost for three tries, and we'd huddle around the machine and plan our attack. We didn't want to waste that two dollars, so we usually took the whole amount of time until our pizza came up, trying to get one of those toys. (Back then, I had my eye on a fuzzy blue monster, and Doug was desperate for one of the teddy bears, but after a while we would've settled for anything.) Aaron, as the oldest, was the designated joystick manipulator, and

Doug, the youngest, would stand at the side and holler when he thought Aaron had the best angle on the chosen toy. I was in charge of strategy.

Mom would sit at the table, waiting for our pizza, and read her book. I think she enjoyed the claw machine even more than we did.

We spent six months trying for a toy in that claw machine. Forty-eight dollars. Never got a single thing. No one else had gotten one either, we could tell. None of the stuffed animals ever shifted position. But we were determined to be the first.

Finally the owner, Sal Jr., made us stop. He said he couldn't in good conscience let us waste any more money. Then he got a key from the back room, and unlocked the side window panel of the claw machine, and showed us.

"See how flimsy this thing is?" he said, poking at the claw. "Here, Trent, have a look." He boosted me up, till I was practically inside the machine, and let me fiddle with the claw, too. After that it was Doug's turn, then Aaron's. "A cheap piece of metal like that," Sal Jr. told us, "it could never grab hold of one of these toys. Not if you had the best aim in the world. Not in a thousand years. And you know why?"

"Why?" I asked. I was mesmerized. I remember.

"I'll tell you, Trent. Because, look." That's when Sal Jr. grabbed hold of the teddy bear's arm. Yanked it hard.

It wouldn't budge. You could hear the bear's stitching rip, just a little.

"They're all packed in together super tight," I said when I figured it out. "There's no room for any of them to go."

"Exactly," Sal Jr. told me. He locked the side window panel back up. "Consider that a lesson in economics, boys."

We got two pizzas on the house that night, with extra everything.

Aaron was so mad about the claw machine, he hardly ate. He said Sal Jr. had been stealing our money from the start, so it didn't matter if he gave us pizza after, he was still a crook. Doug disagreed. He gobbled up his pizza so fast, you'd never even have known he wanted a teddy bear.

Me, though, I was more fascinated than anything. I felt like I'd learned a real lesson, a grown-up one, and it stuck with me. That's the day I figured out that no matter how hard you tug at something, no matter how bad you want it, sometimes it just can't be pried free.

I thought about that claw machine a lot after Jared died. Because there were days—who am I kidding, *every* day was one of those days—when I wished I could lift that moment out of my life, just scoop it up with an industrial-sized claw, and toss it into a metal bin. Remove it from existence, so that it never happened at all.

But I knew that wasn't something I could ever do—and not just because I didn't have a magic claw machine with the power to erase events from history. No, I knew I could never disappear that moment, because just like with the claw machine, there were so many events pushed up around it that there'd be no way to get it to budge. Everything that had happened before, and everything that happened after, those moments were all linked. Smushed together.

Still, I couldn't help thinking that if I had it to do over, I never would've hit that hockey puck.

ONE

IT'S FUNNY HOW THE SIMPLEST THING, LIKE riding your bike to the park the way you've done nearly every summer afternoon since you ditched your training wheels, can suddenly become so complicated. If you let it. If you start to think too hard about things. Usually, when you want to go to the park, you hop on your bike, shout at your mom through the window that you'll be home in an hour, and you're there. You don't think about the pedaling, or the balancing, or the maneuvering of it. You don't consider every turn you need to make, or exactly when your left foot should push down and your right foot should come up. You just . . . *ride.*

But suddenly, if you get to thinking about things too hard, well, then nothing seems easy anymore.

When I'd left the house, with my baseball glove tucked into the back of my shorts, and my ball in the front pocket of my sweatshirt (next to my Book of Thoughts, which I wasn't going to take, and then

I was, and then I wasn't, and then I did), the only thought in my head was that it was a nice day. A good day for a pickup game in the park. That there were sure to be a few guys playing ball already, and that I should get going quick if I wanted to join them.

And then I got to pedaling a little more and I thought, *Do* I want to join them?

And just like that, the pedaling got harder.

Then the steering started to get hard, too, because I started thinking more thoughts. That was the problem with me. I could never stop thinking. I'd told Miss Eveline, my old counselor back at Cedar Haven Elementary, that, and she'd said, "Oh, Trent, that's silly. Everyone's *always* thinking." Then she gave me the Book of Thoughts, so I could write my thoughts down instead of having them all poking around in my brain all the time and bothering me. I didn't see as how it had helped very much so far, but I guess it hadn't hurt either.

Those guys had been playing pickup all summer, that's what I was thinking on my way to the park. I'd seen them, when I was circling the field on my bike. Just popping wheelies, or whatever. Writing down thoughts, because what else was I supposed to do? At first I'd waited for them to ask me to join in, and then I'd figured maybe they didn't know I wanted to, and now here I was wondering if I even wanted to play at all. Which was a stupid thing to wonder, obviously, because why *wouldn't* I want to play? I hadn't swung a bat the entire summer, so my arm was feeling pretty rusty. And what with sixth grade starting in three short days, I knew I better get *not* pretty rusty pretty quick if I wanted to join the intramural team. Because the kids on the intramural team, those were the guys they picked from for the real team in the spring, and the competition was tough, even in sixth. That's what my brother Aaron told me, and he should know, since he landed on the high school varsity team when he was only a freshman. The middle school team, Aaron said, that's where you learned everything you needed to know for high school. Where you practiced your fundamentals. Where the coaches got a feel for you.

But here I was, the last Friday before sixth grade began, not even sure I was up for a stupid pickup game in the stupid park.

This is what I mean about having too many thoughts.

So like I said, it was tough, getting to the park. It was tougher still, forcing myself through the grass toward the field. The grass was only an inch high, probably, but you'd've thought it was up to my waist, what with how slow I was moving.

When I got to the edge of the field, sure enough a bunch of the guys were there, my old group, warming up for a game. A couple new guys, too, it looked like. And all I had to do—I *knew* that all I had to do—was open up my mouth and holler at them.

"Hey!" I'd holler. I could hear the words in my head. "Mind if I join you?"

But I couldn't do it. It turned out opening my mouth was even harder than pedaling. Maybe because the last time I'd opened my mouth and hollered that, well, it hadn't turned out so well.

So what was I supposed to do? I dumped my bike in the grass and flopped down next to it, and just so I didn't look like a creeper sitting there watching everyone else play baseball, I tugged out my

Book of Thoughts and started scribbling. I guess I was glad I'd brought it now.

This one wasn't the original Book of Thoughts. I'd filled up that one in just a few weeks (I don't think Miss Eveline knew how many thoughts I had when she gave it to me). I was on my fifth book now, and somewhere along the line I'd switched from writing my thoughts down to drawing them. I wasn't a super good artist—I never got things on the page exactly the same way I could see them in my head—but for whatever reason, I liked drawing my thoughts better than writing. Maybe because it felt more like a hobby and less like the thing the school counselor told me to do.

Anyway, I drew a lot these days.

After a while of drawing I decided to look up. See how the game was going. See if any of the guys were about to ask me to play (not that I was sure if I wanted to). They didn't look like they were, so my eyes got to wandering around the rest of the park.

I saw the side of her face first, the left side, while she was walking her fluffy white dog not far from where I was sitting on the side of the baseball field. I didn't recognize her at first, actually. I thought she might be a new kid, just moved to town. Thought she had a good face for drawing.

Big, deep, round brown eyes (well, one of them, anyway—the left one). Curly, slightly frizzy brown hair pulled back away from her face. Half of a small, upturned mouth. She was dressed kind of funny—this loud, neon-pink T-shirt blouse thing with two ties hanging down from the neck (were those supposed to do something? I never understood clothes that were supposed to *do* something), and zebra-print shorts, and what looked like a blue shoelace tied into a bow in her hair. The kind of outfit that says, "Yup. Here I am. I look . . . weird." But that wasn't the first thing I noticed about her—her weird outfit. The first thing I noticed was that the left side of her face was awfully good for drawing.

Then she tilted her head in my direction, and I saw the rest of her.

I recognized her right away. Of course I did. Fallon Little was a very recognizable person.

The scar was thin but dark, deep pink, much darker than the rest of her face. Raised and mostly smooth at the sides, with a thicker rough line in the center. The scar started just above the middle of her left eyebrow and curved around the bridge of her nose and down and down the right side of her face until it ended, with a slight crook, at the right side of her mouth. That was where her top lip seemed to tuck into the scar a little bit, to become almost part of it.

Fallon had had the scar for as long as I'd known her. She'd moved to Cedar Haven back in first grade, and she'd had the scar then. Some people thought she'd been born with it, but no one knew for sure. If you asked, she'd tell you, but you knew it was a lie. A different story every time. Once I'd been sitting next to Hannah Crawley in chorus when Fallon described how she was mauled by a grizzly while trying to rescue an orphaned baby girl.

(Hannah believed her, I think, but Hannah was pretty dense.)

Fallon Little saw me looking at her, from across the grass.

And she winked at me.

Quick as a flash, I turned back to my notebook. Not staring at Fallon Little and her fluffy white dog at all.

Drawing. I'd been drawing the whole time.

Still, while I was drawing my thoughts on the paper, I couldn't help wondering how I'd never noticed the rest of Fallon Little's face before. It was like I'd just gotten to the scar, and then stopped looking.

Like I said, it wasn't a terrible face.

I guess I was concentrating on my drawing pretty hard—I do that sometimes, get lost in my Book of Thoughts—because when I finally did notice the baseball that had rolled into my left leg, I thought it was the one from my pocket. Which didn't make a whole lot of sense, obviously, because how would the baseball jump out of my pocket and start rolling *toward* me? Plus, *my* baseball was still in my pocket, I could feel it.

But sometimes my thoughts didn't make a whole lot of sense.

So it wasn't my baseball, obviously. It came from those guys in the field. Which I figured out as soon as a couple of them started walking over to retrieve it. Jeremiah Jacobson. Stig Cooper.

And Noah Gorman.

Noah Gorman didn't even *like* sports, I knew that for a fact. I used to be the one who dragged *him* to pickup games, so what was he doing here without me? Not that I cared. Not that it mattered if Noah wanted to spend all his time with *Jeremiah Jacobson*, the biggest jerk in the entire world.

Jeremiah Jacobson was pretty scrawny (my brother Aaron could've snapped him like a toothpick—heck, give me another month and *I* could do it), but he acted like he was the king of the whole town. His parents owned the only movie theater in Cedar Haven, so he never shut up about how he and all his stupid friends could get in to all the free movies they wanted. Free popcorn and sodas, too. Even candy. I heard that there were pictures up behind the counter of Jeremiah and all his friends, so the high school kids who worked there would always know not to charge them. It might've been a lie, but you never know. Maybe that's why Noah was hanging out with him now—for the popcorn.

Anyway, it didn't take a genius to figure out that when those guys came to get their ball, they weren't going to ask me to join the game.

"Hey, you," Jeremiah said, as soon as he was within hollering distance. "Give us back our ball."

Seriously, that's what he said. "Give us back our ball." Like I had *stolen* his idiotic ball or something, instead of him practically chucking it at me, which is what happened. Didn't even use my name either. Trent Zimmerman. We'd lived in the same town since we were *babies*. And it was a small town.

Well.

As soon as he said that, I got that fire in my body, the one that started like a ball in my chest, dense and heavy, then radiated down to my stomach, my legs, my toes, and out to my neck, my face, my ears. Even all the way to my fingernails. Hot, prickly fire skin, all over.

I snatched the ball out of the grass and clenched it tight in my fiery hand. Then I stood up so Jeremiah could see just how tall I was.

Taller than him.

"This is my ball," I told him as he and the other guys got closer.

That was a lie, obviously, but they were ticking me off. And when I started to get ticked off like that, soon the fire would be up to my ears and down to my toes, and well, then I wasn't exactly in charge of what I said. "Go find your own."

I didn't look at Noah. Who cared what he thought about anything? He was hanging out with Jeremiah Jacobson. His thoughts didn't matter anymore.

Jeremiah cocked his head to one side. "You serious?" he said. "That's our ball. Don't be a turd." Only he didn't say "turd." "Give it back."

"Yeah," Stig said, "give it back." Stig Cooper was the fattest kid in town. Dumbest, too. Not to mention an enormous jerk.

Noah stood just behind the two of them, shrugging at the ground, like he didn't really care if he got the baseball back or not.

"Make me," I told them.

I think Stig might've actually tried to fight me, and even though he was thick like an ox, I bet I could've taken him easy. Quick and mean, that's what Dad said about me when he was teaching me how to defend myself. He meant it as a compliment.

Stig didn't get the chance to get pummeled, though, because Jeremiah Jacobson, for all his faults, was a lot smarter than Stig was, and he could always find a way to get to you that didn't involve punching.

My Book of Thoughts. I'd left it in the grass, like some kind of moron.

"Hey, look," he told the other guys, snatching the book off the grass, "I found the little girl's *diary*." And he held it over his head and started flipping through the pages. Even though I was taller, I couldn't grab at it, because Jeremiah's bodyguard, Stig, kept blocking me. "The little girl's an *artist,*" Jeremiah said as he flipped. Stig hooted like that was the funniest thing he'd ever heard, and Noah Gorman didn't laugh and he didn't help with the bodyguarding, but he didn't go away either. The ball of fire in my chest was getting hotter and hotter, till I almost couldn't stand it. But I couldn't get that notebook.

Then all of a sudden, when Jeremiah had flipped through maybe five or six pages, he stopped flipping. He didn't give back my thoughts, though. Instead, his eyes went wide at me and his face went long and he said, "What's *wrong* with you?"

Well.

"Give it back," I said, still trying to pummel through the Wall of Stig to get my notebook. "It's mine."

"What's in it?" Stig asked.

Jeremiah went back to flipping. "He's like, sick, or something," he said. "It's all messed-up stuff."

It's not messed up, I wanted to say. *It's just my thoughts.* But of course I didn't say that.

"It's all, like, people getting attacked," Jeremiah went on. Still flipping. "A guy getting eaten by a shark, a guy smushed under a tree, a guy falling off a building."

It was a tightrope, like in the circus. The guy was falling off a tightrope, not a building. I knew I was no great artist, but that seemed obvious.

The grass on this end of the park must've been super fascinating, because that's what Noah was staring at.

"What's wrong with you?" Jeremiah asked me again.

It was the kind of question you really couldn't answer.

"Leave him alone."

Well. *That* was a voice I hadn't expected to hear.

"Go away, Fallon," Jeremiah told her. Like he was in charge of the whole park.

She stood right in front of him with one hand on her hip, her fluffy white dog yanking at its leash. She didn't look afraid of him in the slightest. "Not until you give Trent his notebook back." Her little dog yapped.

The fire was up to my hairline now. "I'm *fine,*" I told her. I didn't need a *girl* defending me.

"Go away," Jeremiah told her again. "This has nothing to do with you."

"Yeah," Stig agreed. "This has nothing to do with you."

Noah looked like he was going to write a love poem to the grass, it was so interesting.

"It does too have to do with me," Fallon argued. Her dog yapped again. (I really wished he'd take a chunk out of Jeremiah's leg. But it wasn't that kind of dog.) "Those are drawings of me."

"What?" Jeremiah said, flipping his gaze from the pages to Fallon and back.

"What?" I said, even louder.

"Yeah," she said. "I asked Trent to draw some theories about how I might've gotten my scar, because I don't remember. Amnesia," she explained, as though we'd even asked. Her little dog yapped. "So he made some pictures."

Jeremiah looked at the notebook one more time. A drawing of a guy standing at the very tip of an exploding volcano. "Is that true?" Jeremiah asked me. "You drew all these pictures of *her*?"

On the one side of me was Jeremiah Jacobson, standing with his bodyguards, holding my Book of Thoughts. And on the other side was stupid, nosy Fallon Little and her yappy dog. And what was I supposed to say? Those drawings *weren't* of Fallon, that was for sure. But if Jeremiah and Stig and Noah knew the truth, they'd think I was even sicker than they already did.

"Yeah," I said. "That's what it is." And while Jeremiah and Stig were busy hooting with laughter, and Noah was still focused on his love affair with the grass, I managed to snatch back my Book of Thoughts and stuff it safely into the front pocket of my sweatshirt. "Take your stupid ball," I told Jeremiah, tossing the baseball at him. He caught it easily.

Fallon was grinning big, like she'd helped me out so much. "You boys can leave now," she told them.

Jeremiah just rolled his eyes. "Tell your girlfriend there's something on her face," he told me. And then he and his bodyguards walked away.

When they were safe back on the field, I jumped onto my bike and was ready to pedal my way home when I heard Fallon say, "You're welcome, by the way."

I didn't turn around. "I didn't say thank you, by the way," I grumbled.

I could almost *hear* her shrug. "You owe me one now."

"Whatever," I replied. I pushed my right foot down hard onto the pedal.

"Trent?" she said.

I sighed and stopped pedaling. Did turn around, then. "I'm going home," I told her.

She didn't seem to care about that. "What are the drawings of, really?" she asked. She had scooped up her yappy white dog and was staring at me now, those two big brown eyes, one on either side of that deep pink scar.

"None of your business," I replied.

She nodded, like that was true. Her little dog yapped. And I pedaled away for real. "See you later, Trent!" she called after me.

"See you," I told her. But I didn't mean it.

The pedaling home was hard, harder than it had been on the way to the park, because my whole body was fire now, all over. I couldn't believe I'd let anybody see my Book of Thoughts. That was just mine, and no one had ever looked at it before, not even Miss Eveline at school. *Stupid,* I told myself, with every push of the pedals. *Stupid, stupid, stupid, stupid.*

Those drawings weren't of Fallon and her lame scar. I wished they were. I'd rather have thoughts about that. Instead my thoughts, every page, the whole five volumes, were all about nothing but Jared Richards.

The kid I'd killed in February.

TWO

I DIDN'T DO IT ON PURPOSE, OBVIOUSLY. KILL Jared Richards, I mean. Miss Eveline said I shouldn't say that, that I killed Jared, because it was an accident, what happened, and that wasn't the same thing at all. But accident or not, Jared Richards died, and I was the reason, so what was the difference? Either way, I killed him.

I hit the hockey puck at a bad angle, that was what happened. We were out playing on Cedar Lake last February (February 12, if you're counting, but who is?). I'd heard that some of the guys needed another player to make it even, so I'd asked if I could join them. I wasn't the best skater, but everyone knew I was a pretty good athlete all around, so they said sure.

Funny thing was, when it started, I thought it was going to be a really good day.

Anyway, I hit the hockey puck at a bad angle, and Jared was standing where he shouldn't have been standing, and it got him—

whack!—right in the chest. Which probably wouldn't've been so bad—I mean, I got him hard, it would've hurt anybody, but it shouldn't've *killed* him—but it turned out Jared had a bad heart. A "defect," that's what they said. No one knew about it before. Only found out when it was too late.

One bad shot, that's all it took. One bad shot and one bad heart.

So can you blame me if I drew pictures sometimes? If my thoughts were full of Jared? One thing was for sure: If Jared Richards really *had* fallen off a tightrope, instead of getting whacked in the chest by yours truly, no one would even have to ask if I wanted to join their pickup games.

Anyway, I was thinking about all that, and about Jeremiah and Noah and the park, too, on the way to dinner with Dad and Kari on Friday night. Which was probably a bad idea, because it was making me hot-mad all over again, and at dinners with Dad and Kari it was best to start cold as ice, because that was the only way to get through it.

It wasn't going to be a good evening, that's all I'm saying.

"You all right, little brother?" Aaron asked me as we turned the last corner before the diner. I could see his eyes in the rearview mirror, worried and sympathetic. (Doug had called dibs on the front seat, and normally I would've Indian-burned him into giving it up, because technically as second oldest I had permanent dibs, but I wasn't in the mood, so I let him have it.)

"I'm *fine,*" I told Aaron. Ever since Aaron got his license last year, he'd suddenly started acting like he was the dad in the family, which was ridiculous, because he was only four years older than me and six years older than Doug, and anyway, the last thing any of us needed was another dad.

We pulled into the parking lot of the St. Albans Diner just after Dad and Kari, apparently, because Dad was busy helping Kari out of the car. It looked about as easy as leading a beached whale back to water.

"What if she has the baby at dinner?" Doug asked, whipping off his seat belt and turning around to talk to me with his knees up on the seat. "What if we have to help her deliver it in a taxicab?"

"Why would we get in a taxi if Dad has his car right here?" I asked.

"She's not even due for three weeks," Aaron told Doug. "Get your feet off my seat."

"These aren't my feet," Doug said. "These are my knees. See? *Kneeeees.*"

Aaron sighed a big fatherly sigh. "Let's go inside, okay?"

"You think if Kari did have her baby right now, we'd still make it home in time to watch the game?" I asked. Aaron rolled his eyes at me in the rearview mirror as he pushed his door open. "What?" I said. "We're playing the Diamondbacks tonight, and I want to see it." The Dodgers had been on a losing streak for the past week, but their top pitcher was making his first start after coming off the disabled list, so they were going to turn it around for sure.

"Let's go."

"Hey," Dad greeted us when we beat him to the door. (Kari walked pretty slow these days, on account of the baby.) "You're on time."

"Good to see you," Kari said, which was not very convincing. I was surprised she'd come tonight, to be honest. She skipped out on dinner most nights, to give us more "male bonding time."

Aaron and I buried our heads in our menus as soon as we sat down, even though both of us got the same thing pretty much every time we came. Doug got to work scrunching up his straw wrapper from his water glass, and dropping water on top to turn it into a wrapper worm. Dad checked his phone, and Kari pretended to admire the curtains.

Aaron squinched up close to me in the booth and whispered, "Three, two, one . . ."

"So, how's school?" Kari asked.

I fist-bumped Aaron under the table. He had Kari *down*.

"It's still summer," Doug answered, engrossed in soaking the table with water. "School doesn't start till Monday."

"Oh," Kari said. "Right. I knew that." She laughed a trilly little laugh. "Pregnancy brain."

"Wait, you're *pregnant*?" I asked, in my best incredulous voice. Under the table, Aaron kicked me.

"Trent, please," Dad said, setting his phone on the table. "Must we?"

Doug finished with his wrapper worm, and Kari handed him a wad of napkins to mop up his mess.

We got our second-favorite waitress, Claudia, who clearly had a thing for Aaron even though she was probably in her twenties. "You all ready?" she asked us. She gave Aaron a little smile, no one else.

We were all ready.

No matter how good a restaurant is, if you go there for dinner three nights a week for a full year, you're going to get a little sick of it. And the St. Albans Diner wasn't very good to begin with. When Mom and Dad first got divorced, back when I was five, Dad used to drive out to Cedar Haven every Monday, Wednesday, and Friday night to have dinner with us there. Sometimes he'd eat dinner at the house with us and Mom, which was weird but sort of nice, too, but usually we'd go to one of the restaurants in town. He'd take us to the arcade after, or out to a movie even, if there was something we could all agree on. But after Aaron got his license, Dad decided he was sick of the hour drive each way, so we met in the middle. And the only thing in between Cedar Haven and Timber Trace, where Dad lived, was the St. Albans Diner. So that's where we went.

"How's the, um . . . ?" Aaron started after Claudia left to put in our order. I could tell he was searching for something to talk about. I wasn't sure why he bothered. "The construction going?"

"Oh, we finished that weeks ago," Kari said. She sipped at her tea—decaf, for the baby—and smiled at us. "The room looks just darling. Pink walls and carpet, too. We'll show you next time you're out."

"Can't wait," I said.

"Trent," Dad warned.

What I should have said was that it was news to me that the remodel had been done for weeks. The whole reason we'd been skipping our every-other-weekend overnight visits lately was that Kari thought the construction would disturb us. I guess now that it was over, she still thought we were disturbed.

"Your father's company picnic is coming up soon," Kari told us, the smile stretched too wide across her face. She rubbed her belly.

“We’ll see if this one holds out a little longer so we can all make it. I hope so. It was so much fun last year, wasn’t it, egg-race champs?” She aimed her smile first at me, then Dad.

“Yeah,” Dad said. “It was.” And for a second I thought he was about to smile or something, but I must’ve been making it up, because Dad never smiled at me. Anyway, he went right back to looking at his phone. So I’d definitely been making it up.

Last fall, at Dad’s company picnic that we were forced to attend every year because Dad wanted to convince all his coworkers that he had his own big loving family to brag about or whatever, Kari got the bright idea that it would be “super fun” if Dad and I entered one of the races together. Which is how the two of us ended up with our legs tied together by a purple handkerchief, our hands gripped tight around the handle of a plastic spoon balancing an egg, for the three-legged egg race, which was somebody somewhere’s idea of a good time. Anyway, turns out we won, because apparently we’re both pretty good at not splatting raw eggs into the grass. We got a trophy and everything—Dad kept it on the bookshelf in his and Kari’s living room. To be honest, it wasn’t the worst time I’ve ever had in my life, winning that race with Dad. But even last fall, being joined at the leg to my father by a handkerchief wasn’t exactly on my top ten list of things to do with myself, and now it *definitely* wasn’t.

We were all quiet for a while after that, waiting for our food. Dad started answering a message. Doug went to unscrewing the lids of the salt and pepper shakers, which he obviously was *not* supposed to do, but no one stopped him.

"Me and Annie and Rebecca are going to make cookies tomorrow," Doug told no one in particular. "With Annie's old lady friend Mrs. Finch. She makes good cookies."

"That's nice," Dad said, still checking his phone.

"You've been spending a lot of time with those girls lately," Kari said, smiling that stretched-out smile of hers.

"Yeah," Doug said. "It's . . ." He looked like he was thinking about something for a second, but then he shook his head and returned his focus to the salt and pepper shakers. "They're nice."

I didn't know why Doug had to suddenly start spending all his time with two girls, especially *those* two girls. Rebecca was fine, whatever. Her dad, Dr. Young, was our family doctor. But Annie . . . Annie Richards was Jared Richards's little sister. And for the life of me, I couldn't figure out why Doug felt it was necessary to become her best friend in the entire world. He'd been friends with her in day care, back when it made sense to be friends with whoever happened to sit next to you during snack time on the first day, and then they'd sort of grown apart, which made sense, too. But in the last few months, Doug had been acting like it was his personal mission to spend every waking second with her. Back in July he'd even turned our entire front yard into an obstacle course that he built just for her, made mostly out of pool noodles that he stole from Aaron's lifeguarding job.

I mean, it's not like I thought they sat around talking about how I killed her older brother or anything. But what *did* they talk about?

I just didn't get why they had to be friends, that's all.

"Doug, don't mess with the salt," I told him, once I figured out what he was doing. Pouring a thin layer of pepper into the top of the saltshaker, so you'd reach for salt, but get pepper on your fries instead. "They're going to kick us out."

"You're not the boss of me," Doug snapped back.

"I'll show you who's the boss of you," I told him, making a fist across the table.

"Boys, settle down," Dad barked at us. "Can't we have one dinner where you don't fight?"

"But Doug's trying to prank people," I argued. I didn't know why I bothered. Everyone knew that Dad's favorite kids went: Aaron, Doug, me. And I was only on the list because you had to put all your sons on there *somewhere*. "And you hate pranks."

Doug did a lousy job of screwing the lid back on the saltshaker, and then he slid it across the table back to where it went next to the ketchup. "You ruin all my best pranks," he pouted at me.

"You don't have any best pranks," I told him. Seriously, Doug was the world's worst pranker. Aaron was good, and I wasn't too shabby either, but Doug never managed to pull anything off without botching it somehow. Last week, Aaron had pulled probably his best prank ever, which was covering the toilet bowl with Saran Wrap, so that when Doug went to pee, the stream went *everywhere* and Doug thought he'd gone crazy. It was pretty funny until Mom had a supreme fit and said that if she was going to live in a house full of animals for the next several years, they were at least going to be hygienic animals, and if we ever pulled another prank again, she was going to string us up by our toenails and leave us for the coyotes. I was pretty sure she'd do it, too. So no more pranks ever, for as long as we lived, that was Mom's new rule.

That had pretty much *always* been Dad's rule.

"So," Dad said and then cleared his throat. Next to me, Aaron *"Three, two, one"*-ed at me again, and sure enough the next thing out of Dad's mouth was "What did you all get up to today?"

I gave Aaron his second fist bump.

Aaron told Dad and Kari about his day at Swim Beach, where nothing happened at all because lifeguarding was about the most boring job you could have, apparently. Doug told them about riding bikes and playing Monopoly with his two new best-friends-forever. And when Dad remembered he had a third son and asked me about my day, I said, "Nothing." Because what was I supposed to talk about? How I drew a bunch more pictures of the kid I killed and didn't play baseball and a girl with a scar thought I owed her one?

"Do you think our food's going to come soon?" I asked. "I want to get home in time for the first pitch."

"Trent, be civil," Dad said. "We're having a nice dinner."

"I'm just saying," I told him. I felt my chest warming up again, not quite fire, but on its way, and I wasn't sure why. I scooched lower in my seat and crossed my arms in front of me. I could feel my Book of Thoughts pressing against my stomach from the front pocket of my sweatshirt. Why hadn't I left that idiotic thing at home? "It's the Diamondbacks tonight, and I want to watch it."

"We'll be done when we're done," Dad said. "Just enjoy your dinner, all right? Some kids don't spend any time with their fathers."

"Some kids are lucky," I muttered.

Well. The table got quiet then, let me tell you.

"What did you say to me?" Dad asked. He was all squinty eyes and anger.

"Nothing," I said.

Fire, hot fire in my chest.

"You listen to me, young man," Dad started. Aaron and Doug were staring down at their place mats. They were smarter than me when it came to Dad, always had been. "I go out of my way, three nights a week, to make sure I have a healthy relationship with you boys, and you could not be more ungrateful. I just want to have a pleasant dinner with my three sons, is that too much to ask?" I did not look up at him. "Trent, just do me a favor and don't say anything for the next five minutes, you think you can do that?"

That's when Claudia brought our food. I might've been making things up, but it seemed like she put my burger in front of me extra gently. "There you go, sweetie," she told me.

"Your father had a hard day at work today," Kari decided to say as she dug into her salad.

Dad rolled his eyes but didn't say anything.

I picked up my burger and stared at it. "All I said was I wanted to watch the Diamondbacks," I told him.

"For the love of—!" Dad shouted, slamming his fork down on his plate. "Trent, just shut up for five minutes, would you?"

"You don't tell me to shut up!" I shouted back. The fire was prickly hot now. In my neck, my ears, my everything. "You're my *dad*.

Dads can't say shut up." My heart felt like it was beating in my stomach—*pound pound pound*—right up against my notebook. Thoughts thumping everywhere.

"Stop shouting, Trent, you're causing a scene."

"*You're* the one causing a scene," I told Dad. "*You* stop shouting."

Under the table, Aaron was squeezing my leg, trying to calm me down, I guess, but it wasn't working. It never worked with Dad. Doug was devouring his pancakes, pretending like he was deaf. Kari looked like she wished she could have the baby right then and there and end the whole argument.

Dad glared at me for a good long time, with his Angry Father face. I was pretty sure he'd invented it just to use on me. Aaron and Doug never got to benefit from it.

"Well, you're not going to watch that game tonight, that's for sure," he said at last. And he looked like he was real proud of himself for coming up with something so clever.

I gave him my Angry Son face right back. "Oh, yeah?" I asked him.

"Trent, quit it," Aaron hissed at me.

"Yeah," Dad said.

"Interesting," I said. And just like that I set my burger back down on my plate, not even one bite taken out of it, wiped my fingers clean on my napkin, and slid myself out of the booth.

"Just where do you think you're going?" Dad asked me.

I didn't answer. Kept on walking. Walked right on out of the diner, the bell on the door clanging behind me.

I heard the bell clang again when the door reopened. I was

already on the far end of the parking lot by that time. Took him long enough to get out of his seat. *"Trent!"* Dad hollered at me. I picked up my pace. "Trent Zimmerman, you get your ass in here this minute!"

"I'll be fine!" I shouted over my shoulder. Still walking. "Don't you worry about me. I've got a game to catch!"

I thought he'd run after me then. Grab me by the shoulder, maybe, make me stop. But he didn't.

I'd been walking for a good ten minutes before someone finally caught up to me. I was walking down the highway, clenching and unclenching my fists to try to work some of the fire out of them. Thinking what a moron I was and wishing I had Aaron's cell phone at least so I could call Mom and make her come pick me up, because it was a long walk to Cedar Haven and no way was I turning around now. My Book of Thoughts thumped against my stomach inside my sweatshirt with every step. *Thump thump thump.* Those stupid thoughts I couldn't stop thinking, pelting me the whole way. *Thump thump.*

"Trent." I heard my name before I heard the tires rolling across the pavement behind me. "Trent."

It wasn't my dad.

"Leave me alone," I told Aaron as he pulled up beside me and slowed to a near stop. Cars whizzed around him down the road, honking as they passed. "I'm fine."

"You gonna walk home, idiot?" Aaron asked me. "It's twenty-five miles." Doug was in the passenger's seat beside him. "Get in the car, Trent."

What else was I supposed to do? I got in the car.

"You're a real jackass, you know that?" Aaron told me as he checked his mirrors and pulled back onto the road. Then he reached behind his seat and handed me a Styrofoam box. I opened it.

My hamburger.

"Thanks," I said. Aaron said nothing.

For once, Doug was quiet, too.

The Dodgers lost to the Diamondbacks that night—13 to 2, a real pummeling.

THREE

BEFORE I STARTED WORKING WEEKENDS AT the shop with Mom, I never would've imagined that there were so many people awake at 7:15 on Saturday mornings. But the line at OJ's Doughnut House proved that there were.

"Morning, Trent," Calvin, the head baker, greeted me. "What'll it be today?"

"Two glazed twists and one blueberry cake doughnut," I told him.

Calvin raised an eyebrow. "*Two* glazed?" he asked. I guess Mom and I had been coming here long enough that he was getting used to our regular order.

"Mom says Ray's been jealous of us eating doughnuts without him," I explained. "She wants to surprise him."

Calvin smiled. "Large coffee and an orange juice?" he asked me.

"Thanks."

Weekend mornings, I was in charge of grabbing the doughnuts

and prepping Mom's coffee while she waited in the car. She claimed that before she got caffeine in her, she only had enough energy to drive to the doughnut house, nothing else. Anyway, I didn't mind. I liked prepping the coffee. Mom always said I did it exactly right—half a sugar packet and just enough cream that it *splooshed* up to the top while you were pouring. Two quick stirs and it was perfect.

"My favorite child," Mom gushed as I plopped into the car. (That was what she called any of us kids who handed her a cup of coffee.) She held the cup close to her face and took a giant whiff before bringing it to her lips.

"You know, Doug and Aaron and I *bought* you a coffeemaker for Christmas," I reminded her.

She took another long sip of coffee. You could practically see it surging through her body, filling her with happiness. "Not nearly as good," she told me. She took one more sip, then set the cup in the cup holder and shifted the car into reverse.

"Can we return the coffeemaker to buy video games?" I asked as Mom slowly backed out of the parking spot.

She laughed. "We'll talk about it."

Ray was surprised about the doughnut. "Oh, wow, thanks," he said when I handed him the bag. He rubbed the top of his bald head, which was a habit of his. "I love glazed twists."

"It was Trent's idea," Mom said from the stockroom across the store as she locked her purse in the filing cabinet. "He said it seemed like you were getting jealous."

"Well, thanks, buddy," Ray told me. "I appreciate it."

I didn't know why Mom said that, about the doughnut being my idea. But sometimes moms were weird.

I'd been working with Mom at Kitch'N'Thingz since last March, and the truth was it wasn't the worst way to spend a weekend, even if four dollars an hour was definitely *not* minimum wage (apparently Mom and Ray didn't care too much about child labor laws). I enjoyed the cash, anyway, and Ray was probably the best boss you could hope for, even if he never did answer my comment in the comment box about correcting the spelling of the store name. Mom had offered Aaron and Doug jobs, too, but Aaron was busy lifeguarding, and Doug always seemed to have better places to be. Girly new friends to ride bikes with and bake cookies with and play Monopoly with. He didn't have time for practically-slave-labor.

The only downside to working at Kitch'N'Thingz was that the movie theater was directly across the street, so sometimes Jeremiah Jacobson and his buddies would come into the shop after movies let out and scarf down all the pretzel sticks that Mom and I put out every morning to sample the artisanal jams and mustards. (For the record, if I ever turn into somebody who spends a trillion dollars on a jar of *artisanal mustard,* I hope someone has the good sense to knee me in the groin and throw me into a ditch.) When Jeremiah and his friends came in, I usually found something that needed restocking, and I usually didn't find it in the storeroom until I heard Mom tell them, "All right, boys, you know the rule. Two samples per customer," and they all left.

That Saturday, the second-to-last day before sixth grade started, was shaping up to be a good one. It was still plenty warm, but there was a breeze, if you were feeling for it. And Mom was in a good mood, too, which was only surprising because I figured Dad would've called her to rat me out for my "behavior" at the diner the night before. But either he decided not to or she decided she didn't care, because she hadn't said anything about it, and I certainly wasn't going to bring it up. When the game came on at one o'clock, Ray let us put on the radio that he hid under the counter, since there weren't too many customers in the shop.

That was one thing I liked about Ray—he understood about baseball. He was an even bigger fan than Mom, maybe, which was saying something.

The announcer, Vin Scully (who was about a million years old—Mom said he'd been doing the play-by-play for the Dodgers since before she was born), kept going on and on about how the ump's strike zone was all over the place. When the ump called a third strike after the Diamondbacks' pitcher threw a pitch that was practically in the dirt, Mom totally lost her cool.

"Get your eyes checked, ump!" Mom started screaming at the radio. There were a couple of customers in the store looking at her funny, but most of the regulars were used to her by now.

I was so engrossed in the game that I didn't even notice Doug until he popped his head above the counter during a car commercial.

"My favorite child!" Mom greeted him, since he was holding a cup of coffee. It was a cup he'd poured from the coffeemaker in the stockroom, but it didn't matter to Mom. "I thought you were hanging out with Annie and Rebecca this afternoon."

"Still am," he said. "Rebecca's at Lippy's getting baking supplies with Mrs. Finch, and Annie's right outside."

"Well, tell her to come in," Mom said. "I'd love to say hi."

Of *course* Mom said that.

"Annie!" Doug called out the door. He was so loud that an old lady by the potholders actually clutched at her heart. *"My mom says to come in here! I bet she'll give you some jam if you want!"*

I don't know why I was looking out the door to where Doug was shouting—I definitely had better things to do with myself than find out if Annie Richards was going to come inside to sample jam—but anyway, I was. So I saw it.

Annie Richards poked her head inside the door, her bike helmet smushing her dark brown bangs down over her eyes. And I swear I didn't make it up, but when she saw me—looked right at me, then darted her gaze away quick—she scowled an angry scowl and stomped over to the far end of the sidewalk.

Inside my chest, I felt a sharp, sudden prickling of heat, but I squashed it down.

"Guess she doesn't want any jam," Doug told our mother. "Anyway, I just came over because I had a question for Trent."

Mom took a sip of coffee, and then noticed Doug raising his eyebrows.

"It's a *secret* question," he told her.

"Ah." She stepped out from behind the counter. "Well, then, I think I see some place mats that need refolding." She nodded toward the radio. "Trent, give me the play-by-play if I miss anything, will you?"

Ray looked from Doug to Mom to me. "I, uh, have a strange urge to Windex the counters. I'll be back if there are any customers."

"Sure," I told him. I turned to Doug, then clacked buttons on the register like I was doing something important, even though I knew I'd have a ton of voids to do later. "So," I said. I did not look out the door, where I was pretty sure Annie Richards was still scowling. "What's this big prank of yours?" I knew it was a prank Doug wanted to talk about, because if he was bribing Mom with coffee, it wasn't the world's biggest secret. "And be quick. The commercial's almost over."

Doug leaned across the counter to talk to me, and lowered his voice like he thought we were partners in some big bank heist. "It's only going to be the *best prank in the entire world,*" he told me. "Look." And he plopped a paper grocery bag on top of the counter.

I peeked inside. The bag was filled with travel alarm clocks. At least a dozen.

"So it has to do with alarm clocks," I guessed.

"Yep," he said. "This is going to be *way* better than the saltshakers. I still have to get Aaron back for the toilet thing. You want to help?"

I thought about it while the announcer on the radio talked about switching brands of coolant. "What's the plan?" I asked. I maybe snuck a glance out the door then. Sure enough, Annie Richards was still out there with her arms crossed over her chest. She was glaring at Doug now instead of at me, only a whole lot of good that was doing her, because Doug had no idea he was being glared at. (Doug hardly ever had any idea about anything.)

"Okay," Doug said, bouncing from foot to foot as he spoke.

Doug always bounced when he was really excited about something. "We're going to set the alarm clocks to go off at all different times." Bounce on the left foot, bounce on the right. "Like, two in the morning, three in the morning, all different times." Bounce, bounce, bounce. "Then we're going to hide them in Aaron's room while he's sleeping, so that he keeps waking up all night and going, 'Gah!' It'll drive him crazy."

I thought it over. It wasn't a bad prank, really. But Doug's problem was that sometimes he got so excited, he forgot to think through all the details. "Don't you think we should hide the clocks *before* Aaron goes to sleep?" I asked. "If you do it after he's already in bed, he might wake up, and then he'd be on to you."

Doug's bouncing slowed a little. "That's pretty smart," he said. "Plus, then Annie can come over and help. She said she'd do a prank with me soon."

She was still out there, I could see her. She'd pulled her bike off the bike rack and was hacking away at the kickstand like *that* was the thing she hated.

"I don't want to help," I told Doug, and I went back to clanging at the register. Ignoring the prickling in my chest. Completely ignoring it. "It's your prank. Do it yourself."

"But . . ." Doug was clearly disappointed. I hated when Doug was disappointed. His lip stuck out like a little baby's.

"You gotta go now," I told him. "The game's coming back on. Sorry."

I didn't watch as Doug grabbed his grocery bag full of alarm clocks and slunk out of the shop, back to his best friend in the whole world, but I'd bet that his lip was sticking out the whole time.

Big baby. We weren't supposed to be pulling pranks anymore, anyway. The fire in my chest slowly settled back to a warm simmering, and I went back to listening to the game.

It was close, but the Dodgers won, 6 to 4. "And you were worried," Mom teased, grabbing me around the neck and giving me a motherly smooch that I would immediately have to rub off. When games got close, Mom was the one who freaked out, not me. She refused to sit as long as they were behind by more than one run. Given the Dodgers' record so far this season, I was surprised her feet hadn't fallen off.

Ray went to the front to help a customer, and Mom snapped off the radio and got to the business of grilling her middle child.

"So," she said, "you excited about middle school on Monday?"

It sounded like she was asking seriously, which was weird.

"I thought you hated middle school," I told her.

She stuck her tongue in her cheek, thinking. "I did?"

"Yeah, you said that to Aaron once. You said that you didn't even know why they *had* middle school, that there ought to be some government program where, as soon as kids graduated elementary school, they got scooped up and sent to a lab where scientists could put them in a deep freeze until they were old enough for high school. For their own sake, that's what you said. Because middle school sucks so much."

Mom laughed. "Well, I probably didn't say 'sucks.'"

I held my hand up like I was pledging an oath. "That's what you said," I told her. "I heard you."

"Ah." She straightened out some business cards on the counter. "So, are you looking forward to it? It might be a good chance to make new friends."

Mom had been on my case about making new friends for a while now. She must've asked me about Noah Gorman a million times since February. "I haven't seen him in ages," she would say. "Why don't you invite him over for dinner tonight? It would be nice to catch up, don't you think?"

I didn't.

What I should've told Mom, so that she'd stop harassing me about what a friendless loser I was, was that it wasn't like I'd ever had buckets of friends to begin with. I had Noah, and sometimes I'd hang out with some of his friends, but only if Noah was there, too. And there were the guys I played pickup with—Mike Jessup, Steve Bickford, Tommy Lipowitz.

Jared Richards.

But I was never really *friend-friends* with those guys. That's what I should've told my mom. They were just sports-playing friends. Noah would play sometimes, too, when I could drag him along.

After Jared, though, some of the sports guys didn't want me to join them anymore. Not all of them, just some. It's not like I could blame them, really. That's what I should've told her.

I should've told her, too, that Noah did keep calling me, for a while. He even offered to go out on the lake with me once (even though he was a worse skater than I was), because of me not being able to play hockey with those other guys. But back then, right after it happened, just looking at my skates made the skin on my arms clammy, like I was sweating something terrible, no matter how cold it was outside. Made it hard to swallow. Hard to breathe.

And I guess I should've told my mom that I was the one who'd stopped calling Noah. That I'd said I'd let him know when I wanted to hang out again, and he'd said okay. And I thought I might want to soon, really, but for a while there, thinking much of anything got pretty tough. For a couple of months the drawings in my Book of Thoughts freaked me out so bad, I had to hide them at the back of my closet while I was sleeping. That's how stupid I could be back then—afraid of my own thoughts. The stuff I drew for a while, it made my shark-eating drawings seem like happy little unicorns munching on cupcakes. What-ifs about it not being Jared that day on the lake, that's what I drew for a while. What-ifs about it being someone else instead. So I guess I just never did feel like hanging out with Noah Gorman again.

Eventually Noah had stopped calling. That part I did tell my mom. I just left out the stuff beforehand.

It was too much to tell, anyway.

"Intramural baseball starts in a couple weeks, right?" Mom asked me, poking me in the side with her elbow. I guess she could tell I wasn't going to talk about friends, so she'd moved on to other ways to try to get me pumped about middle school.

I shrugged. "Three, I think."

"Just think," Mom said. "Soon I'll have *two* baseball stars. When you join the Dodgers, just make sure you sign a big enough contract that I can afford the mansion *and* the butlers." I bit the insides of my cheeks to stop from smiling, but it was no use. Sometimes Mom got a little loopy around her sixth coffee or so. "People always forget about the butlers."

"I'll see what I can do," I promised.

When things started to get really slow in the store, about four thirty or so, Ray went to the back to answer emails, and Mom took to dusting, and I didn't do much of anything because I only got paid four dollars an hour. Mom said I could "man the fort" and holler if any customers showed up. So when I was sure no one was looking, I pulled out my Book of Thoughts and started scribbling some more.

I know it was disturbed or something, to draw somebody getting attacked by sharks. Especially if that somebody was dead already. A somebody that you yourself had killed. It was probably disturbed, too, to draw the stuff Jared might be doing that very second if I hadn't hit him with that hockey puck—Jared sleeping, Jared drinking hot chocolate, Jared doing his homework, Jared watching TV with Annie. The nightmares were disturbed, too, I guess. But drawing those kinds of thoughts on paper turned out to be better than keeping them in my brain, because when I kept them in my brain, they sort of jabbed at me like pointy sharp knives, and when I put them on paper, at least they stayed there. Left me alone afterward.

Anyway, like I said, they used to be a lot worse.

"You never told me what the drawings were actually of."

I was so startled by the voice, I jumped off my stool. Actually jumped.

"Hey!" I shouted. I slammed my notebook closed. "What are you doing here?"

Fallon Little smiled a crooked smile at me. The tip of her lip that tucked into her scar, I couldn't decide if it made her look cute or sinister. "I came to see you," she said. Like it was so obvious.

"How did you know where I worked?"

"You don't have to be, like, a detective, Trent. It's a small town. Also, I've been in here about nine times with my parents and seen you."

I guessed that was true. "Where's your dog?" I asked, hoping she'd forget about the notebook and whatever it was she came in to talk about.

"Squillo? He's at home. Where else would he be?"

"What do you want?"

Today Fallon was dressed even weirder than the day before—neon-yellow shorts and a giant green-and-white-striped polo shirt with "#1 Golfer" embroidered on the pocket. Her hair was up in a bun, frizzing out at every angle, and there was what appeared to be a chopstick poking through it. "I want the favor you owe me," she said.

My mom was still dusting, on the far side of the store, with her back to me. I wondered if I concentrated hard enough I could get her to turn around and force me to refill the mustard cups.

"Are you okay?" Fallon asked me. She waved her hand in front of my eyes, breaking my concentration. "Trent?"

Mom actually *did* turn around then, but she totally failed at being a mother, because instead of rescuing me, she just gave me and Fallon a cheerful wave and moved on to another corner of the store.

I turned back to Fallon.

"I don't owe you any favors," I told her.

"Sure you do," she said. "I practically saved your life."

"You did *not* save my—"

"I want a picture."

"What?"

"A picture," she said again. She pointed at the notebook, which I was doing a terrible job hiding under the counter. "You're a good artist, I saw. And I want you to draw me a picture."

"I'm not going to draw you a picture."

She blinked at me. One blink, then another. "You want to hear the real story?" she asked me.

This girl was nuts times a million. "What are you talking about?" I said.

"The real story about my scar," she said. "Everyone always wants to know how I got it."

I couldn't help myself—I was kind of curious. "Sure," I said. "Whatever."

"It happened when I was three," Fallon said. She examined my face closely while she told me. "I was playing Frisbee in the park with my dad, and the Frisbee whacked me"—she slammed a hand up as though re-creating the scene—"right between the eyes. Crazy, huh?"

I may not be the smartest kid in the universe, but I know you can't get a scar like that from a Frisbee.

"Huh," I said. I pretended to think about that, pretty hard.

"You don't believe me?" she asked. She seemed mad that I didn't believe her obvious lie about her scar. Like she'd told me just so she could get mad at me for not believing her.

"No," I said slowly. "I believe you. It's just that it wasn't what I was expecting, that's all. I thought it was something even crazier. I thought maybe you got it in a nuclear power plant explosion." Fallon raised an eyebrow. "And that now you have mutant superpowers or something."

"Ooh, I *like* that one," she said. She pointed to my notebook again. "That's the one you should draw."

"Sorry?"

"That's what I want a picture of," she told me. "How I got my scar. And that's my favorite story yet."

"I'm not drawing that," I said. My notebook wasn't for weird lies about Fallon Little's scar. My notebook was for thoughts. *My* thoughts. "Leave me alone, all right?"

"Not till you draw me a picture."

"I'm going to get my mom to come over here," I threatened. Which, all right, was pretty lame, but what was I supposed to do? I couldn't even leave the stupid register.

"Oh, please do," Fallon said, leaning way too far over the counter, so that I had to step back and almost tripped. "Moms *love* me. Hey, Mrs. Zimmerman!" she called over to my mom, who turned around and gave another friendly wave. "Is it Mrs. or Ms.?" Fallon asked me. "Your parents are divorced, right?"

"Go away now," I answered.

I thought maybe Fallon would stay in the store until we had to drag her out by her frizzy hair just so we could lock up, but just as quickly as she'd appeared, she decided to leave. "You're going to draw me that picture, Trent," she told me as she backed her way toward the door. "Just you wait and see. I'm going to keep bugging you until you do."

"Can't wait," I muttered.

Mom came back to the counter right after Fallon left, which just showed what terrible instincts she had as a mother.

"She seems nice," Mom said. "Friend of yours?"

"Not even a little," I told her.

And then Mom smiled at me in this way I could only interpret to mean that she thought Fallon and I were in love or something, and wasn't that just the cutest? And I had to roll my eyes at her, because that was the only way to stop myself from barfing in my own mouth.

Mom joined me behind the register. She sat on top of her stool and examined the sheet of voids.

"How do you think she got that scar?" she asked me, still reading the voids sheet.

I looked at her. I was surprised, I guess, that she would wonder, too. That even a mom could be so curious about a thing like that.

"Maybe it's none of our business," I said. As soon as I said it, I felt like I'd figured something out about Fallon Little. Something real. "People must ask her about it all the time," I said, running a finger on the edge of my stool top. For all that Fallon talked about her scar, I realized, she didn't really want anyone to know the truth. "I bet it gets really annoying."

Mom looked up from the voids sheet and smiled in that way she did when one of us scored really well on a test. “You’re a pretty good kid, Trent, you know that?” she said.

I shrugged. I wasn’t nearly half as good a kid as Mom thought. Because even though Fallon didn’t want me to know the truth about her scar, I still wondered about it. Actually, the fact that she didn’t want me to know made me wonder even more. It was like that enormous, mysterious scar across Fallon’s face was the end of some great, interesting, terrifying story. The very last line of a book. And now that I’d seen what the last line was, I was desperate to find out how the story started. It was only natural to wonder about a thing like that.

Still, for some reason I couldn’t quite explain, I felt like a real jerk for wondering it.

FOUR

MY FIRST CLUE THAT SIXTH GRADE WAS GOING to suck worse than Mom had predicted was when I walked into my homeroom, Room C-78: Ms. Emerson.

Ms. Emerson was a wrinkled old crone. You could tell, as soon as you looked at her, that she'd been teaching for about a million years, and she'd hated every second of it, and that she was most definitely going to hate *you*. Her room, too, was like a wrinkled old crone's lair. Instead of desks, the room was filled with long rows of tables with stools in front of them. And the rows, no joke, had *ovens* inside them. Real ovens, like if you got mouthy, the wrinkled old crone would turn up the heat and shove you inside and roast you. (The knobs on the ovens had been pulled off, and the doors were sealed shut with duct tape, I guess so no sixth graders could roast each other. But I had a feeling the wrinkled old crone knew a way around that trick.) At the very front of the classroom, where there should be the big teacher's desk, was a huge bank with a long row of stovetops (knobs removed there, too), and a giant industrial sink.

It was weird.

Anyway, I was standing in the doorway, staring at the creepy homeroom with the ovens, when somebody—turned out it was Sarah Delfino—knocked past me into the room and said, "Hey, move it already. Some of us are trying to sit down." And when she knocked me, my elbow rammed into the shelf beside the door, which just happened to be holding an enormous potted plant, and the thing started sliding off the shelf and probably would've crashed to the floor and smashed into a thousand pieces, but thankfully I'm pretty fast and I caught it.

Ms. Emerson, that wrinkled old crone, she saw the whole thing. She snapped to attention at the front of the room. "Hey, there!" she called over to me. And I knew, I just *knew*, she wasn't going to thank me for my super-fast plant-catching moves, or ask me if my elbow was okay. And I was right. Because instead she shouted at me, "You be careful with that plant! It's very special to me." Which was idiotic, because how could a plant be special? And also, once I looked around the room, I realized that she had about four bajillion potted plants, stuck on shelves along every wall, against the windows in the back, even tall ones up front. So what was this stupid plant so special for?

I didn't ask, obviously. I shoved the plant back in place, where it wouldn't smash to the ground and shatter (even though I sort of wanted to watch that happen, just to see the old crone's face), and found a stool no one was sitting on yet. And I sat.

Well, I'd never had a homeroom before, so I didn't know what to expect. But it turned out it was about as exciting as every other class I'd had in my whole life, which is to say, not very. Ms. Emerson took roll and then went over the rules with us (the usual: No hitting, no talking out of turn, show respect, blah blah blah). And I stared at the wrinkled old crone and pictured how I'd draw her in my Book of Thoughts, if I ever felt like doing that. She'd have bat wings, like the bat she was, and an old-lady cane, and a speech bubble coming out of her mouth that said, "Potted plants are my very best friends!"

Okay, it needed a little work.

I was tired, anyway, because Doug and his stupid friend Annie Richards had tried to pull their alarm clock prank the night before. Too bad for them Aaron figured out what they were up to before he went to sleep (probably because they didn't hide the clocks in his room very well—I would've given them plenty of good places to hide them if I'd been helping, but I wasn't), and he re-hid them all in *Doug's* bedroom. Which was actually pretty funny, what with Doug waking up at 11:30 at night, and then 12:06, and then 2:27, and all through the night, going, "Gah! Gah!" and tearing through his room searching for the beeping. But the problem was that Doug's room was right next door to mine, instead of Aaron's, which was across the hall, so I *heard* all of that, and I didn't get much sleep either.

At breakfast while Doug and I poured our cereal all blurry-eyed and did *not* talk about alarm clocks so Mom wouldn't know we'd been pulling pranks, Aaron just smiled and drank his orange juice.

"Get some good sleep before the first day of school, little brother?" he asked Doug.

Doug glared at him.

When Mom ruffled all our heads and went upstairs to finish getting ready, Aaron turned to the two of us and said, "Remember, we're leaving for St. Albans at four fifty, sharp. Not a second later, all right?" He looked specifically at me when he said that. "Four fifty, and we're out of here, so be ready or I'm leaving without you."

"And wouldn't that be the worst," I muttered, because after Friday I definitely was not looking forward to another fun-filled dinner with Dad the Jerk.

Anyway, so that's what was rolling around in my tired brain when that wrinkled old crone Ms. Emerson was droning on and on about homeroom rules, listing them all on the board with their corresponding "consequences."

1. *Verbal warning*
2. *Written warning*
3. *Detention*

I squinted at the list and made up my mind.

"So all we have to do is screw up three times and then we get detention?" I asked. I asked it pretty loudly. Didn't raise my hand, either. "That seems easy."

Ms. Emerson swiveled around from where she was writing at the board. Her black crone eyes zoomed in on me.

The room went silent.

Slowly, Ms. Emerson glanced down at the roll-call sheet on her stovetop desk.

"Trent, is it?" she asked me. She didn't have to ask it. She knew full well. In this town, everyone knew.

"Trent," I confirmed.

She took a slow, wrinkled breath. "Trent," she said. "I'm happy to discuss any concerns you may have with my rules after homeroom ends, but just at the moment we have some very important things to discuss that pertain to the whole class, and not much time to do it. Furthermore"—her black eyes darted to the list of rules she'd scribbled on the board—"as we've just gone over, talking out of turn is not permitted in this class. As I've mentioned, rule breaking may be grounds for detention."

And with that, she moved on, to ask Sarah Delfino to help her hand out student schedules.

"How long is detention?" I asked, interrupting Ms. Emerson again a minute later, when she had just started in about changing periods and lockers.

"I'm sorry?" Ms. Emerson said in that way that indicated she wasn't sorry in the slightest. She narrowed her eyes at me, and everyone in the class sucked in their breaths together. The wrinkled old crone's eyes did *not* look pretty when they were narrowed.

"How long is detention?" I asked again. "How long does it go for?"

Ms. Emerson straightened up her old-crone back. You could almost see the wheels in her head turning, deciding if she should answer me or not. I guess she finally decided she should.

"It lasts as long as I deem appropriate," she told me. I bet she thought she was being really clever, giving me an answer like that.

I nodded, still thinking. "Could it last all the way to five o'clock?" I said. "I mean, if someone did something really terrible?"

"Trent," Ms. Emerson said slowly. Like a dog growling, low and menacing. "You'll be staying in your seat after the bell rings for first period. You and I are going to have a little talk."

Everyone in the class was busy *ooh*ing at that, like I was in so much trouble and they all thought it was amazing. But I knew better.

"No," I said, and I stood up. "I won't be doing that," I told Ms. Emerson. "But I will see you in detention." I walked to the door. And I swung my elbow wide.

And then, just as the bell rang—I couldn't have timed it better if I'd tried—the wrinkled old crone's precious potted plant smashed to the ground, and I swept through the door into the hallway.

It wasn't until I checked my schedule on the way to first period that I realized I had Ms. Emerson for nearly every class.

Lucky for me, first period was *not* with Ms. Emerson. First period was P.E.

I'd always been good in P.E.

Fallon was in my P.E. class, I noticed (I couldn't *not* notice—she waved at me and jumped when she saw me, like we were best friends in the whole world, and I had to pretend I'd never seen her before). But thank goodness they split us up boy-girl, with the girls on the other side of the gym. Different P.E. teachers, too.

Our P.E. teacher was named Mr. Gorman. He was thick, with legs like tree trunks, and you could tell his brain was probably filled with moss. But I didn't actually figure out how much I was going to hate him until he started roll call and called everyone's name, first and last, like teachers always did, and got to Noah Gorman and just said, "Noah," no last name. And Noah shrugged up at him from where we were all sitting on the floor, and Mr. Gorman marked him present, and that's when I noticed that Mr. Gorman looked a whole heck of a lot like Noah's dad.

That's right: My P.E. teacher was my ex–best friend's uncle.

Fantastic.

Mr. Gorman spent ten full minutes telling us the rules of his class, which were pretty much exactly the rules of homeroom. Then he started talking about intramural teams. He went through a bunch of them—hockey, football, tennis. Finally he got to baseball, and I sat up a little straighter.

Okay, I admit it. I was interested. My arm was aching just *thinking* about swinging a bat. I guess I'd missed it. I really had.

"Intramural baseball is starting late this year," Mr. Gorman said, holding tight to his clipboard as we sat around him on the gym floor, staring at him about crotch level. (I have never understood why gym teachers always insist on standing when all the kids are sitting on the gym floor.) (Also, why do gym teachers always have clipboards? What do they even *do* with them?) "Three weeks from today. Anyone who wants to can join the team, and from that group we'll be selecting players for the team in the spring. Intramurals is for learning the ropes. It's a lot of fun, but it's no place for sissies. We meet every day, rain or shine, and we play hard." He looked around the circle. "Any questions?"

When I raised my hand, I thought I heard a few kids from my homeroom snicker, like they thought I was going to be a smart-ass or something. But I wasn't going to be a smart-ass.

"Yes?" Mr. Gorman called on me.

"*Anyone* who wants to can join an intramural team?" I asked.

You could tell some kids were disappointed that I hadn't been a smart-ass.

"Anyone," Mr. Gorman confirmed. "Skill level is not important in intramurals. It's an opportunity to learn."

I nodded at that. If anyone could join, that meant no one could freeze you out. No one could decide you didn't belong.

The day was looking up.

After that, Mr. Gorman broke us up into teams for basketball, and I'll admit I was kind of excited about it. I was really good at basketball, and it wasn't even my third-favorite sport. I leaned forward on the balls of my feet while Steve Bickford dribbled the ball, looking who to pass it to. I loosened up my shoulders, rolling them forward then back, watching the action on the court. I'd missed this, being on a team. It had been a long time.

Too long.

We were pretty far into the game before I got my hands on the ball. Zak Halmeciek passed it to me because I was wide open and had a great angle on the basket, and we both knew it. So he passed me the ball, and I caught it. It felt perfect in my hands. Solid.

I turned to the basket. Bent my knees to shoot.

And then, I don't know why, my arms got clammy. Sweaty, even though it wasn't that hot in the gym. I could see tiny droplets of water beading up on my skin. And as soon as I saw that, for no reason at all, it got hard to swallow. Hard to breathe.

Before I could figure out what was going on, the ball was suddenly snatched out of my hands, and the guys on my team were groaning. "Trent!" Zak shouted. "What's the matter with you? Why didn't you *shoot*?" And I turned around and there was Noah Gorman, dribbling my stupid ball across the court.

Noah didn't even *like* basketball.

I barreled over to him, fast as I could, and got my hands on the ball easy, because Noah had no idea how to guard himself. Noah tried to yank the ball back, but I wouldn't let him.

"Foul!" Noah cried as I tried to wrench the ball from his grip. "Trent, quit it. *Foul!*"

But it was my ball. I had it. I *had* it. I ripped the ball completely out of Noah's hands, and Noah fell to the floor like a sissy, and I turned to scram back down the court, but everyone on Noah's team was suddenly yelling "Foul!" at me, too, like I'd done something wrong, which I hadn't.

"Shut up!" I shouted back at them. But even as I shouted, my skin grew clammier, my throat got tighter. I didn't like it.

I didn't like it.

"Shut *up*!" I shouted again. And then, to show everyone how wrong they all were about me fouling, to show them that I didn't even *care* about stupid basketball anyway—it wasn't even my third-favorite sport—I threw the ball as hard as I could, across the gym. It smashed into the rack of soccer balls on the far end. Broke it. Balls everywhere.

"I didn't foul *anyone*!" I shouted. My breath was coming back, just a little. "Just shut up!"

Which is about all I got out before fat Mr. Gorman ripped me off my feet and practically threw me into the bleachers. Everyone was staring at me with their eyes wide and their mouths open. Except for the people whose eyes had gone tiny, squinting. I glared at them all. What did they know?

"Your nephew was the one who fouled me," I told Mr. Gorman, breathing in deep now that I had air to breathe again. Even with Mr. Gorman inches from my nose, his face angry and purple, his eyeballs practically bugged out of his head, it was easier to breathe here on the bleachers.

Mr. Gorman just kept shaking his head at me, not saying a word. He really did look pretty mad.

The girls were trickling in from running their laps outside. I kept an eye out for Fallon, but I didn't see her. Good.

Finally, Mr. Gorman must've gotten some words in him. "Everybody, to the locker rooms," he said. And the guys started, slowly, to head over. "Not you, Trent," he told me when I tried to get up. "You stay." Great. On their way to change, the guys all kept looking over their shoulders at me, then turning back to each other and saying something.

Well, Noah didn't look.

"I guess having a P.E. teacher for an uncle doesn't make Noah any good at not fouling people," I told Mr. Gorman.

Mr. Gorman pressed his fat lips together. "Let's get something straight, all right, Trent?" he said. He did not sound like he was about to tell me some sort of a joke. "In this class, I'm Mr. Gorman , the phys ed teacher. You got that? I am not anybody's uncle. I am not anybody's husband, or son, or second cousin. I am your *teacher.* I'm Noah's teacher, too, plain and simple. Noah knows that, and I need you to know that. You got it?"

"Sure," I said. The bell rang. Fallon still hadn't come back inside, I noticed. I stood up. "Thanks for the lesson."

"Sit your ass back down, Trent," Mr. Gorman told me. "I'm not even close to done."

He said that. He said "ass." I'm pretty sure teachers aren't supposed to say "ass."

"But the bell rang."

The look Mr. Gorman gave me then—well, I knew in that instant there was a reason he'd become a P.E. teacher. I bet he could've wrestled a bear and won.

I sat my ass back down.

"You listening now?" he asked me.

I nodded.

"Good. Because I need you to hear something. In this class, I am your teacher, and you are my student. I met you today, in this gym, and that's the kid you are when you're here, you got that?" I blinked at him. I didn't say anything. "I don't care who your friends are or aren't, I don't care who you're related to, I don't care if you've robbed a bank or won the Pulitzer Prize. When you're *in this gym,* you're the kid I see *in this gym.*" He poked his first two fingers in the air, pointing at me, every time he said "in this gym." "So you get to decide who you are *in this gym,* no one else. It's up to you. You got that, Trent?"

I shrugged.

"You got it?"

I was pretty sure that if I didn't get it, he was going to poke his fat fingers all the way through my brain, so I got it.

"Yeah," I said. "I got it."

"Do you want to tell me a good reason you broke my soccer rack?" Mr. Gorman asked me.

I did not. *Because my skin felt clammy* did not sound like a good reason.

"Trent?"

"No, sir," I answered.

Mr. Gorman looked at me a long time after that, not saying anything. The guys started to leave the locker room, in their regular clothes, and some of them were milling around, waiting for something truly terrible to happen to me on the bleachers, and still Mr. Gorman kept staring.

Finally he nodded, like he'd made up his mind about something. "Today didn't happen," he told me. "You get a fresh start tomorrow."

I stood up. Headed to the lockers.

"I want to like the kid I meet tomorrow, got it?" he called to me.

I kept on walking.

I saw Fallon coming in from outside just as I reached the locker room. She was all by herself. I could tell by the look on her face that she hated gym almost as much as I did.

"Hey, Trent," she called over, and she gave me a little wave.

I rolled my eyes and didn't wave back.

I want to like the kid I meet tomorrow.

I knew better than anybody that that was never going to happen.

The rest of the day went about as well as you can imagine. Ms. Emerson glared at me all through language arts. All through literature. All through social studies. The only time she didn't glare at me was when she confirmed that I did, in fact, have detention, young man.

Someone had swept up her precious potted plant. I hoped it was having a very happy life in the garbage can.

During lunch, I didn't feel like getting glared at by anybody, so I spent the whole time in the bathroom, hiding out, scribbling in my Book of Thoughts while perched on the back of the toilet tank. That was about as much fun as you can imagine, too.

Even detention was a disappointment. Ms. Emerson sat behind her sink-counter for a long time, just staring at me, looking like she was going to give me some big lecture or whatever, but she never did. *I* certainly wasn't going to be the first one to talk. Finally she said, "Trent Zimmerman, I have lessons to plan. Why don't you sit there and be silent until I decide you can go home?"

So she planned, and I drew in my Book of Thoughts until she decided I could go home at 4:15, which was way too early. But I walked my bike instead of rode it, and I took four detours, too, so by the time I got home, it was 5:03. There was a note from Aaron on the table.

Trent—

I told you 4:50. We had to leave without you.

—Aaron

I crumpled the note into a ball and threw it in the garbage, and fixed myself some soup for dinner. Mom got home just after Aaron and Doug, and neither of them mentioned that I'd skipped dinner, and Dad didn't call about it either. Mom did say, "Detention on the first day of school, huh?" with her eyebrows raised to the ceiling. And then when I told her that it was an accident, with Ms. Emerson's stupid plant, she looked at me for a long time, studying my face like she was deciding whether or not to believe me. I guess believing me must've been easier, because finally she said, "You can always talk to me, Trent." And I agreed with that, because, duh, I wasn't about to say anything otherwise. And then, thank goodness, Mom turned on the game.

The Dodgers beat the Padres, 5 to 4, so I guess the day wasn't a total loss.

FIVE

AM I GOING TO LIKE THE KID I MEET TODAY?" That's what Mr. Gorman asked me as I walked into the gym on Tuesday morning. He was standing in the doorway, holding his clipboard, like he was waiting for me or something.

"I don't know," I told him. "Are you?"

And I walked straight up to the bleachers—didn't even bother to go to the locker room and change into my gym clothes—and I sat.

"Trent?" he asked me. "You planning on participating today?"

"Can't," I said. "I twisted my arm helping my mom move furniture last night." And I made a big show of rubbing my arm, my right one. "I forgot my note. I'll bring it tomorrow."

Mr. Gorman frowned at me, but what else was he going to do? He couldn't exactly pick me up and force me to play basketball. So he just sort of made an "*Mm-hmm*" noise in his throat, and checked something off on his clipboard. Probably the box that said I was a screw-up.

I spent the whole period watching other kids play basketball, which is not nearly as fun as it sounds.

I spent all of lunch in the bathroom again, which is even less fun than it sounds.

“Am I going to like the kid I meet today?” Mr. Gorman asked me on Wednesday. Still standing at the door. Still holding his clipboard.

“I don’t know,” I told him. “Depends if you like kids who can’t play basketball because of their horrible colds.” I fake-sneezed. I think a little got on Mr. Gorman, which was an added bonus. “I’ll bring my note tomorrow!” I said as I made my way up the bleachers.

Mr. Gorman made a check on his clipboard.

By the time lunch on Wednesday rolled around, I was getting pretty sick of the bathroom. So, even though I really didn’t want to, I went to the cafeteria. Bought myself lunch. Sat down at a completely empty table in the corner.

Guess who decided to sit down next to me.

“Trent!”

I tried to make myself look so large that I took up the whole table, but Fallon found room anyway.

“Hey,” she told me. “You’re here.”

“Yeah.” I held up my tuna sandwich to show her. “It’s lunch.”

“But you weren’t in the cafeteria yesterday,” she said. “Or Monday, either.”

I just shrugged. No way I was going to tell her I’d been hanging out in the bathroom.

"Well, I'm glad you're here now." She opened her chocolate milk like an expert. Took a long swig. "I wanted to tell you something."

I sighed. I didn't want to talk to her about her stupid scar anymore. I didn't want to argue with her about drawing her weird pictures. "Don't you have any friends?" I asked her.

All right. It came out meaner than I meant it.

Fallon froze, halfway to her apple. Hand just frozen in midair, like she'd been zapped or something. But then, just when I thought she was going to burst into tears like a real girl, she unfroze herself and grabbed the apple, like nothing had happened at all. Like the freezing had just been a fritz in my vision. "Don't *you*?" she asked.

Well.

That was a fair point.

I sighed again. "What did you want to tell me?" I asked.

She took a bite from her apple. Today, I noticed, she was wearing a yellow-and-pink-checked dress with a rounded collar, like a four-year-old might wear for Easter. Where did she *get* these clothes? "I was going to tell you the real story of how I got my scar."

Oh, brother.

I still had half a sandwich to finish, plus a whole bag of chips, and I had nowhere to be but a bathroom stall, so finally I gave in. "Fine," I said. "Tell me. *How* did you get that mysterious scar of yours?"

Her eyes lit up, on either side of the scar. It really was a thing to look at.

"Lightning bolt," she told me. "I was standing under a tree during a lightning storm—you know how they tell you never to do that?—and

I got struck." She made a slicing motion with her non-apple-holding hand. "*Boom!* I was out cold for an entire hour. When I woke up, I had this scar."

I focused on my sandwich. A glop of tuna was threatening to fall onto my cardboard tray. I caught it with my tongue. "Were you all by yourself when it happened?" I asked as I chewed. Fallon nodded. "Then how do you know how long you were out for?"

"Good point," she said. She took another bite of apple and chewed slowly. Swallowed. "I'll work on that."

"Don't you ever talk about anything else?" I wondered. I'd been thinking about it, and actually I was pretty sure that Fallon Little wasn't friendless. She wasn't one of the loner kids like Ian Holt, who spent every recess huddled in a corner behind the handball court playing Connect Four by himself. Or even like Mindy Fitzgibbons, who made best friends with the librarian and hung out with her every day for all of elementary school. In fact—not that I'd spent a lot of time paying attention to Fallon, but just on remembering—it seemed like she always had someone to sit with at lunch, always had someone to partner with on projects. But I was pretty sure it was always someone different.

I was starting to figure out why.

"Like what?" Fallon asked. "What else is there to talk about?"

"I don't know," I said. "*Anything.* Baseball. The Dodgers. How about that?"

She took another bite of her apple.

"Have you seen *Field of Dreams*?" Fallon asked me.

Well. I didn't see *that* coming.

"*Field of Dreams*?" I said.

"Yeah. It's a movie. About baseball. This farmer guy hears this weird voice and decides to make a baseball field, and then all these old baseball players who are, like, dead or whatever, come play baseball."

"I know what it's about," I told her.

"But you've never seen it?"

"I saw part of it." I didn't want to tell Fallon that my mom had been trying to get me to watch it forever, because she said it was the best baseball movie of all time, but when she first tried to make me watch it when I was six, I got freaked out by all the creepy whispering—"*If you build it . . .*"—and I screamed until she turned the TV off.

"You should watch *all* of it," Fallon said. "If you like baseball. Or *The Sandlot*. Have you ever seen *The Sandlot*?"

"No." Talking baseball movies was way better than weird scar stories, but I was still trying to figure out which was worse, eating lunch with Fallon or starving in a bathroom stall.

"I have both of them," Fallon said. "You could come over and watch with me sometime."

I choked on the last of my sandwich when she said that.

"You okay, Trent?" she asked. She looked like she was about to start giving me the Heimlich, right there in the cafeteria, so I nodded and downed some apple juice until she seemed to believe I wasn't going to die. "Well, what do you think? Want to come over sometime?"

I was still coughing a little bit, so luckily I didn't have to answer right away.

Here's what I knew for sure: Fallon wasn't asking me over to her house, as, like, a *date* or anything. I'd seen the way girls acted when they liked boys that way (heck, hang out with Aaron for more than three seconds and you'd see plenty of it), and that wasn't the way Fallon seemed to be acting.

She seemed, if I really thought hard about it, like she wanted to be my friend.

But here's the thing I couldn't figure out: Why *me*? Out of all the kids at Cedar Haven Middle, why me? I wasn't particularly funny, or nice, even, and I was good at sports, but Fallon didn't seem to care so much about that.

"Maybe," I told her. "Probably not."

Fallon nodded as she took another bite of her apple, like that was exactly the answer she expected. "Okay," she said. And she grinned, apple flecks showing in her mouth. "Then how 'bout you draw me a picture?"

I thought about breaking another one of Ms. Emerson's plants, just to get detention, but I figured two phone calls in one week might be too much for my mom. Also, the wrinkled old crone would probably just kill me instead. (I'd been ignoring her, mostly, in class. Not answering questions, scribbling thoughts instead of doing homework, that sort of thing. You could tell the wrinkled old crone hated me back, because she didn't seem to mind so much about the ignoring.)

Anyway, there were other ways to miss dinner.

First I went to the Episcopal church on Summit Avenue, because they had the best parking lot for practicing wheelies. Then I biked down Bufflehead Lane (mostly because I really liked the word *bufflehead*) and wound my way in and around the fallen leaves on the street, until an old lady honked her horn at me and told me to stop being a nuisance on her block. Then I biked past the high school, where someone had set up a collection of lawn gnomes from who knows where on the front lawn. After a while I wandered over to Knickerbocker, although I pedaled really fast as I passed the Richardses' house. I soared down Maple Hill, closing my eyes, for just a second, as I went. There was just enough wind pushing me back against the road that between the pushing and the soaring, I could almost believe I was flying.

Floating.

Two tacos, that's what I had for dinner. They were two for five dollars if you got them from the take-out window of Rosalita's. Mom and I picked food up there a lot when we were working late at Kitch'N'Thingz, because it was right down the block, and Marjorie, who ran the window, was always really nice.

"Nothing for your mother?" she asked when she handed me the bag.

I shook my head, sliding five dollars from my shift last weekend across the wood counter. "She might come by later," I said. Which, then, I wished I hadn't said, because maybe it would come true and Mom *would* go over, and then Marjorie would tell her she saw me, and then Mom would be mad that I wasn't having dinner with my dad like I was supposed to on Wednesday nights. But I figured there was no fixing it now. I waited until Marjorie was busy at the fryer, and I turned left instead of right, the way I would normally go to get back to the store. And I hopped back on my bike and headed to the park.

It wasn't the worst, eating delicious tacos on a bench in the park. Even if I was all by myself. And it was a little chilly, too, especially since I was just in my sweatshirt and jeans.

Friday I'd have to remember to wear a jacket or something.

I guess I did a real good job with the wandering, because Aaron and Doug were already there by the time I got home. Aaron slugged me in the arm and called me an idiot, and said that he was done—"absolutely *done*"—covering for me with Mom and Dad, and if I was going to miss dinner one more time, I was going to have to explain it myself.

He didn't say anything about Dad being super sad to miss me or anything, so I could figure out how that went.

Mom had to work late, so it was just me and Aaron watching the game—Padres again. Although you could hardly call what Aaron was doing "watching," because he had his head half buried in his trigonometry book the whole time. Normally Aaron was nearly as fanatical about baseball as Mom, but I didn't bother asking why he didn't feel like watching, because knowing Aaron, he'd only use the opportunity to lecture me about responsibility or something. Doug didn't care so much about baseball. You could tell he didn't care because he spent most of the first inning poking me in the back, saying he needed to talk to me "in private." He was working on another prank, obviously.

"Doug, quit it," I told him. "I'm trying to watch the game."

Doug finally stalked off until Aaron's cell phone rang and Doug snatched it off the table before Aaron could get it and immediately started gushing like a baby. *"Aaaaaarooooon,"* he said, like our brother's name was a million syllables long. "It's a *giiiiiiiiiiiirl* calling you. Who's *Clariiiiiiiise*?"

Aaron hopped off the back of the couch, his trigonometry book tumbling to the floor, and grabbed the phone away from Doug. "Give me that." He went to his room to take the call, and Doug plopped into Aaron's seat beside me.

"You think Aaron has a girlfriend?" Doug asked me.

I shrugged.

"You gotta hear my prank," Doug said. And I couldn't really argue, because it was a commercial anyway.

"Fine," I said. "Shoot."

"Okay." Doug was bouncing already, even sitting down. "Rebecca has a hamster, right? So what if I borrowed it, and me and her and Annie let it loose in Aaron's room, and then while he was sleeping, it would, like, nibble at his toes? It would totally freak him out." I guess he saw me rolling my eyes, because he said, "What? You don't think that's good?"

"That's a horrible prank, Doug. No way will Rebecca let you borrow her hamster. And anyway, it would just get lost or end up in the toilet or something, and then Rebecca would hate you."

Doug stuck his lip out, pouting. But I guess he couldn't really argue with me. "You got any better ideas?" he asked, crossing his arms over his chest.

I did. I had plenty of good prank ideas. Hiding all of Aaron's underwear. Tying his doorknob to the bathroom across the hall, so he couldn't get out of his room. Reprogramming his voice mail to something embarrassing. I was full of ideas. And I hadn't done a good prank in a long time.

But if I told Doug any of those things, he'd just want to do them with *his* friends. With *Annie*.

"The game's back on," I told Doug. And he stuck his lip out again like a little baby, but really, what did I care?

SIX

FRIDAY MORNING WHEN MR. GORMAN ASKED me, “Am I going to like the kid I meet today?” I just shrugged and told him, “Neck cramp” and made my way up to the bleachers. I spent the whole period doodling Jared in a buffalo stampede in my Book of Thoughts. If Jared really had been smushed in a buffalo stampede, I thought, instead of hit with a hockey puck, probably everybody would like the kid they met today.

One thing I knew: Mr. Gorman hadn’t called my mom to ask for any doctor’s notes. I was certain about that, because if he had, Mom would’ve shouted my head off about it. Instead, he just kept adding checks to his clipboard.

I bet I had more “screw-up” check marks than any kid in the history of P.E.

That afternoon I had lunch with Fallon, just like I had the day before, too. It wasn’t horrible. It was sunny outside, so we sat at one of the outdoor tables, the ones with the built-in benches and the tops of grated metal.

"I still think you should come over and watch *Field of Dreams,*" Fallon said, for about the four hundredth time. "I bet you'd really like it."

I didn't know what to say to that, so I didn't say anything. Instead, I poked a finger up through one of the holes in the metal grate of the table and bumped my tray up and down. *"Oooooh!"* I howled, like I was some kind of ghost. The Lunchtime Poltergeist or something. "The tray is *mooooving!*"

It was stupid, but Fallon laughed.

I had to admit, I sort of liked when Fallon laughed.

"Fine," I said at last.

"Fine what?" Fallon asked.

"I'll watch your stupid movie."

Her face lit up. "Really?" she squealed. Actually squealed.

"It's long, right?" I asked. "Like I wouldn't get home till at least five o'clock?"

"We could watch it as soon as we got to my place," she said. "Not even make any snacks. If you need to get home early."

"No, that's okay. Late is fine."

Fallon grinned at me. "Great," she said.

It was the first lunch we'd had together where she didn't bug me to draw any pictures.

I called Aaron from Fallon's house and told him I wasn't going to make dinner with Dad because I was working on a school project with a friend.

"You know, you're not the only person with other stuff going on in your life, Trent," Aaron told me in his best fatherly voice. "But sometimes you have to do the *responsible* thing and show up when you promised you would."

"I'm sorry you're missing a date with your girlfriend or whatever," I said, sounding a whole lot like Doug when I said it—but that's what Aaron got for all his "responsible" talk. "If you're so upset about having to go to dinner, you should whine to Dad, not me."

"You are being completely immat—" Aaron began. But I hung up on him before he could finish his sentence.

Fallon's mom wasn't home, only her dad. He was practically big enough for two people, though. He hardly even blinked at me when Fallon introduced me, just looked me up and down from the doorway with his arms crossed and said, "Mm-hmm."

Fallon rolled her eyes at that. "Dad's a cop," she told me, loud enough for her father to hear. "He likes to be intimidating."

I gulped.

Fallon's dad worked the night shift, so she said he didn't start work until 11:00 p.m., and then he slept while she was at school. Which would explain why he was making eggs and coffee in the kitchen (glaring at me while he did it, I swear).

"We're going to watch a movie in here!" Fallon called to him, tugging me away from the phone in the kitchen. "Don't be weird, okay?" He grunted at her. Fallon started up the movie, and her dad finished cooking his eggs and then sat at the kitchen table to eat them without saying a word. I noticed he had a good eye on us where we were sitting on the couch, through the partition between the kitchen and the living room.

I bet Fallon's dad made an excellent cop.

We didn't so much watch *Field of Dreams* as chatter all the way through it. Well, *Fallon* chattered, bouncing up from the couch every two minutes or so to tell me something interesting. (I mean, something *she* thought was interesting. Sometimes it was an interesting thing, other times not so much.)

"There!" she said, pausing the movie. She ran over to the TV. Her fluffy white dog, Squillo, who'd been sleeping on the couch, jumped up too and started yipping. "You see that? The time on the scoreboard? It says eight forty-one, right?"

I had to squint to see it, because the clock on the scoreboard was so tiny. But Fallon was right. "Yep," I said. (This was one of the not-very-interesting things.) "Eight forty-one."

"Okay, watch this." She unpaused the movie and let it play forward while Squillo ran around in excited circles. Fallon's dad was still pretend-reading his tablet in the next room over—the world's slowest eater of eggs. I tried to focus on the movie.

The shot cut away, to the main character, Ray, and the writer he drags to the game with him, sitting in the stands. Then a second later it cut back to the scoreboard. Fallon paused the movie again. "Look!" she shouted. She was bouncing, hard as Doug. "Boom!"

Squillo yipped.

I squinted. It took me a second to see what she was talking about, but after a bit I spotted it. "The clock says ten thirty," I told her. I was kind of impressed with myself for figuring it out, actually, even though I never would've noticed it in a million years if Fallon hadn't made me look for it.

Fallon grinned at me. "Right? The clock changed two whole hours in a split second. Total continuity error."

I didn't know what a "continuity error" was, but I wasn't about to ask.

"A continuity error is when something doesn't line up from one shot to another," Fallon told me. Like she thought she could read my mind or whatever. She plopped back next to me on the couch, and Squillo followed her and settled down between us. Fallon started the movie up again. "Like clocks flipping back and forth," she went on, "or if a guy's wearing a hat, and then the next time you see him, he's not. Movies have all sorts of stuff like that. It's awesome. Wait, there's another one coming up that's great."

I raised my eyebrows at her. "How many times have you seen this movie?" I asked.

"*Field of Dreams*?" she said.

"No, *Transformers Four.*"

Fallon laughed. "I don't know. A couple times, maybe. I'm really good at spotting this stuff. I'm training myself to be a script supervisor in Hollywood." She scratched Squillo behind the ears. "That's my dream job. It's the person who keeps track of every single take, and what all the actors are wearing, and what the set looks like, and the lighting and everything, and makes sure there are no errors at all." Squillo rolled onto his belly, and Fallon began scratching him there, his paws up in the air like he was really enjoying himself. "I'm going to be amazing at it."

I snorted. Leave it to Fallon Little to go and declare herself amazing before she'd even started something.

But I had to admit she might be right.

"Okay, this one's good," she told me a few minutes later. "Look, you see how the ground is super wet right as Ray and Terence are leaving Fenway Park? Like it's just been raining?"

I leaned forward on the couch. I was pretty sure I knew where she was going. "Only they were just at the game, and it hadn't been raining at all," I said.

"Exactly!" Fallon cried. She looked like she was real proud of me or something.

I guess I was a little proud of me, too.

"You'd think *someone* would've noticed that," I said.

Fallon tucked her hands behind her head. "It's 'cause they didn't have me as their script supervisor," she said.

I didn't think *Field of Dreams* was the hands-down incredible movie that my mom was always claiming it was. Actually, the plot was a little silly (ghosts playing baseball—I mean, come on). And if you thought about it too hard, it didn't make much sense. But it was *way* less scary than I'd thought it was when I was six.

About two-thirds of the way through, Fallon declared that it was time for a snack, so we got up to make popcorn while Squillo stayed zonked out on the couch, making tiny doggie snores. Fallon's dad was still at the kitchen table, reading his tablet, and pretended to ignore us. But a giant, intimidating cop dad can only be so invisible. Fallon pretty much ignored him back, though, so I did too.

"You like the movie so far?" Fallon asked, watching through the window of the microwave as the popcorn popped. It had that amazing fake buttery smell, and my mouth watered. "Grab a bowl from that cupboard, will you? A big one."

I opened the cupboard and pulled out a mixing bowl. Handed it to Fallon. "Yeah," I said. "It's pretty good."

"I love Moonlight Graham," Fallon said. "He's my favorite." And right there in the kitchen, in front of the buzzing microwave, she launched into one of the scenes we'd just watched, where the main farmer guy tracks down an ancient white-haired old ballplayer and asks him what he'd wish for, if he could wish for anything.

"'*That's what I'd wish for,*'" Fallon said. Her voice was dropped low, just like the actor in the movie. Gravelly, like an old man. "'*A chance to squint at a sky so blue that it hurts your eyes just to look at it. To feel the tingle in your arms as you connect with the ball.*'" She even had the exact hand movements down that the guy did in the movie, the perfect rise and fall of his voice. "'*To run the bases, stretch your double into a triple. And flop, face-first, into third. Wrap your arms around the bag.*'" I swear, for a second she wasn't Fallon Little, the girl with the big brown eyes and the dark pink scar. For a second she really was that white-haired old man. "'*That's my wish, Ray Kinsella,*'" she finished. "'*That's my wish.*'"

That's when the microwave beeped—perfect timing.

"Whoa," I said as Fallon pulled the popcorn out with the tips of two fingers to avoid the steam.

"Whoa, what?" she said, not even turning around. But I could see her smiling, just a little, as she tugged open the bag and dumped the popcorn into the bowl. It was sort of annoying, really, asking what when you knew full well.

But I told her anyway. Maybe it was her giant cop of a dad. Maybe it was the smell of the popcorn. Maybe I was just feeling nice.

"That was really good," I told her. "You're really good."

"Oh, I don't know," Fallon replied as she handed me the bowl of popcorn. But that smile was still there, I could see it. Even if a tiny smidgen of it was tucked into her scar. "I've got a thing for movies," she said. "I told you. Want to finish?"

I nodded.

The rest of the movie wasn't bad either. I even found my very own continuity error, when a hot dog is flying out of its bun in one shot, and then when it lands on the ground, it's back inside. (Well, I only found it because Fallon told me there was something coming up, so I should keep my eyes peeled. But it still counted.)

I almost forgot the main reason I'd gone over there until Fallon asked me, "Hey, you want to stay for dinner? Dad's a really good cook. Aren't you, Dad?"

From the kitchen, I heard her father grunt.

I checked the clock. It said 5:05.

"I should probably go home," I said. I kind of did want to stay for dinner, since I was pretty sure whatever Fallon's dad whipped up was going to be better than cereal, which is what I was probably going to end up eating. But the Dodgers were playing the Giants at 7:00, and my mom was coming home early to watch it. Anyway, I was going to be in enough hot water as it was, what with skipping dinner with Dad again.

Better not push it. "This was, um, fun, though," I said. And I wasn't even lying.

Fallon grinned at me. "We should do it again," she told me. "We've got tons more baseball movies. A million, even. We could start a whole club."

"I don't know about that," I said. Fallon wasn't the worst, but I wasn't sure I wanted to be her best friend or anything.

She didn't seem to hear me. "You going to be at the store this weekend?" she asked me. "Maybe I can stop by and we'll plan."

"Um," I said. This weekend was supposed to be a Dad weekend. I guess Kari had run out of excuses for not having us over at their apartment anymore, now that the room was remodeled. But I'd rather work a million free shifts at Kitch'N'Thingz than spend one night there. "Sure. I mean, I don't know. I mean, we'll see."

Fallon laughed and held open her front door for me. "Bye, Trent Zimmerman," she told me.

"Bye," I said.

She shut the door behind me, and I pedaled home, thinking how Fallon Little was about the weirdest person I'd ever met.

And how, if I was being honest with myself, I didn't really mind so much.

When Aaron pulled into the driveway, I was sitting on the front porch, waiting for him.

"Did you tell Dad?" I called to him, leaping to my feet as he opened his door. "About my project?"

Aaron didn't answer till he was all the way up the stairs. Then he slugged me in the arm on his way into the house. "You owe me big, little brother," he said.

Doug followed the two of us into the house like a puppy. "Dad was real mad," he told me. "He said if you aren't ready to go when he picks the two of us up tomorrow morning, you're going to be in awful big trouble. Oh, also, Dad said we could practice games for the company picnic, if it's not raining."

"Wait," I said, turning around on Doug in the doorway when what he said finally sank in. "What do you mean, the *two* of us? What about Aaron?"

Aaron was already in the kitchen, devouring a granola bar like he hadn't just gotten back from dinner. "I have lifeguarding," he explained.

Lucky dog. "Well, I have to work at the store," I said. But even I could hear in my voice what a giant baby I sounded like. "Mom needs me there."

"You think Dad's going to buy that one?" Aaron asked as I joined him in the kitchen. He unzipped his backpack with one hand, still munching his granola bar, and pulled out a textbook, tucking it under his arm. "You think Mom's going to let you work just to get out of seeing him?"

I frowned. Probably not.

"I have to study," Aaron said, pushing past me to get to the hall.

"It's Friday night," I told him.

"Someone has to be the responsible one in the family," Aaron replied just before he shut his door behind him.

"Glad it isn't me!" I called back. But if he heard me, he didn't bother to respond.

All that talk about being the responsible one was obviously garbage, because Aaron snuck out during the game against the Giants, right in the middle of the second inning. "Going out with a friend!" he told Mom as he slipped into his coat. He was out the door before she even got a chance to ask him any questions.

"Teenagers," Mom grumbled at the closed front door. She turned to me and Doug, who was watching with us only because Mom was letting him have ice cream if he did (her attempts to turn him into a baseball fan like the rest of us never worked out too well). "When you two get to be teenagers, don't even think about pulling any stunts like that one," she said, aiming her thumb toward the door. "Your brother knows his butt is toast when he comes home."

"He's out with a *girl*," Doug informed us, raising his eyebrows as he slurped up his ice cream. Doug had a disgusting habit of letting his ice cream melt into soup before he ate it. He claimed it tasted better that way. "I heard him on the phone. It's that *Clarisse* girl again."

Mom sighed. "So it begins," she said, mostly to herself.

Aaron got home a little before midnight. Mom was asleep—tuckered out, she said, from mentally cursing the Dodgers for losing to *those Giants* on a wild pitch. ("A wild pitch!" she kept shouting from the bathroom as she was brushing her teeth.) But I was still awake. I poked my head outside my bedroom door as he tiptoed down the hallway.

"Hey," I whispered to him.

"Hey." He seemed surprised to see me. "You're still awake."

I shrugged. "Were you out with Clarisse?"

He didn't answer that. "You going to Dad's tomorrow?"

It was my turn not to answer. "Mom said she's going to kill you in the morning for not telling her where you were going." I paused. "A *responsible* son probably would've asked first."

He looked down the hall to Mom's closed bedroom door, like he was considering something, then shook his head. "Get some sleep, okay?" he said. He sounded real tired.

I figured if Aaron wanted to secretly date some girl, it was none of my business. I wasn't snoopy like Doug. I just hated when our mom was mad.

"'Kay," I said, giving in. "You too."

Aaron slugged me in the arm. "Good night, little brother."

"Night, Aaron."

SEVEN

MOM HAD ALREADY LEFT FOR WORK BY THE time I woke up on Saturday morning. Dad was supposed to come by to pick us up at 10:30, but while Doug was in the bathroom at 10:15, I snuck out the door and hopped on my bike.

I decided to head over to Swim Beach, which is where Aaron worked as a lifeguard. Unfortunately, Giles, who was at the ticket office, wouldn't let me in even though he'd met me about a bajillion times.

"It's me," I told him, "Trent. I'm Aaron's brother. You've met me."

Giles went on chewing his gum. "Five bucks for a day pass," he said. Aaron once told me that Giles was bitter because he'd dropped out of law school and now he was a fifty-year-old man who worked the ticket booth at Swim Beach. "Park your bike over there after you pay," Giles told me, jerking his head toward the bike rack next to the booth.

"But I only want to talk to Aaron," I argued. "I'm not going to go swimming. I shouldn't have to pay just to talk to my own brother."

"Five bucks for a day pass," Giles said again.

It was no use arguing with Giles, because he always won in the end anyway. He probably would've made a really good lawyer.

I handed over the single five-dollar bill I'd scrounged out of my piggy bank for breakfast money, got my neon-green wristband, and parked my bike in the rack. After that I was allowed inside the gate.

Swim Beach wasn't really a beach at all, since we didn't live on the ocean. It was just a stretch of Cedar Lake that was good for swimming, and years ago someone had hauled in a bunch of sand from somewhere and lined the shore with it, so if you squinted really hard, it sort of *felt* like a beach, except without waves or salt water or whales. There were lake fish, though, and sometimes they'd swim right up to you while you were in the water. Once when Doug was little, we told him they were piranhas, and he wouldn't go in the lake all summer. Mom was pretty mad about that. Anyway, this past summer Aaron worked there as a lifeguard every day, and now that school had started he was there on weekends until it got too cold for anyone to want to swim. He said it paid pretty well and was good practice for when he went to college at UC San Diego and could maybe lifeguard for real.

I found Aaron right away. He wasn't hard to spot, because he was one of only three people wearing a bright red hoodie that said LIFEGUARD on the back. I walked over to the lifeguard stand where he was sitting, watching the water. Since I hadn't known I was going to end up at Swim Beach when I'd hopped on my bike, I wasn't wearing my bathing suit or flip-flops, so I had to walk slowly so not too much sand would catch in my sneakers.

"Hey," I called up when I reached the bottom of the stand.

Aaron flicked his eyes down at me, then quick back to the water. He took his job very seriously. "Trent," he called back, like he was super disappointed in me. A really nice welcome for his little brother. "Why aren't you with Dad?"

I checked the imaginary watch on my wrist. "Just missed him," I said. "So sad."

Aaron sighed. I could tell he was trying to figure out what he was supposed to do, as the big brother, in this situation. But I knew he didn't have a whole lot of options. It wasn't like he was going to ditch his job to wrestle me into his car and drive me all the way to Dad's house, kicking and screaming.

"You're going to have to see him sometime, Trent," he said at last.

"Not if I can help it," I replied.

Aaron continued to stare at the water. I stared too.

This was the first summer Aaron had lifeguarded, and he'd gotten really tan. You could hardly even tell he was related to Doug and me. He was muscly, too. I bet all sorts of girls at school were in love with him, even before they found out he was funny.

"What time is it?" he asked me, eyes still on the water.

I checked my imaginary watch again. "Probably, like, ten forty-five," I told him.

"I'm on bathroom duty at eleven," he said, "and then I get a break. Want to hang out with me then?"

"Sure," I said. And then I left him to his job, because Aaron didn't like to chat too much when he was on the stand.

Since I didn't have a towel to sit on the sand, I found a seat over by the snack stand. The tables weren't too crowded today, since the summer was over.

"Hey, Trent!" the girl at the snack stand, Melinda, called over to me. I turned to look at her, and she checked to make sure her boss wasn't looking and then tossed me a bag of chips. She smiled and held a finger to her lips, like I should keep it a secret.

Thanks, I mouthed. She nodded. At least *someone* here was nicer than Giles.

While I munched on my chips and waited for Aaron, I watched the swimmers in the lake. It was mostly little kids, but there were some parents with them, too. They all stayed in the area that was marked off by buoys. There was a floating platform you could swim to if you felt like it, and some girls about my age (but the ones who would never talk to me, ever) were hogging it, lying on top sunbathing and shooing away the little kids who wanted to dive off the edge.

Far in the distance, way beyond the buoys in the larger part of the lake, was a tiny island, just big enough for about a hundred trees. Sometimes I thought about what it would be like to swim all the way to the island. What you'd find there, besides the trees. Aaron said sometimes the lifeguards went there in their off time to explore, even though they weren't supposed to, but I liked to imagine that the island was one of the few places on earth that no human being had ever set foot on. We could see it, but it was still completely unexplored. A mystery.

Aaron came and got me before he had to do bathrooms, and I went with him to the cleaning shed, where we picked up the mop and the bucket and the other supplies. Aaron strapped on a pair of thick purple gloves and went inside the men's room first, and I set up the yellow CLEANING IN PROGRESS sign outside and talked to him through the open door.

"Did you have to rescue anyone today?" I asked Aaron through the doorway. I had to speak loudly, because of the sloshing and water running.

"No," Aaron called back. "Thank goodness."

So far Aaron hadn't had to rescue anyone. He'd had a few times, he said, when he'd had to leap into the water because it looked like someone was in distress, but they'd all been false alarms, except for once when another lifeguard got to the person before him and Aaron didn't have to do CPR or anything.

I know Aaron didn't actually want to need to save anyone, because that would be incredibly scary. But I always secretly hoped that he would. Because, for one thing, I knew that he could do it. Aaron was an amazing swimmer, and he'd aced his CPR class, too. And for another, well, I know it didn't actually work that way, but I couldn't help thinking that if Aaron saved somebody's life, maybe it would even things out with me and Jared.

"Oh," I said. "Yeah. Thank goodness."

While Aaron was in the women's room, I had to shoo away three moms with little kids, because apparently having a little kid who's screaming that he's about to pee himself makes you incapable of reading big yellow signs. They just ended up using the men's room, which I didn't tell Aaron in case they messed it up and he'd have to clean it again.

After cleaning the bathrooms, it was Aaron's break. We went to the snack stand, where Melinda tried desperately to give us free nachos, even though Aaron insisted he didn't want to ruin his appetite for lunch. In the end, I got the nachos, because I didn't care about my appetite, but Aaron made me refuse the free soda.

"I think Melinda has a crush on you," I told Aaron when I was pretty sure she was out of earshot.

He flicked a chip at me, so I ended up with cheese on my shoulder. "You're the one with the free nachos," he said. "Maybe she likes *you.*" But I noticed his cheeks had gone a little pink. "Anyway, she has a boyfriend."

I wiped the cheese off my sleeve with a napkin. "She could have a boyfriend and still have a crush on you," I said. I knew about this stuff from TV.

Aaron didn't say anything to that.

"Does she know about Clarisse?" I asked.

"What?" Aaron said, all innocent.

"Your *girlfriend,*" I told him. "Everyone knows, Aaron. It's not a secret."

"Oh." Aaron shook his head. "Uh, no. Probably not." And then he wouldn't talk about Melinda or Clarisse anymore.

When we were finished eating, Aaron said that as long as I was visiting, he might as well see if he could take an early lunch, so he got one of the other lifeguards to cover for him and ended up with a full extra hour of break. He told me he was going to use that time to take me out in one of the rowboats and work on my rowing. I was terrible at rowing, because I didn't have nearly as much upper-arm strength as Aaron, but I liked the movement of it. Dip the oars, swipe through the water, up, across, repeat. It felt like good hard work, not like cleaning counters at Kitch'N'Thingz or counting money or something wussy like that. There was something about it, when the lake was still and you were far enough from the shrieking children that you could pretend you couldn't hear them, that made you feel calm and sweaty at the same time.

"Can we row to the island?" I asked Aaron.

He thought about it. "Sure," he said. "But just around in a loop. No getting off, because my boss'll get mad."

"Okay." That was fine with me.

We rowed around the island, a slow circle. Aaron made me do most of the work while he studied how I held the oars. Occasionally he'd give me pointers, and I'd correct my grip. We were on the far side of the island, blocked completely from Swim Beach by the trees, when Aaron decided to say something.

"You've got to stop being so hard on Dad," he said.

I nearly started choking at that one. "*I'm* hard on *him*?" I asked. Maybe all that tanning had gotten to Aaron's brain.

"Weren't you guys supposed to practice your championship egg racing this weekend?" Aaron said, by way of an answer. "It seemed like Dad was looking forward to it."

"It's not that hard to keep an egg on a spoon," I replied. "You just, like, don't drop it."

Aaron looked into the water, at the ripples from the oar as they grew into larger and larger circles. "I just think you could bother to show up to dinner sometimes," he said. "Dad misses you when you're not there."

"Fat chance," I told him. "Dad doesn't care about anyone but himself."

You know what Dad said to me, after Jared? He said, "Well, it happened, I guess. And there's nothing you can do about it now. No use thinking about it."

I didn't listen to anything Dad had to say anymore.

"Watch your thumb, there," Aaron told me, pointing. "You're going to get blisters."

"I already have blisters," I muttered, but I moved my thumb anyway.

When we'd made a full circle around the island, Aaron said we should probably start heading back, so I rowed us the whole way to shore, all by myself. I didn't mind, because it meant I got to watch the island as we left it, getting smaller and smaller, more and more mysterious.

Once we reached the shore, Aaron hopped out of the boat without hardly making a splash and dragged me back in. I managed to lurch out onto the sand without getting my sneakers wet, and then I hauled up the front end, with my arms straining like they might burst, and Aaron picked up the back end, like it was the easiest thing he'd ever lifted in his life, and together we walked the boat back to the rack and slid it into the bottom slot.

"I'll tie it up later," Aaron told me. He glanced over at the lifeguarding stand, where his boss, Zoey, was waving him over. Zoey had graduated high school last year, but she acted younger than the other lifeguards half the time, that's what Aaron said about her. "I gotta get back to the stand. You heading out?"

"Yeah." It didn't make much sense for me to spend the rest of the afternoon at Swim Beach, even if I had paid five dollars for a day pass. "I'll see you later. Dodgers are playing the Giants at seven."

"You should call Dad," Aaron said.

I stuck my hands into my back pockets. "I probably won't," I replied.

Aaron glanced at the lifeguard stand, then he turned back to me. "This was kind of nice," he told me.

"Yeah?"

"Yeah," he said. Then he slugged me in the shoulder. "Don't make a habit of it, little brother." And he raced off to the lifeguard stand, kicking up sand with the back of his wet flips as he went.

Mom was clearly surprised to see me when she walked in the front door that evening.

"Trent!" she cried, clutching her chest like she'd thought I was some sort of robber. "What are you doing here? You're supposed to be at your father's."

I clicked off ESPN. "I sort of, um, missed him," I said.

She tossed her purse onto the couch and flopped down next to me. "Oh, Trent," she said. She felt my forehead with the back of her hand like she thought I might have some sort of fever. "What's going on with you two?"

I shrugged. "I hate him."

Mom nodded at that, like it was a perfectly normal thing to hate your father. "Okay," she said. "But he's still your dad. Growing boys need their fathers. It's, like, science." She peeked into the kitchen. "Are your brothers here too?"

"Doug's spending quality time with Dad like a good little boy," I said. "And Aaron's out. He didn't tell me where he was going. Probably with Clarisse." I nodded back toward the TV. "Game's on in ten," I said. "Want me to heat up two potpies?"

Mom bit her lip for a second. "Yeah," she said at last. "Sounds good. Let me just make a phone call." Then she dug her phone out of her purse and started dialing, walking toward her room to talk.

I could only hear her a little while I pulled the potpies out of the freezer and started up the oven. She was canceling plans, probably with her friend Barbara, from her book club. Part of me felt bad for being such a terrible delinquent that my own mother had to cancel the one night to herself she'd probably planned in eons. Aaron would glare at me for sure, if he knew. But then I realized that if my mom was canceling plans, that meant she'd *made* plans. On a night the Dodgers were playing the *Giants,* second in a series after a losing game. As far as I knew, Mom hadn't missed a single game against the Giants since the day she was born.

I was going to ask about it when she came back into the living room. But she was smiling, really smiling, and she looked happy as she flicked through the channels to the game and said, "Ready to pummel some Giants, Trent?" She pulled our two baseball caps from the coat rack and smooshed mine onto my head. *"Let's go, let's go, let's go!"* she hollered.

And I wasn't about to mess up a good mood like that. So I didn't say anything at all.

EIGHT

SUNDAY MORNING MOM LET ME GO WITH HER to the store. I guess she figured I'd already missed out on going to Dad's for the weekend anyway, plus I could tell she was feeling pretty happy after we pummeled the Giants the night before (there was nothing that made Mom happier than pummeling the Giants—not even coffee). So she decided I might as well make a couple bucks working.

"Trent!" Ray greeted me when we walked into the store. "Good to see you."

"There's one for you in here," I said, holding out the bag of doughnuts. I guess it was becoming a regular thing, Mom getting an extra doughnut for Ray on the weekends, because Calvin at the doughnut shop didn't even blink this time when I asked for it.

"Chocolate glazed," he said, peering into the bag, then back up at me. "My favorite person."

I laughed. "You sound just like Mom," I told him.

It was pretty slow at the store, so I spent most of the morning drawing in my Book of Thoughts.

One of the pictures I drew was a good one, maybe my best yet. Me in my house, on that cold February day, right after Doug came inside with his friend Brad and told me that the guys at the lake needed another hockey player. It looked pretty close to how it had happened in real life. Only in the drawing, as soon as I tossed the skates over my shoulder to go outside, one of the blades hit the wall behind me and snapped off. Broke, right in two. Unusable. And everyone knew you couldn't play hockey with only one skate.

"How are your thoughts?" Mom asked, sliding onto the stool next to me. She didn't try to sneak a peek at my book. Mom didn't do that.

"Fine," I said, closing the book.

She nodded. "How's school?"

Well, let's see, I thought. My homeroom teacher hates me. My gym teacher hates me. I hate everyone else. But at least I don't spend lunch in the bathroom anymore.

"Fine," I said.

"You making friends?"

I guess Fallon counted as a friend, if you didn't mind that she was half wacko. "Yep," I told her.

Mom smiled at me. A real, Giants-pummeling smile. Then she slipped my Dodgers cap onto my head. I don't know where she'd been hiding it. "Excellent," she said. She nodded toward my closed Book of Thoughts. "Now stop all that thinking you're doing, because it's time for serious things." She put on her own cap, then pulled the radio out from under the counter. "Ray!" she shouted across the store. Our only two customers whipped their heads around, but Mom didn't seem to care. "It's starting!"

I stashed my Book of Thoughts under the counter. The third game in the series against the Giants was not something to be missed.

It was a rough game, tight the whole way through, but going into the ninth we were up 3 to 1. Which is of course when the Dodgers' idiot closer came in, walked the bases loaded, and then gave up a bases-clearing double. So in the bottom of the ninth we were losing 4 to 3.

With men on second and third, Mom and Ray and I all had our rally caps on (which were just our regular baseball caps flipped inside out) when they announced who was stepping up to the plate.

"Come on, Slumps McGhee!" Mom hollered at the radio. ("Slumps McGhee" was her favorite nickname for any player having an off week.) *"You can do it! We all believe in you!"* She was standing in front of her stool, clutching the sides of the counter. A couple of customers were up at the front and shouting, too. I was pretty sure some people had left the store when they heard all the shouting and stomping, but it didn't look like Ray and Mom cared too much at that point.

All we needed was a single to win the game.

"You can do it!" Mom screeched again. I held my breath.

The guy struck out.

The Giants won.

"Nooooo!" Mom screamed, falling back onto her stool.

"You've *got* to be kidding me!" Ray shouted.

Me, I just whipped off my baseball cap. Tossed it onto the counter and turned to the customer in front of me, who was holding two whisks. "I'll ring you up," I told him.

I didn't even know why I bothered getting my hopes up about anything anymore.

I thought the Dodgers getting pummeled by the Giants that afternoon was going to be the worst thing that happened that day.

It wasn't.

Aaron cornered me as soon as we got home.

"Doug's going to prank you," he told me, checking over his shoulder to make sure that Mom was safely in the kitchen and couldn't hear. Pranking was still completely off-limits.

I hung up my useless Dodgers cap on the rack by the wall. "Why's he trying to prank *me*?" I asked. "I thought he was trying to get you."

Aaron smiled at that. "I guess he figured it's useless trying to prank the master. Anyway, he said he's mad at you because you keep ruining all his best pranks."

"Doug ruins them all by himself," I said. "He's just mad because I won't help him."

"Regardless," Aaron went on (sometimes Aaron liked to use big words because he thought it made him sound smarter, but it didn't, because he always emphasized them a lot so you'd be sure to hear exactly how smart he was), "we're going to reverse-prank him."

"We are?"

"Let's go to your room and I'll give you the scoop."

This was the scoop: Doug was going to put hot sauce in my food at dinner. That was it. That was Doug's whole big prank. But obviously, because he was Doug and he was terrible at pranks, he'd gone and made the thing as complicated as possible. Which was why he'd turned to Aaron for help.

"So first I have to help him convince Mom that he's going to cook dinner for the entire family, simply out of the goodness of his heart," Aaron told me, rolling his eyes.

"She's going to be suspicious for sure," I said.

"It's not a great plan," Aaron admitted. "But it wouldn't be a Doug prank if it was a good plan."

"True."

"So he's going to make soup," Aaron continued.

"And put the hot sauce in my bowl," I figured. It was too obvious, really. "So what's the reverse prank?"

"Simple," Aaron said. "After Doug puts the hot sauce in your bowl, I'm going to secretly switch it with *his*. He'll be so eager to see you burn your tongue off that when you just eat it, no problem, he'll be really freaked out."

"And then," I said, catching on, "when he goes for his *own* bowl, steam will come out his ears and he'll lose his mind. And he won't even be able to say anything, or he'll get in trouble for pulling pranks."

"Precisely."

It wasn't a bad reverse-prank, really. And on Doug, it would definitely work.

"I'm in," I told Aaron.

I decided to spend the rest of the time until dinner attempting to sort of live up to being the great-at-school non-screw-up my mom thought I was turning into, so I stayed in my room and tackled some math homework. It wasn't too hard. When Doug came home from Dad's, I heard him holler at Aaron, "I bought lots of soup! Don't tell Trent!" Which probably would've ruined the prank if it hadn't been ruined already. I just got up and shut my door so I wouldn't hear anything else and Doug would still think his prank was running smoothly. I didn't come out until Mom shouted at me that it was time to set the table.

"What's for dinner?" I asked as I came into the kitchen. Playing it totally cool. Doug was at the stove stirring an enormous pot of soup with a wooden spoon, a potholder on each hand. He pushed me away with the spoon, flicking me all over with soup dribbles.

"It's a surprise," he told me. "Get away."

Mom laughed from where she stood at the counter, inspecting a salad I guess Doug had been making. It looked like bagged lettuce with some salad dressing poured over the top. "Doug insisted on making dinner himself tonight. Isn't that sweet?"

I squinted at Mom for a moment, to see if she actually thought it was sweet or was just humoring him. She definitely didn't know about the prank, I decided.

"The sweetest," I told her. There were seven empty cans of chicken noodle in the recycling bin. So no need to guess what kind of soup we were having.

"Now why don't *you* be the sweetest," she said, "and help set the table? Aaron, you're on napkins."

"Aye, aye!" Aaron replied with a salute.

While Aaron and I set the table, and Doug stirred his soup, Mom put two loaves of Italian bread in the oven to heat. Everyone was in such a good mood, laughing and talking and having a good time, that I was actually starting to look forward to the reverse prank.

And then I heard the voice from the hallway behind me.

"Doug, I didn't see the badger anywhere," the voice said. "Maybe you lost it."

I whirled around.

Standing there, in my own home, was a short little squirt of a girl. Brown hair, bangs, wearing white-flowered shorts and a shirt with dogs all over it.

Annie Richards.

I gripped my hands into tight fists, and did my best to breathe normally. What was *she* doing here?

"What's *he* doing here?" Annie asked, glaring at me. Her hands were gripped into tight fists, too.

"I thought you knew he was going to be . . . ," Doug said slowly. He seemed confused.

Annie kept glaring at me. Wouldn't look away. "I thought we were doing it to your other brother," she said.

"Doing what?" Mom asked.

I could tell Aaron was just as surprised about Annie being there as I was. He grabbed the wooden spoon from Doug, to help with the stirring. "Boy, this soup sure smells good!" he said a little too cheerfully.

Doug was biting his lip as he glanced from Annie to me, both of us with our fists clenched tight. He looked really upset. Probably worried that his big, wonderful prank was going to be ruined. "It'll be fun," he told Annie. Practically begging her. "I promise. Please, you *have* to stay."

"I could use some help tossing the salad," Mom said to Annie.

Annie turned to Doug and tugged at the ends of her hair for a bit, like she was busy making up her mind. "Okay," she finally said, and Doug let out a deep breath. She moved to the counter to help my mom with the salad.

"Wonderful," Mom told her, giving her a squeeze around the side.

I guess I was the only one who wished Annie Richards would leave. The way she looked at me—like she *knew,* and she hated me for it—I didn't like it. Not at all. Because I couldn't blame her, for looking at me like that. That's the way I'd look at me, too, if I were her.

When the salad was tossed and on the table, and the bread was warmed, and Doug finally declared the soup stirred enough for his satisfaction, he told us all to sit down. "I'm the server," he told us. "I'll bring you your soup."

"Let me just put the pot on the table," Mom said. "Our bowls are already here."

"No!" Doug shouted, too quickly. "I mean, that won't work. It's like a restaurant, it needs to be like a restaurant."

Aaron was doing his best not to laugh. "I'll help," he said, and he picked up two bowls off the table and brought them to Doug at the stove. "Everybody stay seated. Doug is the chef and I'll be the waiter." He winked at me.

"What nice boys I have," Mom said.

I made my way to my seat, and so did Annie. She sat as far from me as she possibly could, glaring at me the whole time. I folded and unfolded the edge of my napkin, doing my best to pretend I couldn't see her.

"No one eat till I get there!" Doug shouted at us as Aaron brought the first two bowls of soup to Mom and Annie. "I want to see everyone eat it!"

"Are chefs supposed to be so bossy?" Mom asked. But I noticed she didn't touch her soup.

If anyone ever doubted that Doug was the worst pranker in the history of the universe, the job he did getting the hot sauce into the soup would've proved it. Mom couldn't see, because lucky for Doug she was sitting a bad angle and attempting to have a conversation with Annie besides. But I had a perfect view of Doug ladling out the last bowl of soup, then making Aaron walk to the fridge with him, then taking out the giant bottle of hot sauce, then slowly, slowly tearing off the plastic on the lid (he hadn't even taken the plastic off the lid yet? Doug *really* needed some work on his pranking), then hiding behind the fridge door while he dumped it in. "That one's for Trent," he told Aaron. Didn't even bother to whisper it.

I couldn't tell what Aaron said to Doug then, because he was better at whispering than Doug was, but it seemed like he told him to sit down at the table without him while he stirred the hot sauce into the bowl. I'm guessing that's what he said, anyway, because Doug came to the table then, and Aaron got a spoon from the drawer and quick stirred the soup.

Aaron put one bowl in front of me, and one at Doug's place. "Bon appétit," he told me as he sat.

"Thank you so much for this delicious meal," Mom said to Doug.

"You're welcome!" he replied happily. His eyes were glued to me.

Annie's eyes were glued to me, too. If glaring was a subject in school, she'd have an A+. Heck, she could teach the class.

Mom started digging into her bowl right away, with super-loud *mm!*s and *delicious!*es to make Doug feel good about his soup stirring. But Doug and Annie and Aaron were all focused on me and my bowl of soup.

I made a big show of it. If I was in for a reverse prank, I was going to be *all* in. I unclenched my fists and then rolled up my sleeves, one at a time.

And I reached for my spoon.

"You want some bread?" Aaron asked me just as I dipped my spoon into the bowl.

"Aaron!" Doug shouted. "Let him eat his soup!"

"Oh," Aaron said. He could barely contain his laughter. "Sorry."

I lifted the spoon full of soup to my lips. One noodle lay in the center, next to a single slice of carrot. In my head, I visualized exactly the face I was going to make. Flat, like I was playing poker. I'd take one huge swallow, tilt my head to the side like there was some flavor in the soup I couldn't quite put my finger on, and then look right at Doug and say, "This is great!" and then take another spoonful. It would freak him out. Wouldn't even occur to him that *his* was the one with the hot sauce until he took his own bite.

"Doug, aren't you going to eat your soup?" Mom asked across the table. He still hadn't started.

Doug shook his head above his hot sauce–laced bowl. Aaron had stirred it well, I had to admit. You couldn't even see the hot sauce in it. It looked almost the same as my normal bowl. "Trent, take a bite!" Doug shouted at me.

"Boys are weird," Mom said to Annie beside her.

I opened my mouth wide, and stuck in the spoonful of soup.

OhgoodnessholyswampcrittersfromAlabama. That was *hot!*

I shot eyes at Aaron, who smiled a wicked smile at me. Why, that *little* . . . That fink had swapped the bowls on me. I had fallen for the classic double-reverse prank.

"How's the soup?" Doug asked me eagerly as the burning liquid roared its way down my throat. I could feel it heating my cheeks, my chest, my shoulders. Next to Doug, Annie was watching me, too. Glaring.

I didn't like it.

I was stuck, I realized. I couldn't say anything about the hot sauce, or we'd all get in trouble for pranking. And I couldn't get up and dump my bowl in the sink either, because Mom's rule about never leaving the table before you'd finished your dinner was even more serious than her rule about pranking. No way I was going to put myself on double lawn-mowing duty because of Doug's stupid hot sauce idea.

I was stuck. And I was stuck in front of *Annie Richards.*

As far as I could figure, there was only one way out.

I held my spoon out to the side and slowly tilted my head, like there was some flavor in the soup I couldn't quite put my finger on. I looked right at Doug, then at Aaron, who were both smiling smugly like they were so *positive* they'd gotten me better than ever. I did *not* look at Annie, who I'm sure was still glaring. And I said, "This is great!"

Then I took another spoonful.

Doug's mouth fell open. Aaron coughed so hard, he nearly choked on his own soup. Annie probably still kept glaring—I don't know—I wasn't looking. But I kept smiling, even as the hot sauce worked its way into my nose, into my eyes, into my hairline. I could feel every individual taste bud on my tongue screaming at me. I blinked away the tears that were forming in the corners of my eyes.

Swallowed the soup on down.

"Is something going on?" Mom asked, finally looking up from her bowl and noticing everyone else watching me eat soup like they were watching the World Series. "Trent, what are you doing?" She narrowed her eyes at me. "Are you pulling some sort of prank? You know what I said would happen the next time one of you pulled a prank. . . ."

"Me?" I said. I spooned more soup out of the bowl and brought it to my face. "I'm not doing anything. I'm eating soup."

And I downed that bite, too, while everyone watched. "Tastes great," I said. "Thanks for making dinner, Doug."

Doug scowled. I bet if Aaron hadn't betrayed me and we actually *had* reverse-pranked Doug, Doug would've been a real baby about it. He would've ratted us all out for his stupid prank, and he would've done it with his stupid lip sticking out, too. I took another spoonful of soup.

Slowly, everyone turned their attention away from me and back to their own bowls of soup. Mom asked everyone how they were liking the school year so far, trying to start up a conversation.

And me, I kept eating soup. One spoonful at a time. Burning, burning, burning, with every bite. It was making a trail of fire down to my stomach now. I could feel exactly where my intestines were inside me. If I paused for even a second, I knew I'd give up for good, never get going again. So I didn't stop. Didn't talk. Didn't look at anybody. I just kept on dipping my spoon. Bringing it to my mouth. Swallowing the soup on down.

Dip, mouth, swallow.

There was a crack in my lip I hadn't noticed before. It was raging with pain, and licking it didn't help.

Dip, mouth, swallow.

I could feel a trickle of sweat threatening to roll down my forehead.

Dip, mouth, swallow.

My body was one large flame.

Dip, mouth, swallow.

And my chest. My chest. I shifted in my seat.

Dip, mouth, swallow.

Maybe ten spoonfuls left. I could do it. I really could. Man, I was going to get Aaron and Doug back *good* after this.

Dip, mouth—

A bubble of hot sauce must've been trapped in a noodle or something, because there was a burst of fiery flame on my tongue that was hotter than anything I'd tasted before. I started choking.

"You okay, sport?" Mom asked. "You need some water?"

I couldn't stop choking.

"It's the hot sauce," Annie said. First thing she'd said in five minutes, and she said it with that glare of hers. "Doug put hot sauce in his bowl. Tons. Trent's been eating it the whole time."

Three spoons, clanging into three bowls, that's what I heard over the sound of my choking.

"Doug did *what*?" my mom cried.

"What's *wrong* with you?" I said to Annie. Maybe I shouted it, I don't know, but I didn't care, either. Because maybe I deserved the glaring, maybe I did, but I didn't deserve to get into trouble for some stupid prank. "I was doing *fine*!" I said. I was up on my feet before I planned on getting there. The fire in my chest was burning hot. "I was going to *finish* it!" And I swear I didn't hit it, but somehow my bowl flew across the table, those ten remaining spoonfuls sloshing everywhere. Doug's napkin. Annie's hair.

"Trent!" Mom shouted. She was on her feet, too. "Go to your room!"

"Already going!" I shouted. I still had a couple of chokes left in me, but I wouldn't give anyone the satisfaction of hearing me cough. I stomped off to my room and slammed the door closed, throwing myself across the bed. My insides were fire, from hot sauce or what, I wasn't sure.

I could hear them in the kitchen, muttering about me. Clanking my bowl off the floor. I couldn't tell what they were saying, but I guess I could figure it out well enough.

My Book of Thoughts was on the floor by my bed, but I didn't pick it up. Just stared at its black cover as I listened to the sounds of dinner being finished, cleaned up. Of Annie going home. I didn't feel like drawing anything. My thoughts were so screwed up anyway, what was the point?

Mom let me out of my room, once, about eight o'clock, when Dad called me to yell at me for missing my weekend with him and being such a screw-up. Too bad for him I already knew what a screw-up I was so I didn't need him telling me.

"This is my *time* with you," he said into the phone. "It is my *right* as your *father* to *see* you. You can't just skip out on dinners and weekends when you feel like it. You don't get to choose those things. *I* choose. I am your *father.*"

I let him yell at me, because sometimes with Dad the best thing to do was let him yell. He wasn't going to finish until he felt like it anyway, no matter what you said. While he yelled, I decided to count all the things he *didn't* say.

1. I really like spending time with you.
2. I've really missed seeing you this week.
3. How are you doing, Trent, really?
4. Anything you'd like to talk about?

When he was finished yelling, he did say the fourth thing, actually. Well, almost.

"What do you have to say for yourself, Trent?" he bellowed into the phone. Not quite yelling, but close. "I'd really like to hear it."

"I can't come to any more dinners," I told him. "Not for the rest of the school year."

"Oh, yeah?" He was back to yelling now, for sure. "Is that so? And exactly why not, Trent?"

"Because," I said. I kept my voice as calm as possible. The exact opposite of yelling. "I'm in a club now. The Movie Club. And unfortunately, it meets Mondays, Wednesdays, and Fridays." I paused, waiting for him to yell some more, but I guess he was too surprised by that, because he didn't. "Sorry," I said. "I'm *really* going to miss spending time with you."

And I hung up the phone.

DO YOU WANT TO TALK ABOUT WHAT HAPPENED last night?" Mom asked the next morning while I didn't eat my cereal at the breakfast table. I had my Book of Thoughts open in front of me, but I didn't draw anything, just sort of stared at the white page. I guess I wasn't really having any thoughts worth drawing.

"No thanks," I said. I shut the book and went back to staring at my bowl of cereal.

Mom came over to the table with her half-eaten bagel. Aaron had left early that morning—he said he had before-school tutoring, although if I had to bet on it, I'd say the only person he was probably tutoring was *Clarisse.* Doug was in the bathroom, taking forever to get ready, like usual.

"*I'd* like to talk about what happened last night," Mom said, pulling out a chair and settling herself on top.

"Then why'd you bother to ask me what I wanted?" I muttered.

Mom gave me a *look* then, so I quick scooped a bite of soggy cereal into my mouth. My insides hadn't quite recovered from the hot-sauce soup the night before, but I figured cold cereal and milk would probably be good for me.

"Trent." Mom put her hand on my arm, but I didn't look at her. "Let's forget about the pranking for now. I already spoke to your brothers about that, and I know it wasn't your prank. That's not really the issue at the moment."

"Then what's the issue?" I asked. Not that I wanted to know.

She sighed, which was definitely not a good sign. "Have you ever heard the phrase *shooting yourself in the foot*?" she asked.

I didn't blink or nod or anything. I didn't like where this was going.

"Sometimes lately," Mom said slowly, "sometimes it feels like you're being nasty to people on purpose. Mean. Just to give them a reason to hate you."

I didn't move a muscle. Not a twitch of my mouth.

"But the thing is, Trent," she went on, "I don't get why you do that. Because you're not a mean person. I wish you could just let everyone see the side of you that *I* know. How good and kind and sweet you are."

I darted my eyes up to Mom then. But I still didn't say anything. Because she was wrong about me, dead wrong.

Good and kind and sweet kids didn't make their mothers look the way she was looking right now.

"I should get ready for school," I told her. I got up from the table to dump my soggy cereal down the sink.

"Are you really in a movie club?" Mom asked.

I turned around. "Yep," I said. "It meets Mondays, Wednesdays, Fridays, after school. In Ms. Emerson's room." I added that last part because I'd heard once about lying that the more details you added, the more realistic your lie would sound. But then I sort of wished I hadn't, because if my mom decided to call the wrinkled old crone to ask about it, then I'd really be toast. "We watch movies," I said. That part, at least, wasn't a lie. "Fallon Little's the president." That could've been true, I guess.

Mom's face lit up at that last part. "That nice girl who came into the store the other day?" I nodded. "Well." She was thinking. I could tell she was thinking. "I don't like the idea of you missing your time with your dad," she said after a minute. "We're going to have to figure out something about that. But"—my heart began to lift, just a little, when she said that *but*—"I'm really glad you're making new friends, Trent. That's important."

"So I can be in the club?" I asked.

"Why don't you try it out for a few days, and we'll see how it goes? I'll talk to your father."

That was good enough for me. "Thanks!" I said, and I rushed off to my room to get ready for school.

"Hey, Trent?" Mom called when I was already halfway down the hall. I stopped, turned. "Try not to shoot any of your feet today, will you? I'm afraid you'll fall over."

I did my best not to shoot any of my feet all day. I didn't talk at all in any of the wrinkled old crone's classes, even when she called on me, but that was probably for the best, because if I *did* talk, who knew what

I would say. I didn't participate in P.E. either, but that was probably the best thing, too. I didn't yell at anyone, no one yelled at me, I didn't smash any plants, I didn't get detention. Overall I think Mom would've been proud.

Fallon was so excited when I told her I could go over to her house to watch a movie again that she practically did cartwheels at the lunch table.

"You want to watch *The Sandlot*?" she asked. "That's baseball, too. Wait, you've seen *The Sandlot*, right? You *have* to have seen it. Tell me you've seen it, or I might just die."

"I've never seen it."

Fallon pretended to die, right there at the lunch table. She gagged and coughed and even kicked one leg up in the air. A few kids from the next table over scrunched up their faces like the whole thing was so disgusting, but I couldn't help it. I laughed. Fallon sure knew how to be dramatic.

"We're watching it today," Fallon told me, popping up from her seat, alive and well again.

I was pretty sure I wouldn't have any trouble convincing her we should meet every Monday, Wednesday, and Friday.

"Well, you are the president," I told her.

Fallon didn't even ask what I meant by that. She just grinned huge, the corner of her mouth tucked up inside her scar, and said, "President. I like that."

Fallon was right. *The Sandlot* was a good movie. It didn't have too many continuity errors, but the ones it did have made Fallon extra-excited.

"Wait, there's one right there!" she shouted, hopping up from the couch to pause the movie. It was hard to get used to, watching a movie with so many interruptions, but I didn't mind as much as you'd think I would. She stood right next to the TV and pointed at the characters on the frozen screen. "Look, you see how Benny's making his killer play right now, sliding into home base?" I nodded. It was hard to miss. "Okay, but check this out." She rewound the movie just a few seconds. "Look right there, on the TV screen behind Smalls's head." I looked where she was pointing.

"The TV shows him sliding home before it even happens!" I said, hopping up from the couch too. I couldn't help it. Finding this stuff actually was kind of fun.

When the movie was over, Fallon craned her neck to peer into the kitchen, where her dad was hanging out, pretending he wasn't being really weird reading his tablet at the table when he could've been anywhere else where there weren't two loud kids watching a movie.

"What're we having for dinner?" she called over.

He didn't look up from his tablet. "Pork chops," he answered. Which might've been the first time I ever heard him speak.

"You want to stay for dinner?" Fallon asked me, without even bothering to check with her dad if it was okay. (If he were *my* dad, I sure as heck would've checked first.)

"I can't," I said. "Have to get home by five-ten." The Dodgers were playing the Rockies tonight. They were two games out of first place and with the season coming to an end, they were running out of time to make up ground.

Fallon checked the clock on the wall. "Want to help me take Squillo for a walk?" she asked me.

I still had some time before I missed dinner with my dad, so I said okay.

"Dad, we're taking Squillo out!" Fallon called to the kitchen as she scooped her dog up from where he was napping on the couch. "Be back in a sec, 'kay?"

Her dad grunted in reply.

We took Squillo on the walking path through the park, since Fallon only lived two blocks away. Squillo was a cute dog, but he liked to tug at his leash.

After Squillo did his business in the grass (which was disgusting, by the way—first time I was ever thrilled I didn't own a dog), Fallon asked me to take his leash so she could scoop his poop with the plastic bag she'd brought. And I *thought* I was holding on good and tight—I mean, how tough could it be to keep a grip on a tiny fuzzball like that?—but before I knew what had happened, Squillo had tugged so hard that the leash flew out of my hands. He probably would've been halfway across the state before we caught up with him, but luckily Fallon was paying more attention than I was, and she stepped on his leash, jerking him back.

"You've got to hold on *really* tight," she told me as she handed back the leash. "Wrap it around your hand. He's stronger than he looks."

I tried to wrap the leash around my hand, but I guess I didn't really get what Fallon was talking about, because she rolled her eyes at me and said, "You're *killing* me, Smalls," like the fat kid in *The Sandlot*—I mean, exactly, same ups and downs to her voice and everything—and rewrapped it for me. I didn't want to admit it, but it did seem much sturdier that way.

She went back to picking up the poop while Squillo sniffed at the grass.

"You're really good at that, you know," I told her.

"What?" Fallon asked, tying up the bag and looking around for a trash can. "Cleaning up dog poo?"

"No." I laughed. Squillo decided it was time to get moving again, so he tugged and we followed. "Saying lines and stuff. From movies. You always say it exactly like the person. I could never do that."

"Oh." Fallon shrugged as she tossed the plastic bag into a trash can. "Thanks. It's fun, I guess."

"Maybe you should try to be an actress," I told her. "Instead of a script person. You'd be really good at it, I bet."

Fallon wrinkled her nose.

"What?" I asked her. "You don't like acting?" But as soon as I said it, I knew the answer. I could see it in her face. In her eyes. You couldn't hide a thing like that.

"You think you can't do it," I said. I didn't mean to say it out loud. But then once I said it, there was no stopping. "Because of your scar." What a moron I am, I thought, telling Fallon she should be an actress. She probably wanted to be an actress, more than anything else in her life. But.

But.

You couldn't be an actress with a giant scar across your face. What parts would she play? Girl with a Scar? Other Girl with a Scar?

I felt like a real jackass.

I was just opening my mouth to tell her what a jackass I was, hoping she wouldn't be too mad and we could just forget about the whole thing. But before I got a chance to say anything at all, Fallon said something first.

"Why doesn't anybody ever get hungry at the beach?"

That's what she said.

"Huh?" I asked. Squillo stopped to sniff at the roots of a tree, so I stopped too.

"Why doesn't anybody ever get hungry at the beach?" she said again. She was tugging at the bottom hem of her sweatshirt (it was bright green, with cartoon peas all over it, and said "Visualize Whirled Peas"). Suddenly it occurred to me.

A joke. She was trying to tell me a joke.

"Um, I don't know," I said. "Why?"

Fallon bent down to scratch Squillo behind his ears, her head tilted up to look at me. "Because," she said, raising her eyebrows at me like this was about to be the most hilarious joke I'd ever heard, "of all the sandwiches there."

I wrapped the leash tighter around my wrist. "What?" I said.

"Get it?" she asked, even though very clearly I hadn't. "Because of all the *sand which is there*?" She enunciated each word. "At the beach?"

I blinked at her. "That's the dumbest joke I ever heard."

Fallon laughed out loud at that. She was pretty when she laughed, actually, because she had this way of throwing her head back, and her whole face got into the act, not just her mouth the way some people laughed. "Yeah," she said. She wiped at her eyes. "Right? It's so terrible!"

I was pretty sure she was losing her mind.

"My uncle used to tell me that joke," Fallon said, "when I was a kid. Uncle Steve. And I mean, he told it to me *every single time* I saw him. Christmas, Easter, birthday parties, whatever. Over and over and over. And I'd laugh, every time, just to be polite. Finally on my ninth birthday I told him, 'Uncle Steve, you already told me that joke.' And he said, 'Yeah, I know, I was just waiting till you said something.'" She snorted, then looked off to the far end of the park, where some kids were throwing a Frisbee. Then she looked back at me, shrugged, and said, "I know it's not funny, it just sort of cracks me up still, you know?"

I tugged at Squillo a tiny bit, until he gave up on the tree and was ready to start moving again.

We walked a few minutes in silence.

There was something about Fallon, I'd noticed, that wasn't what it seemed. Something sad. She was like Mom's coffee—it always *smelled* sweet, and then you took a sip and realized it was nothing but bitter.

"It's a pretty funny joke," I told her at last.

"You still owe me a picture, you know," she replied.

I sighed. "No pictures," I said. "I don't even have my notebook anyway."

"Liar." She tapped the front pocket of my sweatshirt, and my Book of Thoughts let out a hollow thud. "You always have it."

"Well, I'm not drawing you any pictures anyway. I don't draw stuff for other people, just for me."

She snorted like she didn't believe me. "Just wait till you hear the *real* way I got my scar," she said. She flipped around backward so she could face me as the two of us walked together. "Then you'll be dying to draw it." I sighed again. I didn't even have to wait to hear it—I knew it was going to be another weird lie. I couldn't say why for sure, but I hated when Fallon told stupid lies about her scar.

But Fallon clearly didn't care about my sighing.

"I was deep-sea scuba diving," she started, "and this manatee came up to me, swimming right side by side. It was so cool, you can't even imagine. Just me and nature. And then all of a sudden, he turned his head to look at me, and I saw that he had this *look* in his eyes, like he was a soulless beast. And before I could swim away, he *whacked* me with his flipper, right here." She karate-chopped the air, right between our two faces. I flinched, and she howled with laughter. "You like that one?" she asked, spinning back around to walk forward again. She almost tripped over Squillo. "'Soulless beast'?"

There were kids playing baseball, over on the ball field. I steered us left so we wouldn't pass them.

"Hey, Fallon?" I said, after a minute or two.

"Yeah?" She was walking just a few feet to my right, plucking leaves off the trees as we passed underneath and shredding them between her fingers. She didn't look at me. I wondered if she knew what I was going to ask.

"How did you get your scar?" I said. "I mean, for real? No stories."

I didn't have to see her face then. I knew, by the way her breath stopped, for just a beat, that I shouldn't have asked. She was mad.

"I'm sorry," I said softly.

"It's okay," she said. She was trying to sound like it didn't matter.

It mattered.

"You don't have to tell me," I said.

"I know," she replied. "I'm not going to."

"Okay."

She grabbed Squillo's leash then, right out of my hands, and the two of them were in my way, stopped still, so I had to stop, too. "Not because it's some big secret or anything," she told me. "That's not why I'm not going to tell you. It's too boring, the real story. Not interesting at all. And once you know, then that's it." She poofed one hand out in front of her, like she was performing a magic trick. "No mystery." She smiled that lopsided smile at me. "And where's the fun in that?"

"Yeah," I said. Because I knew that's what I needed to say. "I'd rather have the mystery."

"Exactly. Promise me you won't ask again. It would ruin it."

"I promise," I told her. And I meant it.

She turned back around, and started walking back toward the house. I waited a second before I followed her.

That night, during the first inning, one of the Rockies hit a fly ball, straight to shallow center field. It should've been an easy catch, only something wasn't right. The centerfielder had his glove raised high, but he wasn't moving towards the ball.

"What's he doing?" I shouted, scooching forward on the couch to yell at the TV better. "What's he—?"

That's when the ball sailed right over the guy's head—and I mean, *right* over. He still had his glove extended, just hanging out there, useless, in the air, while the ball zipped past him, only a few inches away.

"He missed it!" I slapped my leg, angry. "It was right there, and he totally missed it!"

Next to me, my mom just shook her head. "He couldn't see the ball," she said. "It must've been lost in the sun." And that's when I realized that the centerfielder hadn't been trying to catch the ball at all—he'd been using his glove to shield his eyes.

"But it was right *there,*" I whined, watching the centerfielder turn around and chase pathetically after the ball as it rolled all the way to the warning track. "He *had* it. If he'd just shifted even a little, he would've caught it easy."

Mom shrugged. I thought she'd be more mad about missing the out—usually she screamed at the players louder than anybody. But this time she only said, "You can't catch what you can't see, Trent." And we went back to watching the game.

The Dodgers lost by one run. *One run.*

Stupid sun.

TEN

THERE SURE WERE A LOT OF MOVIES ABOUT baseball. Over the next week and a half, Fallon and I watched *A League of Their Own*, *Bad News Bears*, *42*, *Rookie of the Year*, and *Angels in the Outfield*.

(I caught an error in that last one that even Fallon didn't see: After Ray Mitchell hits his home run at the end, he totally doesn't touch home plate, which means the run wouldn't even count! Fallon was pretty impressed with me for that one.)

Fallon said we could keep going for a thousand years if we wanted to, but I knew we'd have to stop soon. The first day of intramural baseball was on Monday, and once that started, I'd have to give up Movie Club. Which I never expected I'd be sad about, but it turned out I sort of was.

On Friday after the movie ended, we took Squillo for a walk again, and I was trying to figure out how to tell Fallon about intramural baseball without her getting mad at me, but she started talking as soon as we stepped outside the door, so I didn't really have a chance.

"My birthday's tomorrow." That's what she told me.

"Oh," I said, surprised. I don't know why. A person can have a birthday any old day, obviously. "Happy birthday."

"Thanks," she said. "Want to come to my party? We're going to Castle Park." Castle Park wasn't too far away, and they had miniature golf and video games and bumper cars and a couple of roller coasters, too. It was pretty fun. Fallon stopped walking while Squillo peed on a tree. "You have to come," she said. "It's going to be really fun."

"Tomorrow?" I asked. She nodded.

Tomorrow was Dad's company picnic. He would murder me if I tried to bail.

"Okay," I told Fallon.

"Yeah?" Her eyes lit up on either side of her scar.

"Yeah." I'd've wanted to go anyway, even if it didn't mean turning my dad into a raging lunatic. It turned out Fallon wasn't too bad to hang out with.

But the raging lunatic dad part was a plus, I have to admit.

"Be at my house at nine," she said. "My parents are driving."

"Fine."

That's what my dad said when I told him I couldn't join him and Doug and Kari and the company picnic that weekend because of a "Movie Club field trip." No screaming, no scolding. Just . . . "fine."

"Fine?" I asked. I guess I was a little surprised.

"Fine," he said again. "You don't want to see me, Trent? Then I don't want to see you. Tell your mother."

That was it. He hung up the phone.

I guess I wasn't too sad I didn't get screamed at, but still. You'd think most dads would've done a little bit of screaming.

I was the only person at Fallon Little's birthday party. Well. Besides Fallon, obviously. And her parents.

"Where's everyone else?" I asked when we piled into the car. Fallon was wearing the ugliest pair of jeans I'd ever seen, with glittery flowers all over them. Her top was normal, though—plain blue. Her hair was pulled back into two frizzy pigtails. "Are they meeting us there?"

"You're the only person I invited, nimrod," Fallon told me.

I guess I should've been flattered by that, but instead I was kind of confused. Why didn't Fallon have any friends? She was nice. And funny. Weird, but you know, who wasn't?

Well. I guess she had *one* friend.

"Did you bring me a birthday present?" she asked as her dad started up the car.

"Fallon!" her mom scolded, shifting around in the front seat to face us in the back. Fallon's mom wasn't intimidating like her husband. She was short and skinny, with long curly brown hair, like Fallon's, but like she'd figured out how to unfrizz it. She seemed really friendly, too.

"What?" Fallon answered. "It's my birthday. I'm supposed to get presents."

I stuck my hands underneath me so I was sitting on them, then realized that was weird and moved them. "I forgot," I said. "I mean, you didn't give me much time."

Fallon stuck her lip out. "That's fine," she said, after a second of thinking about it. "You owe me a cotton candy then."

"Sure," I said, because that sounded fair to me. But Fallon's mom turned around again and rolled her eyes in that teasy mother way and said, "You don't owe her anything, Trent. We're very glad to have you."

When we were on the highway and the wind was whipping through the sliver of open windows in the front seat so her parents couldn't hear, Fallon leaned across the gap in the seat and told me, "You *owe* me a cotton candy."

I just laughed.

Fallon's parents pretty much left us alone once we got to Castle Park, which was good, I thought, because I wasn't really looking forward to hanging out all day with a gigantic silent cop who looked at you like he could kill you with his eyeballs. They gave Fallon and me a wad of ride tickets and Fallon another wad of cash, and told us where to meet up with them later.

"What do you think they're going to do all day?" I asked Fallon as we raced off to the Viking Voyage roller coaster. (Fallon, as it turned out, was nuts for roller coasters.) "Play video games?" I couldn't exactly picture that.

"They're probably going to do miniature golf," Fallon told me. "Because they're old and boring, and that's the most boring thing in the park. Or people-watching. Mom likes to people-watch."

It was still early, so the line for Viking Voyage wasn't too long. When we got through the turnstile, Fallon grabbed my arm and raced me to a seat on the far end. "You get to see the most over here," she told me as she strapped herself in. "This is where it's the scariest."

Fallon was right about that. The Viking Voyage whipped us up sideways like a swing—higher, higher, higher—until finally we were completely upside down, and then it left us there, hanging, for what felt like ten minutes. I could feel the blood draining into my head as we hung there. Next to me, Fallon's frizzy hair was hanging wild.

"Isn't this awesome?" she called over to me while we were still upside down. Her scar was darker than normal, bright eggplant purple, from all the blood in her face, I guess.

She was grinning like it was the best day of her life.

I laughed. I'd never met anyone who looked so at home on a roller coaster as Fallon Little.

By the time we were ready for lunch, we'd done all the roller coasters twice, and the Killer Vortex four times. We got in line for hot dogs, and while we were squirting ketchup and mustard on our dogs at the condiments stand, Fallon said, "You know where I really want to eat lunch? On the bumper cars."

I thought eating lunch on the bumper cars was weird enough. But when I followed Fallon's gaze over to where she was looking, I thought it was even weirder.

"The bumper cars are closed," I told her. There was a rope over the entrance part, and a sign that said CLOSED FOR REPAIRS—SORRY!

"Oh." Fallon waved a dismissive hand at the sign and rewrapped her ketchup-ed hot dogs in foil. Grabbed her soda off the stand. "They'll never notice."

"But—" I began. We couldn't just *break into the bumper cars*. But I didn't want to say that, because that would sound lame.

"What's the worst that could happen?" Fallon asked me.

"Uh, we could get kicked out of the park," I said. "They could call the cops on us."

Fallon only shrugged at that. "We've already gone on every roller coaster," she said, like that was a good argument. "And my dad *is* the cops. Come on. It's my birthday."

She grabbed my arm so quick, I barely managed to take my hot dogs and soda with me.

It was surprisingly easy to sneak into the bumper car cage. We waited until no one was looking, and then we stepped over the rope and scuttled over to the farthest car, against the fence, squeezing ourselves inside.

"Cheers," Fallon said, clinking her soda against mine.

"Happy birthday," I told her.

"You still owe me a cotton candy," she replied, taking an enormous bite out of her hot dog. Then she turned to look at me, ketchup and mustard smeared all over her chin. "Do I have something on my face?" she asked, pretending she didn't know.

I laughed.

It might've been the best birthday party I'd ever been to.

"So," Fallon asked me as I bit into my first hot dog. "What movie do you want to watch on Monday?"

I frowned. "About that . . . ," I said. She waited, head tilted to the side, for me to answer.

It was a little weird, being squeezed in so tight inside a bumper car with someone when you weren't actually *going* anywhere. Not bad, exactly. Just . . . weird.

I sighed. It was time to tell her.

"I think I'm going to start intramural baseball on Monday," I said.

"That's great!" Fallon said. I guess I must've looked surprised at that, because she said, "I mean, not great about Movie Club. That stinks. But great for you, because you like baseball." It seemed like she was studying my face for a moment. "Wait. Why do you *think* you're going to join? If you want to do it, just do it."

Like it was that simple. Like everything in Fallon Little's world was so simple.

"I'm going to," I told her. "I will." I took another bite of hot dog. Swallowed. "I mean, I want to."

"So *do* it, nimrod. It's intramurals. You don't even have to try out. They let, like, monkeys on the team if they want to play. Anyway, you're good at sports, so what are you worried about?"

I squinted an eye at her over my hot dog. It was no use trying to explain things to Fallon. No one who felt so at home on a roller coaster would ever understand being petrified of something as stupid as clammy arms.

"How do you know I'm good at sports?" I said instead.

She swallowed. "Small town," she reminded me.

"Oh."

I finished up my first hot dog, then wadded up the foil into a tight ball. Fallon grabbed it from me and threw it at the trash can across the bumper car lot. She missed by a mile.

"*You,*" I told her, "are *not* good at sports."

She laughed.

We ate our second hot dogs without talking. When we were finished, Fallon tried to toss all the foil wrappers, one by one, into the trash can. She missed every shot. After that she grabbed the wheel of the bumper car and pretended we were driving for a while, making *vroom-vroom!* noises and *beep-beep!*s and crashes and *Get outta our way!*s.

All at once, she set her hands in her lap.

"Is it because of what happened with Jared?" she asked me.

Just like that, I could feel tiny dots of sweat beading up on my arms.

"What?" I asked, tugging the sleeves of my T-shirt down as far as they would go.

Fallon was looking at me, right in the eyes. Not mean. Just thoughtful. Curious. "Is it because of what happened with Jared Richards last year?" she asked. "Is that why you're afraid to play sports now?"

It wasn't last year, I wanted to tell her. It was this past February. Just seven and a half months ago. Not even long at all.

But what I said was "You wouldn't get it."

Fallon returned her hands to the steering wheel. But she didn't make any fake bumper car sounds. "It was an accident, right?" she said, tilting her head again to study my face. I nodded. Cold sweat, clinging to my arms. I wished I knew how to stop the sweating. "Then, Trent." She shook her head, like she'd made up her mind about something for good. "It's okay. That could've happened to *anybody.* It's not like you did it on purpose."

I looked at her hands on the wheel. Calm hands. I bet Fallon wasn't afraid of anything. "It doesn't matter if it was on purpose or not," I told her softly.

I don't know why I told her that.

I hadn't meant to tell her.

"Of course it matters!" Fallon said. She said it so loud, I had to inch away from her in the bumper car, just to save my ears. She lowered her voice a little. "It's not like you walked up and stabbed somebody, Trent. You hit a hockey puck while you were playing hockey. People do that all the time. You didn't do anything wrong. You got unlucky."

I shook my head. She didn't get it. No one ever got it. My mom didn't. My dad sure as hell didn't. Miss Eveline never had a shot at understanding. "But I still *did* it," I said. "If I hadn't been playing hockey that day on that lake at that second, then Jared Richards would still be alive. Annie would still have an older brother. His parents would still have a son. Who knows, maybe he'd grow up and solve world hunger or something. There's one less person in the world, all because of me."

"Yeah, but you don't really *know* all that," Fallon said.

"What do you mean?"

"I mean"—she drummed her fingers on the steering wheel—"if you hadn't been there, if you hadn't hit that hockey puck, maybe Jared would've fallen through the ice the very next second and died anyway. Or maybe, if Jared hadn't been there, and you *had* hit that hockey puck, you would've hit someone else, and blinded *that* person for life. You can't know. You just can't know what would've happened."

She was sounding like my Book of Thoughts. Like a list of what-ifs. But in the real world, there were no what-ifs.

"I know what *did* happen."

What Fallon was going to say next, what everyone always said next—Mom, Miss Eveline, everyone who'd ever tried to talk to me about it since February—was that I had to stop thinking about it so much. That I had to stop making myself feel guilty, because I wasn't guilty, not really.

So I stopped her before she could get there.

"I did a bad thing," I told Fallon. Staring off at the foil hot dog wrappers littering the floor by the trash can. Trying to ignore the tightness in my throat. "Whether it was on purpose or not, I did something bad. Somebody *died*. And if I just . . . stop thinking about it, if I don't even feel *bad*, then what? If you do something bad, you're *supposed* to feel awful."

Fallon shook her head. "I think you're wrong," she said. Like that was that. Like she just *knew*.

I squinted at her. "What do you know?" I asked, folding my arms over my chest, rubbing them dry against the front of my shirt. I didn't know why I'd even *told* her. "Just shut up about it, all right? I don't want to talk about it anymore."

I figured Fallon was going to get mad then, about me telling her to shut up on her birthday. But she didn't. She took a deep breath, through her nose, and let it all out through her mouth.

"Sometimes," she said, staring off at the same trash can where I'd been looking a second before, "bad things just happen, and it's not anyone's fault." Outside the bumper car cage, kids were laughing and screaming, running around. Probably eating too much cotton candy. "And you can't go on forever, thinking and worrying and feeling bad about something that just *happened*. It's over, Trent. Let it be over."

My arms were mostly back to normal, then. But I guess *I* wasn't.

"Is that how you got your scar?" I asked her. I knew she didn't want to talk about it, not really, even though she talked about it all the time. "Did that just happen too?"

Fallon stared off at the trash can for what felt like a century.

"No," she said finally. "Someone did that on purpose."

And that was all she told me about that.

We sucked on our sodas till they were just ice and someone who worked at the park finally noticed that there were two kids inside the closed-down bumper cars.

"Hey!" the guy shouted at us, super angry. "Get out of there! What are you *doing*? Can't you read?"

Fallon grabbed my arm again and we lit out of the bumper car lot, ducking under the rope, laughing the whole time.

"Sorry about the trash!" Fallon called over her shoulder.

After that I decided to buy her a cotton candy. I knew I didn't technically have to, like Fallon kept saying, but I guess I sort of wanted to anyway.

The Dodgers lost to the Cubs, 7 to 6. Which meant that they missed the playoffs by one stupid game. Which meant that their season was over. Kaput.

And that wasn't even the worst thing that happened that night.

Just after ten o'clock, when I was already in bed getting ready to sleep, Mom knocked on my door and then came into my room. "For you," she said, holding out her cell phone. I took it, and looked at the screen.

Dad.

Mom waited in the doorway while I put the phone to my ear.

"Hi," I said.

I didn't really mean it.

"Trent. Nice to finally talk to you."

"Why are you calling so late?" I asked.

All the way off in Timber Trace, my dad sighed. I probably could've heard it even if he hadn't been on the phone.

"I thought you'd like to know," he said slowly, "that you have a baby sister. Jewel Annabelle Hoffsteader Zimmerman. She was born at seven fifty-six p.m., and she weighs seven pounds, four ounces. Both she and Kari are doing fine. Doug's here too. He got to be at the hospital for the birth. Kari went into labor at the picnic."

Dad said that like he thought it was such an amazing treat, about Doug being there for the birth. Like I should feel bad that I was riding roller coasters all day instead of sitting in a stinky hospital, waiting for a baby to be born. I would've bet a million dollars Doug would've gone for the roller coasters if he'd had the choice.

"Trent?" my dad said.

I ran my tongue between my teeth and my gums. Looked at my mom in the doorway. She was trying not to look back.

"Was there anything else?" I asked.

He sighed again. A pause. Then another sigh. "I just thought you'd want to know, Trent. About your sister." He paused again. "Most people say congratulations."

"Congratulations," I said. I felt bad for the baby, that was the truth. She had my dad for a dad and she didn't even get my mom. She had *Kari*. "Did you and Doug win the egg race?" I don't know why I asked that last part. What did I care?

"No," Dad said. And then he must've been finished talking to me, because he said, "I'll talk to you later, Trent." And he hung up the phone before I had the chance to say "Bye."

I pressed End on the phone, and Mom came to retrieve it from me.

"Good news, huh?" she said. But I couldn't tell if she believed it or not.

"Sure," I said.

"Having a sister will be nice."

I shrugged.

Mom kissed me on the forehead. "Your father loves you, you know."

"What kind of name is *Jewel*?" I asked.

Mom smiled a real smile then. "I love you too."

"Sucks about the Dodgers."

"Yeah. There's always next year. Get some sleep, all right, mister? We're leaving for the store bright and early tomorrow."

"Okay. Night, Mom," I said.

"Night."

"Mom?"

She turned.

"I love you too," I told her.

ELEVEN

AS I WALKED INTO THE GYM FOR P.E. FIRST period on Monday, Mr. Gorman was standing in the doorway as always, holding his clipboard. "Am I going to like the kid I meet today?" he greeted me.

"Your guess is as good as mine," I told him.

I couldn't play tennis, since I had a pulled muscle in my neck from all the roller coasters on Saturday. That's what I told Mr. Gorman. Anyway, I figured I better save my strength for intramurals that afternoon.

I wasn't really in the mood for drawing thoughts, so while everyone else pretended to be having a great time whacking tennis balls with rackets, I sat outside in the dirt by the tennis courts and read Mom's latest *Sports Illustrated* that I'd snagged from home. I wondered who the intramural coach would be, if it was a teacher I already knew. Anyone had to be better at leading a team than Noah's uncle. All he did was look up from his clipboard occasionally and say, "Great! Keep hitting the ball!" Like if he didn't say that, maybe they'd start swallowing it instead.

Where did the school *find* these people?

Mr. Gorman didn't particularly seem to like the kid he met that day, but I didn't bother to ask.

During social studies, the wrinkled old crone handed me a stack of worksheets and asked if I would hand them out for her. I could tell just by the look in her eyes that she expected me to say no (or worse). Maybe she *wanted* me to say no (or worse), because I hadn't had detention since the very first day of school, and she was probably just itching to see me suffer.

But I didn't tell her where she could stuff her stupid worksheets. Partially because that was probably exactly what she wanted me to do, and partially because I had intramural baseball after school, so I didn't need her dumb detention anyway.

"Sure, Ms. Emerson," I said, smiling. It really freaked her out, you could tell. "I'd *love* to."

So anyway, the day was going pretty well.

And then it was time for lunch.

All the outside lunch tables were taken by the time Fallon and I got there. Totally filled. The one we usually sat at, that one had people at it, too. Three people.

Jeremiah and Stig and Noah Gorman, to be exact.

I grabbed Fallon's elbow so hard, she almost dropped her tray.

"Come on," I said. "Let's eat somewhere else." Noah had already spotted us—I saw him look at us, just ten feet away, then shoot his eyes down to the table. Jeremiah's back was to us, and I didn't think Stig had seen us yet either.

"There's nowhere else to eat," Fallon said. "Let's just sit down." She yanked her elbow free. "It's a big table."

What was I supposed to do, just let her go? Of course not. Those guys would eat her alive if she didn't have me with her, I didn't care *how* brave she thought she was. So I followed her.

There may have only been three of those guys, but they were spread all the way around the table, taking up the whole thing, like they thought they added up to twelve people. Maybe they did think that, for all I knew. They were all morons.

"Hey," Fallon said to Jeremiah and the other guys. Pretty nicely, too, if you ask me. "Would you mind scooching over, please? Thanks."

Jeremiah turned around, to see who was talking to him. When he saw it was Fallon, with me behind him, he rolled his eyes. "Get lost," he told us.

"No," Fallon said carefully. She blew a lock of hair out of her eyes. "I don't think we will." All I wanted to do was stare at the lumpy mashed potatoes on my tray. I could feel the heat in my chest starting up. But I didn't stare at my potatoes. I kept my eyes focused on Fallon.

"Fallon," I whispered, "we should go."

Fallon ignored me. "Scooch over," she told Jeremiah again.

By this time, obviously, Stig had noticed us, and Noah couldn't pretend he hadn't. But they were clearly waiting for the boss man to tell them what to do.

I was surprised, I guess, by what he said.

"You heard her," Jeremiah said to his buddies. "Scooch over."

They looked as surprised as I felt by that, but I guess when the Boss Moron tells you to do something, well, you do it. So they scooched, and Jeremiah scooched, and suddenly there was plenty of room for us.

"Thanks so very much," Fallon told them.

I saw it before she did. And I tried to stop it, I really did. But there wasn't time.

Just before Fallon sat, right next to Jeremiah, looking so nice and friendly you just knew he was up to something, Jeremiah let out a fake sneeze and plopped a heaping forkful of mashed potatoes on the seat next to him, exactly where Fallon was about to sit. And there was no time to stop it from happening—not for me, because I was too far away, and not for Fallon, who was halfway to sitting when she must've figured out what was going on—so gravity just plopped her *PLOP!* smack in the pile of potatoes.

The fire in my chest then, it moved on to the rest of me. Felt like my intestines were boiling. My fingertips twitched with heat. I wanted to punch Jeremiah in the face. I wanted to pull him off that bench by the collar of his shirt and smack him between the ears. I wanted to throw him on the floor of the cafeteria and kick him and yell at him and tell him to pick on people who actually ever *did* something to him, and not the one nice person in this whole stupid town. And then when I was done beating the crap out of Jeremiah, I wanted to beat the crap out of his friends, too.

I swallowed the rage down.

Instead, I turned to Fallon. "Are you okay?" I asked. Which was a stupid question, because it wasn't like she sat on a firecracker and her butt exploded. She sat in a pile of mashed potatoes. She wasn't bleeding. She didn't need a bandage. She needed a washing machine.

Fallon was swallowing down her own chestful of rage, I could tell just by looking at her. Her face was red and blotchy. She looked like she might cry, even. Her hair, if it was possible, looked even frizzier than it had three seconds ago. She took a deep breath. She turned to look at me, eyes purposefully not on Jeremiah.

"I'm fine," she said. "Let's eat lunch."

"But—" I started. She had potatoes on her weird plaid skirt. Smooshed all into the fabric, probably seeping over the hemline onto her leg.

"I *said,*" she snapped—and it was the first time I had ever seen her even the slightest bit angry—"I want to eat *lunch*. I'm *fine*."

Well, what was I supposed to do? I sat.

I set my tray on the table, still trying to control the fire in my stomach, while Jeremiah and Stig just laughed about the potatoes, like it was the funniest thing they'd ever seen. Noah pretended he was super interested in something at the bottom of his backpack, and definitely did *not* look at me. Fallon worked on yanking her plastic utensils out of their package. Spork, knife. Individual salt and pepper. She pulled each piece out calmly, slowly, like there wasn't a wad of potatoes mucking up her skirt. But her face was still red. Her scar was purple. And her hands were shaking, just a little.

I tried to ignore that boiling rage on my insides. I tried so hard. Because obviously Fallon didn't want me to do anything, and she was the one with mashed potato on her, so that's what I knew I should do—nothing.

I curled my hands into tight fists.

"Where did you even get that stupid skirt?" Jeremiah said to Fallon. She slowly opened her container of chocolate milk. "You know it looks dumb, right?"

"It's a shame you think that," Fallon told him. I had to admit, her skirt was particularly weird today. Like something you'd have to wear at a private school, only it didn't exactly fit her very well. The waist was rolled over at the top, and she was wearing a piece of rope as a belt. "I think it would look really nice on you." She took a swig of milk. "It would show off your legs."

If you hadn't been able to see her—her red face and her shaking hands—it would've been really funny, Fallon telling Jeremiah he'd look nice in a skirt. But from where I was sitting, it wasn't so funny.

You could tell Stig didn't know from funny, though, because he hooted like it was hilarious.

"Shut up," Jeremiah told him.

Noah was still searching inside his backpack for who-knows-what.

"If you want," Fallon said, sticking her spork into her mashed potatoes, "you can come over sometime. My mom has some blouses that would really bring out your eyes."

"You're so lame," Jeremiah shot back. Which was pretty much the lamest comeback on earth, but when you were a bully like Jeremiah, with lackeys who'd do whatever you asked them to, I guess you didn't have to be too witty with the comebacks.

Anyway, I could already tell this wasn't going anywhere good. "We should go," I whispered to Fallon. "I'm not really hungry anyway." But she just shook her head and dug into her potatoes, glaring at Jeremiah the whole time.

So it wasn't like I was going to leave her there or anything.

"You're ugly." That's what Jeremiah said to Fallon next.

Fallon took another bite of potatoes. "Aw, shucks," she said, batting her eyelashes. "I didn't know we were writing each other love poems yet. It seems like that shouldn't be till the fifth date at least."

I couldn't take it anymore. My toes were tingling now. I had to *do* something.

While Jeremiah stared at Fallon, confused, I decided what I needed to do.

Fallon was halfway through her potatoes already. "Well, here's one for you then," she said. "Just so we're even."

With my hands hidden under the table, I *slooooowly* began to push my tray, through the metal weave of the mesh top. Invisibly. So you couldn't see it was me.

"You have the brains of a wet turkey," Fallon said with a smile. She was clutching her hands to her chest, like a lovesick girl in a romantic movie. All swoony.

I inched the tray closer to Jeremiah's lap. Closer. Mashed potatoes with gravy. Open container of milk. Glops of meat loaf. Closer and closer I pushed the tray. The key was doing it so slowly that Jeremiah wouldn't notice it moving.

"And the wit of a dead sloth," Fallon said.

Closer and closer.

"Whatever," Jeremiah shot back. Which was a terrible comeback, again. But I bet he was so busy thinking it up that he still hadn't looked at the table. He still hadn't noticed the tray.

"I'll write it down for you," Fallon said with a smile. "In case you forget it. You can hang it in your locker."

And then, just as the tray was two inches from perfect topple territory, Fallon—without even looking my way—picked up her spork and smashed it handle-first into my arm through the tabletop.

"Ow!" I shouted. I pulled my arm out from under the table.

The tray remained untoppled.

"What was that for?" I hissed at Fallon.

She snatched her lunch tray off the table. "Let's go," she told me.

"But—" I said, my eyes darting back to my own tray. I'd *had* him. I'd totally *had* him, and Fallon had stopped me.

Jeremiah and Stig and Noah just kept looking at us, one to the other, clearly confused.

Heck, I was confused.

"I said," Fallon told me, standing up, "let's go."

So what could I do? I followed her.

"You two are both turd faces!" Jeremiah shouted at our backs as we left the cafeteria. Only he didn't say "turd faces."

I could feel everyone's eyes boring into me.

"Where are you going?" I called to Fallon as we entered the hallway. We were both still holding our lunch trays, and she was walking so fast, I was practically running to keep up. "Why did you stop me back there? I was totally about to mess with him."

Suddenly Fallon spun around to face me. Only I hadn't known she was going to spin around, so I nearly careened right into her. My milk sloshed out of its carton. "I didn't ask you to do that," she told me.

"But I did anyway," I said. "What's the big deal?"

"I was *fine,*" she said.

"I just thought he could use a lapful of lunch food," I said. I was confused. Why was Fallon so mad? All I was trying to do was stand up for her. I was trying to be her *friend.*

"So what would happen then, huh?" she asked me. Her face was redder than it had been before. It was like I'd made her more upset than Jeremiah had. And that didn't make any sense. "He'd still be a jerk, he'd just be a jerk covered in milk."

"That's kind of the point," I said.

Fallon didn't say anything, only stood there, in the hallway, looking around her like she didn't know where to go.

"You're covered in mashed potatoes," I reminded her. It wasn't usually the sort of thing you needed to remind somebody, but she seemed to have forgotten. "You should go to the bathroom and try to clean it off. I'll wait for you." She was still just standing there, clutching her lunch tray. It was weird. I didn't like it. "Then we can go to the library and look stuff up on the Internet or something."

She shook her head. "I can't," she said. Her voice was small. It sounded weird coming out of her mouth. Fallon was not, I realized, a quiet girl.

"Um, okay," I said slowly. I didn't really know why a person wouldn't be able to go to the library, but I wasn't exactly going to argue about that right now. "We can go somewhere else then. We'll find another lunch table. Or go to the blacktop."

Fallon shook her head again. *"No,"* she said. Quiet, but insistent. "Not that. I can't go . . ." She darted her eyes away from me. "I don't like to go into the bathroom at lunch. There's always girls in there. This same group of them, doing their makeup and stuff. I don't . . ."

She didn't need to tell me any more.

"Okay," I said. I wanted to put a hand on her shoulder, or something, to calm her down. But I wasn't sure if that was the right thing to do. How was I supposed to know what to do? "Well, but you can't walk around with mashed potatoes all over you. Why don't you wait here and I'll get paper towels from the boys' room? I'll be right back."

"No, it's okay," Fallon said. She'd stopped shaking. "I know where we should go."

So that's how we ended up outside Ms. Emerson's room. Which is pretty much the last place I wanted to be.

"Why *here*?" I asked. I already had to see Ms. Emerson a million times a day. I definitely didn't want to make it a million and one.

"She has a sink," Fallon said, peeking in through the window of the door, still clutching her lunch tray. "And I know she'll let me use it. I have her for social studies, and she's nice." That was when I started to think that somehow the mashed potatoes had made Fallon go insane. Could mashed potatoes make you go insane? "Good, she's there," Fallon said. "Come on, let's go in."

"Wait, no," I said, tugging on her arm so she'd stop trying to open the door. "Ms. Emerson is awful. There must be another teacher you can go to."

"She's not awful," Fallon told me. "I like her."

"She *hates* me," I said.

"So you stay outside then. I'm going in." And just like that, she left me standing in the hallway.

I guess I could've left. Gone to the library by myself, or gone back to the cafeteria, or even worked on my Book of Thoughts inside the boys' room, if I'd wanted to. But I hadn't told Fallon I was going to leave, and what if when she came out, she wondered where I'd gone?

I waited.

It took fifteen minutes. Or longer, I wasn't sure. I didn't have a watch. Anyway, I stood there, in the hallway, holding my stupid lunch tray, not doing anything. I didn't even finish my lunch. I wasn't hungry. Every once in a while I'd peek through the window. Ms. Emerson was helping Fallon at the sink, handing her paper towels. She didn't look like a wrinkled old crone when she was talking to Fallon, but I knew better. Anyway, I felt pretty weird staring at the two of them through the window, so mostly I stared at my feet. Whenever someone walked by and looked at me funny, I acted like I was opening the nearest locker.

When Fallon came out, she said, "You're still here." And she seemed happy about that. She smiled at me. Her face wasn't red anymore.

I smiled back. "Still here," I said.

"So"—she looked around her—"where should we go?"

"The library?" I said.

"Sure." I tossed my lunch tray in a garbage can in the corner, and we took off down the hall.

"By the way," I said. "I figured it out."

"Figured what out?"

"How you got your scar." Fallon tilted her head to the side, watching me. "When you were born," I told her, "you had a Siamese twin. Joined at the nose. And when they separated you in the hospital, you were left with a giant scar."

Fallon's smile grew even wider. "I like that one," she told me.

The rest of lunch wasn't too bad, after that.

When the final bell rang, it was time. I made my way through the gym, outside to the ball field, where intramurals were meeting. One foot after the other. Slowly. Very slowly. The walking was hard. The thinking about it was harder.

The first thing I saw, when I got outside, was a group of kids, all guys, sitting on the benches that lined the field. My new teammates, I guessed. I took another step. Bend the right knee, bend the ankle, set it down, shift the weight, left leg up. And repeat. Made my way over.

I was almost all the way there when I noticed Noah Gorman, sitting on the very end of the bench.

Noah Gorman. Great.

He was staring at his sneakers, looking about as angry as a person can look. I guess I must've just been standing right in front of him, watching him—which, okay, was kind of weird. Because after a few seconds or so of that, he noticed I was there and lifted his head up and said, "What do you want?" in about the least friendly way you can say such a thing.

"Are you on the team?" I asked him. I didn't mean to say it not-friendly. It just sort of came out that way.

He glared at me. I swear, *glared*. Like he'd been taking lessons from Annie Richards. "Looks that way, doesn't it?" he said.

"Ah!" came a booming voice behind me. "Our old pal Trent!"

I turned around, even though I didn't have to. I knew who it was already, without even looking.

"I didn't think I'd see you here." It was Mr. Gorman himself.

I'm pretty sure my mouth was hanging open. I couldn't help it.

"What are you doing here?" I asked him. Which, okay, was sort of a stupid question.

Mr. Gorman laughed at that. "I'm coaching intramural baseball, Trent," he said. Big smile. Like a wolf. "The real question is, what are you doing here? You joining the team, son?"

I looked around. Everybody on the benches was staring at me. Everybody.

And that's when I heard it, from right behind me. The sharp, distinct *CRACK!* of a bat hitting a ball dead-on.

So I flinched. So what?

"I . . . ," I said. I took a step back. "I . . ."

My arms had gone clammy. That fast, and it had happened.

"I . . ."

"Trent?" Mr. Gorman asked me. He looked genuinely confused. Lowered his clipboard to look at me and everything.

"I messed up," I said. It was hard to swallow. Hard to breathe. "I didn't mean to come here."

Mr. Gorman was not looking less confused.

"I'm supposed to be at Movie Club," I said. And with that, I took off. Back toward the gym. Walked off that field as fast as a person can walk without sprinting.

I missed sprinting.

When I showed up at Fallon's house, she didn't even ask what had happened. She just opened the door and let me inside. Her father barely looked up from his eggs.

Anyway, *Little Big League* was a pretty good movie.

TWELVE

THERE WAS ONE GOOD THING ABOUT JEWEL Annabelle Hoffsteader Zimmerman, at least. Apparently just her being born made Dad and Kari so tired that they couldn't even *contemplate* doing anything else, including spending time with the three children Dad already had. So for almost a whole month, I didn't have to think of a single excuse for missing out on dinners at St. Albans, or weekends at Dad's either. Doug and Aaron got out of it, too, without even trying.

I didn't hear anyone complaining.

I guess I technically didn't have to go to Movie Club all that time, but I went anyway. I figured Fallon would be upset if I didn't go. After a while we got sick of baseball movies (which I didn't know was possible, but I guess it was), so even though there were lots more baseball movies left in the world, we moved on to other types. Mostly Fallon picked the movies, because she was very opinionated when it came to those things, and arguing with her was the pits. But I didn't too much mind most times. *The Princess Bride* and *Coraline* were good. I could've lived my whole life without watching *Little Women*, though.

Anyway, Dad must've finally remembered he had sons, because one Saturday morning, three days before Halloween, I was stuck in the car with Aaron and Doug, heading over to their place Whether I Liked It or Not. (You can guess if I liked it or not.) I thought Mom might give me a break, but she said when it came to meeting my baby sister, she wouldn't hear any excuses. That, she said, was a thing you just *did*.

If you asked me, she was only excited to get all us boys out of the house. She said she hadn't made it to book club in a thousand years.

The baby was a poofed-up pink jellybean of fuzzy fleece, lying in a motorized baby-rocking thing in the living room. That was the first thing we saw when Dad opened the door—the pink baby in her pink motorized rocking thing, with Kari perched on the edge of the couch, cooing at her.

We went over to examine the baby. I'm not sure any of us cared too much about babies, but it just seemed polite.

"Wash your hands, will you?" Kari told us. "Before you get too close. We don't want to give Jewel any germs."

Jewel. Like she was the most precious thing in the world.

"So what do you think?" Dad asked when we were all sitting around the table eating turkey sandwiches. (Aaron and I made the sandwiches ourselves, because Dad said now that we had a baby in the house, we all had to "pitch in." Doug had to vacuum the living room while we were on sandwich duty, though, so I think Aaron and I won.) Well, Kari wasn't eating, because she was rocking Jewel, who also wasn't eating, because she was screaming. She did that a lot. You'd think it would be impossible to hold a conversation with a screaming baby in the room, but spend more than an hour with a month-old infant, and suddenly you're a pro.

"What do we think about what?" I asked, chewing on my sandwich.

Dad laughed. "About your sister."

"Oh." I swallowed. "She's fine." She looked like a fat pink grape with arms, but I didn't think that was the kind of thing you were supposed to say.

Under the table, Aaron kicked me. "She's beautiful," he told Dad.

"We think so," Kari replied from her chair. I noticed she didn't say anything to us unless it was about the baby. *"The doctor said she was the most beautiful baby he'd ever seen. Isn't she the most beautiful baby you've ever seen?" "Do you like those little socks? They're darling, aren't they?" "Don't you think she has your father's nose? I think she has your father's nose."* All sorts of questions that didn't really require answers. "Aren't you the most beautiful baby girl, little Jewel?" She bounced her in her arms, and Jewel gave a little growly squeak and finally stopped screaming. "Aren't you?"

"Can I have your chips?" Doug asked Aaron. Aaron pushed his chips across the table.

I was glad Dad and Kari had a baby to be excited about. Really, I was. Having a baby was probably the best thing ever. Babies couldn't disappoint you.

"What are we going to do today?" I asked. I was just trying to make conversation, really. Not like I really cared what we did. But Dad usually had something planned for the weekends. He'd take us to a baseball game or a football game or a movie, or to go bowling at least. We always "got out of Kari's hair" for a while, and sometimes if you could ignore Dad and just focus on the thing you were doing, it could kind of even be sort of fun.

Dad looked around the room. "This is pretty much it," he said. "Unless you want to go with me on a diaper run later."

It was practically impossible to leave your house after you had a baby. That's what I learned that Saturday.

What we did instead of anything fun was we sat around and stared at Kari staring at the baby. We weren't even allowed to turn on the TV, because Kari said it was bad for Jewel's developing eyes, not like she was even watching it.

I almost said I'd go on the diaper run, just for something to do. But I thought better of it.

About four o'clock, I went to the bathroom (talk about excitement). And I didn't think I was in there that long, but when I came out, Dad and Kari were nowhere to be seen. It was just Doug and Aaron sitting on the couch. And Aaron had Jewel snuggled in his arms.

"Where'd everyone go?" I asked.

"Dad's getting diapers," Doug told me. I should've known. "And Kari decided to take a nap."

I plopped down next to Aaron on the couch. Looked at my little sister in the face, the closest I'd gotten to examine her since we'd arrived. She was a fat pink grape for sure, but she *was* sort of cute, under all that fleece.

"Does Kari know you're holding the gemstone?" I asked.

Aaron shrugged, without disturbing Jewel in his arms. "Kari asked if I wanted to," he told me. "So I said yes."

Watching Aaron hold the baby was pretty much exactly as interesting as watching Kari hold the baby, except that every once in a while Aaron would make fake farting noises at her, so that was better at least.

When Dad got back fifteen minutes later, he smiled at Aaron on the couch holding Jewel and said the two of them looked pretty nice together. He even got out his phone to take a photo. Dad and Kari already had more framed photos of their month-old daughter than they had of me and Doug and Aaron combined. I noticed that the egg-race trophy was still on the bookshelf, though. Half tucked behind a photo of Jewel being held by Kari's mom and dad, but still, it was there.

Probably Dad hadn't gotten a chance to toss it into the garbage yet, what with taking care of his new baby and all.

"Here, Trent," Aaron said, leaning closer to me while Dad went off to the baby's room to put away the diapers. "You take a spin."

And before I could say, "Huh?" there was a tiny baby in my arms.

"Be sure to support her head," Aaron told me. "Yeah, that's good."

I'm not sure what I'd thought holding a baby was going to feel like. I guess I'd never thought about it before. Mostly it was warm. Jewel snuggled herself into my arms like she was getting good and ready to stay there for keeps. She let out a little baby sigh and smacked her baby lips together.

It was kind of nice, actually.

For about three seconds.

That's how long it took before Kari came out of her bedroom, yawning, and said, "Thanks, you guys, for letting me take a little na—"

She stopped as soon as she saw me with Jewel. And maybe I was making it up (only I knew I wasn't making it up), but there was something in Kari's eyes I didn't like.

She cleared her throat, then smiled, a real big smile. She rushed over to me. "Let me just . . . ," she said. "Tom!" she called into the nursery to my dad. "I think Jewel needs a diaper change." And just like that she scooped Jewel out of my arms.

Dad poked his head out of the baby's room and looked at Kari, rescuing their precious baby from his least favorite son. "Oh," he said, like he was taking something in. Something important. "Oh. Um . . . Who wants to learn how to change a diaper?" he asked us.

Aaron said he did. I don't know why. Obviously that wasn't a thing that anyone wanted to learn.

As he got up, Aaron squeezed my knee.

I don't know why he did that either.

I tried to ignore the burning in my chest. It was nothing, I told myself. I was making things up.

Dinner was spaghetti with sauce from a jar and salad from a bag. Kari apologized nine times that we weren't having something homemade, but the truth was that's what we had half the time at Mom's anyway. And it wasn't awful.

After dinner Aaron and Doug and I got ready for bed, even though it was all of eight thirty. And now that Jewel Annabelle Hoffsteader Zimmerman was in our lives, we all had to sleep in one room, in Dad's office. There was one bed in the corner with a pull-out trundle underneath, and one person had to sleep on the floor in a sleeping bag.

"I'll rock-paper-scissors for the bed," Doug said when we were in the bathroom brushing our teeth.

"Don't worry about it," I said, spitting over his shoulder into the sink. "I'll sleep on the floor."

"You will?" Doug sounded surprised. Aaron glanced at me in the mirror. I gargled a mouthful of water and didn't answer. I hated it here anyway, and sleeping on the floor wasn't going to make things any worse.

"If you have to get up in the middle of the night to pee," I told my brothers, "don't step on my face."

"No promises," Aaron said. And then he slugged me in the arm.

When I woke up on Sunday morning, there was a horrible howling sound, like a great tornado gale of wind, swirling around the room. I shot straight up in my sleeping bag.

"*Whoooooooo-eeeeeeeeee!*" the noise went.

"What was that?" I said. The noise was loud but tinny. Like nothing I'd ever heard before.

Aaron was sitting up in his bed, too, on the top part above the trundle. "I don't know." He rubbed his eyes. "It sounds like it's coming from the closet."

"Whoooooooo-eeeeeeeeee!" came the noise again. *"I'm the Ghost of Nightmares. I've come to haunt your dreeeeeeams!"*

Doug. It was very clearly Doug. Who, now that I thought about it, was very much *not* asleep in his bed.

Aaron and I looked at each other, both of us trying not to laugh.

"Oh, man," Aaron said in his loudest voice. "Trent, did you hear that? I think it's a ghost!"

"Yep," I said, just as loudly. "I think maybe"—I pointed—"there's a ghost in the closet."

"I'm not in the closet," the voice said. *"I'm in your dreeeeeeams! Whoooooooo-eeeeeeeeee!"*

It was definitely the closet.

Aaron and I got up at the same time. I unzipped the side of my sleeping bag, and he pulled back his covers. Quietly. We tiptoed to the closet. Quietly. And we opened the closet door.

"Whoooooooo-eeeeeeeeee!"

The surprising thing was that Doug *wasn't* sitting in the closet, howling at us from behind the door.

"Whoooooooo-eeeeeeeeee!"

But that's definitely where the noise was coming from.

"What the . . . ?" Aaron said.

I pointed to the top shelf. There was a small white plastic square of something, with a tiny plastic antenna.

"Whoooooooo-eeeeeeeeee!"

A baby monitor.

Aaron pulled it down from the shelf.

"Oh boy," he said, still super loud so Doug could hear, wherever he was. "What is going on? I think there really is a ghost in here."

"Man, I'm scared!" I shouted. "What should we do?"

"The only way out is to leeeeeeave your dreeeeeeams!" Doug howled on the other end of the monitor. *"You've got to— Hey, what the . . . ?"*

"Doug Zimmerman!" Suddenly Kari's voice shot out of the other end of the monitor. She did not sound happy. *"Just what do you think you're doing? That monitor is not a toy."*

Aaron and I couldn't take it anymore. We broke down laughing.

"Trent and Aaron!" Kari screeched through the monitor. *"You two bring me that right now!"*

From the other room, we could hear Doug pouting like a little baby. *"You totally ruined my prank,"* he told Kari. I'd've bet anything his lip was sticking out, too.

Sunday was about as exciting as Saturday was, which is to say, not very. Aaron said we couldn't leave till five o'clock, which was exactly when Game 4 of the World Series started, and even if it was just the stupid Phillies versus the stupid Orioles, I still wanted to watch it.

Aaron said we could listen on the radio while we were driving.

I must've really been dying for something to do, because when Kari asked me if I wanted to take a walk with her to the corner store, I actually said yes. I thought maybe she'd ask Doug or Aaron, too, since she actually liked the two of them a little, but nope. It was just me and her.

We were mostly quiet on the walk.

I guess on the way back from picking up the milk, Kari decided she was sick of the silence, because she asked me, "So, how's school going?"

I shrugged. "Fine," I said. It was mostly true, anyway.

"I heard you're in a club."

"Yep," I said.

She was quiet some more.

"You know, we're all rooting for you, Trent." That's what she decided to say after a while.

I looked down at my feet. One step after another. Just kept walking.

"I know you had a tough time last year, what with everything that happened. And I know there's a lot of anger in there about all that." She pointed vaguely at my shoulder, like she thought that's where I kept my anger or whatever. "But I just want you to know that we're rooting for you. That we know it's all going to come out all right."

"Uh." It seemed like she wanted me to say something to that, but what was I supposed to say? They were *rooting* for me? It wasn't like I was in the World Series or anything. I was just in sixth grade. So what were they *rooting* for me for? Not to choke and blow my whole life? "Thanks, I guess."

Kari nodded.

When we got back to the house, Dad was washing dishes from breakfast and Aaron was drying. Doug was sitting with Jewel on the couch.

"Hey," Doug said when we came in. "Check this out." And he raspberried, right on the bare part of Jewel's belly, where her tiny shirt was riding up. "Awesome, huh? I think she likes it."

Kari actually smiled a little.

I don't know why I asked it, what I asked next. Because I knew—I *knew*—what the answer was going to be. But I guess there was that warm tingling in my chest, and I was wondering if maybe I was making it up, the whole thing, or if I'd been right.

And Kari *did* say they'd been rooting for me.

"Can I hold her?" I said, walking over to Doug.

"Sure," Doug replied, and he held out his arms, with Jewel inside. But just as I was about to take her, Kari rushed over and scooped her up, and said, "You know what? I think she's tired. Why don't we let her sleep?"

I should've stopped there. I should've shut my fat mouth and gone to Dad's office. Crawled into the sleeping bag and pretended to take a nap.

I didn't.

"Why can't I hold her?" I asked.

Kari glanced at me, then over to my dad, still at the sink in the kitchen. "She needs to sleep," she told me.

"I can help put her in her crib," I said. I was still holding my stupid arms out. Like some kind of moron who couldn't take a hint.

There was that smile again. "Oh, that's not necessary, Trent," Kari said, "but thanks for the offer. Tom!" she called to my dad in the kitchen. "Can you come here for a sec, please?"

Fire. Fire in my chest.

"Why can't I hold her?" I asked again. "Doug got to hold her. Aaron too."

"Trent . . . ," Kari said slowly. She was bouncing Jewel softly in her arms, watching my dad as he scuttled over.

Dad put a hand on my shoulder. "Trent, calm down, all right?" he said.

And I don't know why, but that made the fire burn hotter than ever. "*You* calm down!" I shouted. "All I'm trying to do is *hold* my stupid *sister*. You're the one who made me come here in the first place to meet her, and now you won't even let me *hold* her. How is that fair?"

I was louder than I meant to be. I was louder than I should've been.

Jewel got upset. She started wailing.

"Trent." My dad's grip was hard now. "I said, *calm down.*"

"No!" I said. I was really screaming now. I had to be, to be heard over the baby, because she was really going to town, even with Kari racing her off to her pink bedroom, shutting the door behind her. You could still hear her, wailing bloody murder through the walls, like someone was being unfair to *her*. "What did I ever do? Why can't I just *hold* her? What do you think's going to *happen*?"

"Trent." That was Aaron now, but I wasn't about to listen to him either. Doug had his hands slapped over his ears, like all the screaming and wailing was really getting to him.

My dad's face, you should've seen it. It went from normal to chili-pepper red in seconds. He was *angry*. "You listen to me, you little snot," he told me. And his angry red nose was inches from mine as he spoke, his grip bone-crushing tight on my shoulder. He almost pushed me all the way back on the couch, but I held my ground. "You don't come into *my* house, and upset *my* kid. Do you hear that?" He jerked his red face toward Jewel's closed bedroom door, where she was still wailing like a monster. "*You* did that. *You*. And you wonder why Kari and I won't let you hold her? You are the angriest little . . ." He took a deep breath, but his face was still red as ever. "You are *never* holding that baby, you understand me?"

The fire, it was all the way to the tips of my fingernails. Digging down to the bottoms of my heels. "That's not fair!" I told him. "She's only crying because you guys wouldn't let me hold her. It's not even my fault." I never even wanted to hold a stupid baby. That was never a thing I wanted. "It's not fair."

Dad shrugged then, like there was nothing left inside him but the up-and-down movement of his shoulders. "Sometimes you only get one chance," he told me.

On the way out the door, I took a good hard whack at the milk on the counter. Heard it hit the wall and smack open and slosh everywhere before I slammed the door so hard that even outside, I could hear Jewel start up again. "You said you were rooting for me!" I shouted at the closed door.

But even I didn't know who I was talking to.

No one came outside to talk to me. I sat on a rock on the corner of the road for more than an hour, and not one person bothered to find me. I wasn't going back in there, not as long as I lived.

I guess none of them wanted me there either.

There's nothing you can do about it now. That's the thought that rolled around in my brain, over and over—what Dad had said to me right after I killed Jared on the lake. *No use thinking about it.*

Sometimes you only get one chance. That's what I thought about, too.

What did Dad know?

Someone must've called Mom, obviously. She pulled up to my sad little rock and stopped and rolled down her window. But she didn't say anything, just bit her lip and sighed at me.

I got in the car.

"Oh, Trent," she said as she started on down the road.

I'm sorry. That's what I wanted to say. But I wasn't, not really. Not for what everyone wanted me to be sorry for. I was sorry Mom had to drive all the way out to get me because my dad was such a jerk that I couldn't be in the same house as him for two full days. But I wasn't sorry about the shouting, or the milk. I didn't think I was the one who should be sorry about that.

"What am I going to do with you?" Mom said to me as we drove.

I didn't answer. I didn't have the slightest idea.

THIRTEEN

I DIDN'T DO ANYTHING TO THAT WRINKLED old crone all day on Monday, I swear, but at the last second before social studies ended—the final period of the day, so I was almost free—she looked up from her stovetop desk and said, "Trent, stay after class a moment, would you? I'd like to speak with you."

Next to me, Heidi Hammels whispered, "Ooh, someone's in *trouble*!" Which was not helping very much, but I decided not to pummel her or anything.

I stayed after class. What else could I do?

The wrinkled old crone sat me at an oven station in the front row, in the middle, which wasn't mine for any class. It was usually Pete Trager's, the suck-up. Ms. Emerson sat behind her big bench area with the sink and the stove and everything, and stared at me down her nose. Her chair was really high, so she had to tilt her head a lot to look down at me, which made her look even more wrinkly, even more old, and way too much like a crone.

"Did you know," she began—and I noticed that her *voice* was even sort of wrinkled—"that as your homeroom teacher I am also your sixth-grade adviser?"

I didn't answer that one. It didn't really seem like a question that needed to be answered. I mean, who cared?

She slapped a bunch of papers into an even stack on her stovetop desk. "We've come to midterm review," she said. She tilted her head even farther to examine me—so far I worried her neck might snap (well, I wasn't exactly *worried,* but you know). "And I have been reviewing you."

"Goody," I said. I thought I said it quietly, but I guess not, because Ms. Emerson sniffed.

"In most of your classes you seem to be doing well enough," she told me. "Not wonderfully, but passing." She looked up from the paper on the top of her stack. "Did you know that you do precisely enough homework in each class to earn exactly a B-minus?" She narrowed her eyes at me then, like she thought I was up to something fishy. It wasn't anything fishy at all. If the teacher gave you a rubric at the beginning of the year and told you what you needed to do to earn an A, or a B, and so on, then it wasn't too much of a trick to figure out exactly what would get you a B-minus. B-minuses, I knew from experience, were grades that weren't too tough to make you want to die from homework overload, but were good enough that your parents wouldn't nag you all the time about getting better ones.

"B-minuses sounds pretty good," I said with a shrug.

Ms. Emerson kept her eyes narrowed at me for a long while, then said, "You are clearly too smart for B-minuses, Trent." Then she turned back to her stack of papers. Flipped to one lower in the stack. "But perhaps that is a different matter. What I wanted to speak with you about today," she went on, "is your physical education."

I couldn't say I was too surprised about that one. Still, my heart thudded, right down into my stomach.

"It has come to my attention," Ms. Emerson told me—and was it just me, or was she really enjoying every minute of this? I swear she was even smiling a little bit—"that you have been failing to participate in your P.E. class."

"I show up," I said. "Every day."

"But you fail to participate."

I shrugged. No use denying it.

Ms. Emerson nodded at that. "Unfortunately that's going to prove to be a bit of a problem for you, Trent."

I didn't like how she was talking to me. Like she was so high and mighty, at her stovetop desk. Like she knew everything in the world.

"P.E.'s not even a real class," I said. "It's *P.E.* Half the time we play *dodgeball,* which isn't even a real sport."

"The state of California would disagree with you about P.E. being a real class," the wrinkled old crone said. "According to the state of California, it is in fact very real, and very important. Which means that to Cedar Haven Middle School, it's very important, too. If you don't participate, you cannot pass your physical education class, and if you do not pass your physical education class, you will not pass sixth grade."

My chest was getting hot now. Not quite fire, but almost.

"You mean, I could actually *fail sixth grade* because of not playing dodgeball?"

Ms. Emerson raised an eyebrow. "It's sounding more like a real class now, isn't it?"

I really hated that wrinkled old crone.

"So I'm going to fail," I said, getting up from my stupid oven station. "Thanks for letting me know. Can I go home now?"

"Sit back down," Ms. Emerson snapped at me.

She was kind of scary when she snapped.

I sat.

The wrinkled old crone did not say anything. She just stared at my face, which was about as uncomfortable as you can imagine. I looked down at the missing knobs on the oven, but when I looked back up, she was still staring at me. It didn't look like she was planning on talking any time soon, either.

Kind of creepy.

"Why do you have all these ovens in your class?" I asked. Just for something to say. So she'd stop creepy-staring at me in silence. "Are you going to, like, bake something?"

When she answered, she didn't even blink. So it didn't really solve the creepy staring thing. But at least she was talking, which I suppose was an improvement. "Many years ago," she said, "this was a home ec room. I was the home ec teacher." She jerked her head back toward the large closet behind her without moving her eyes from my face. "There are sewing machines in the closet."

Well. I guess that explained that.

"Do you wish you were still teaching home ec?" I asked. "That sounds way more fun than social studies."

"Trent Zimmerman," Ms. Emerson said with a grand sigh. I could tell she was not about to fall for changing the subject. "I know you were seeing a counselor last year at the elementary school." She glanced down at her stack of papers. "Miss . . ."

"Eveline," I said, gripping my hands into fists at my sides. "Miss Eveline."

The wrinkled old crone looked up at me again. I wished she wouldn't. "Did you find speaking to her helpful?"

I shrugged.

She nodded at that, like that's what she'd been expecting—a shrug. "Unfortunately," she went on, "because of budget cuts, the middle school no longer has its own counselor. But you are welcome to speak to any of our other instructors, anyone you trust." She started the creepy staring thing again, grilling me with her eyeballs, and I swear, if she'd suggested that I come talk to *her* like I talked to Miss Eveline, I would've laughed right in her face.

But she didn't. She just stared.

"Okay," I said at last. "Can I go now?"

"No."

I really wished that I could go. Fallon was probably waiting at the front of the school for me to go to Movie Club. She'd probably been waiting there since the bell rang. She was probably getting mad.

"You are required to receive a physical education," Ms. Emerson said, still staring down her old-crone nose at me. "But seeing as how you refuse to participate in your physical education class, Mr. Gorman has come up with two alternatives for you."

"What if I couldn't participate in P.E.?" I asked. "What if I had a note from my doctor? What if I broke my arm?"

Ms. Emerson pursed her wrinkled old-crone lips. "Are you planning on breaking your arm?" she asked.

I thought about it. "No," I muttered at last.

"No," she repeated. "Because that would be a fairly dimwitted idea, wouldn't it?"

"I don't think you're supposed to call your students dimwits."

"Do you want to hear Mr. Gorman's alternatives," she asked me, "or do you want to fail?"

It wasn't a real question.

"Mr. Gorman has suggested," she went on after a brief pause of more creepy staring at my face, "that you might make up your poor grade by joining a sport. He generously offered to let you into intramural baseball, although it started several weeks ago. He said he would make an exception for you."

I gripped my fists tighter.

"What's the other alternative?" I asked.

"You don't like baseball?" she said.

I creepy-stared at her until she started talking again.

Ms. Emerson sighed a deep sigh and dug another paper out from her stack. She glanced at it, then pushed it toward me.

"There's a community program starting up this year," she said, "on Saturdays. A basketball program, to get the younger elementary school kids who might not be the best athletes interested in sports at an early age. They are looking for older volunteers."

I got up from my seat and walked around the oven station to take the flyer. I read it. Volunteering to help uncoordinated babies every Saturday for the rest of time. Wonderful.

"Is Mr. Gorman in charge of it?" I asked. Because I was sensing a trap.

"To the best of my knowledge, he has no involvement."

"I'll do this one," I said. And I scooped my backpack off the floor and unzipped it, stuffing the flyer inside. "Can I go now?"

"You may. And Trent?" I turned around, already at the door. "There are plenty of teachers at this school who'd be happy to speak with you, when you feel like talking."

"Are you going to call my mom?" I asked. "And tell her? About P.E., I mean?"

"Of course," Ms. Emerson said.

There was a new plant, in a pot, right on the shelf by the door, at my elbow. I wanted to break it. I wanted to break it so badly.

I slammed the door hard, but the plant didn't fall off the shelf.

Fallon was waiting for me outside the school, just like I thought.

"What took you so long?" she asked.

I didn't answer. The fire was still licking at the neck of my T-shirt, and I was having enough trouble pushing it down. Talking about it wouldn't help.

"What movie do you want to watch today?" Fallon asked as we walked. I wheeled my bike next to her.

I shrugged again.

We ended up watching *Iron Man,* which was one of my favorites, but I couldn't concentrate. I kept thinking about Fallon's dad, in the kitchen reading his tablet. I wondered if the reason he always had his eyes on us was that he thought I was a screw-up. I wondered when the wrinkled old crone was going to call my mom and tell her what a screw-up I was. I wondered if she was calling her right then.

"I have to go," I told Fallon, standing up suddenly, right in the middle of the movie. "I don't feel good."

"You okay?" she said, squinting at me.

"I don't feel good," I said again. Because I didn't. I felt like a screw-up.

"My dad can drive you home," Fallon told me. Sure enough, her father was already getting up from the kitchen table, grabbing his keys.

The last thing I needed was a ride from Fallon's dad. A cop and a screw-up in a car together—that could go wrong fast. "I'll be okay," I said. "I promise."

Fallon squinted at me even harder. "You sure?"

I nodded.

"Okay," she said. "Um, see you tomorrow?"

I nodded again.

I didn't know what I was planning to do when I got to Kitch'N'Thingz. Telling Mom about P.E., maybe, before the wrinkled old crone could get to her. Grabbing a snack from the back room and doing some homework, so I could look like a *not* total screw-up, and Mom wouldn't hate me and we could listen to Game 5 of the World Series together.

I didn't do any of those things.

I saw them through the window as I was chaining my bike up out front. I saw them. No one else was in the store but Mom and Ray, and I guess they didn't think anyone could see them through the window, but they were wrong, because I did.

Ray kissed her. My mom. Not on the mouth, but on her neck. Slowly, and kindly, and Mom smiled when he did it.

It didn't look like the first time it had happened, either.

Four things I knew, right then, in that one split second through the window:

1. Ray liked my mom. A lot.
2. My mom liked Ray. Just as much.
3. If they weren't officially dating, then they were going to be, one day soon. And probably for a long time.
4. They had decided not to tell me.

It all made sense, really, I thought as I quick stuffed my bike chain back into my backpack and sped on down the block. One through three, those things all made sense. My mom was great, and Ray, he was pretty great, too. He loved the Dodgers more than anybody. I was glad they'd found each other. I was glad they seemed so happy.

But number four, that one didn't make so much sense. Why

wouldn't they want to tell me? Had they told Aaron and Doug already? Did they think I would *care*?

The fire coursed all through me as I pedaled back to the house, wondering why my mom would decide not to tell me something so important.

Wondering if it had anything to do with me being such a screw-up.

FOURTEEN

I DIDN'T TELL MOM I KNEW ABOUT HER AND Ray. I was going to. I was going to tell her that it was great, I didn't care, I was happy for her, only why hadn't she told me? But by the time she got home, after Game 5 was well over and the stupid Orioles were the stupid World Series champs, she wasn't exactly in the mood to talk to me.

That's what she said to me as soon as she walked through the door and I opened my mouth to tell her I knew. "I'm not exactly in the mood to talk to you, Trent," she said to me. "Do you know who I got a phone call from at work today? Your teacher," she said, like I couldn't guess. "Ms. Emerson. Why didn't you tell me you were failing P.E.?"

Why didn't you tell me you were kissing your boss? That's what I wanted to say. But I didn't. I can be smart sometimes.

So I stood there, and I listened to her yell at me. Listened to her tell me that there was no way a smart kid like me was going to fail sixth grade. That she'd drag me to that basketball program kicking and screaming every Saturday if she had to. That wasn't I lucky I had such wonderful teachers who cared about me as much as Ms. Emerson and Mr. Gorman, that they'd go to all that trouble to find a makeup program for me when I couldn't even be bothered to get my rear end off the bleachers and play *dodgeball*?

I listened to it all. Didn't say a word, because I wasn't supposed to. Then I went to my room, because Mom was too mad to look at me. And when Aaron and Doug got back from dinner with Dad, I didn't much feel like looking at either of them, so I stayed in my room.

If I could've stayed in there for the rest of time, I would've. But even screw-ups have to leave their rooms sometime.

The next day was Halloween, and I think Mom really wanted to "ground the living tar" out of me, but since she wasn't going to be home, she decided to drag me with her to the store to hand out candy. I wasn't complaining. It was pretty much the world's best grounding.

Cedar Haven, California, didn't have a whole lot going for it 364 days of the year. But Halloween, that one it did right. All of Main Street shut down to traffic, from about four o'clock on. Not a single car was allowed through, only people. And all of the shop owners stayed open late, handing out candy to trick-or-treaters. Not the cheap kind of candy, either—Blow Pops and cracked peppermints with their wrappers half melted off. No, every single one of the shops handed out real candy, the good kind. Snickers. Kit Kats. Twix. Skittles. M&M's.

A kid could make out like a bandit on Halloween in Cedar Haven. I was too old to go trick-or-treating anymore, but I got to keep one piece of candy for every twenty I gave away, that was Mom's rule, so I still made out like a bandit.

This year I was the only one helping Mom because Aaron was out with Clarisse (even if he *still* kept trying to insist they weren't dating), and Doug had decided he *wasn't* too old for trick-or-treating, and was out with his two favorite girls in the entire world, Annie and Rebecca.

I thought I was in for an evening of handing out candy and pretending I didn't know about Mom and Ray, because it didn't exactly seem like the right time to bring it up, what with Mom practically wanting to murder me and all. But just about six o'clock, after I'd handed one kid ten whole pieces of candy just so I could eat a mini Twix, Fallon showed up.

"Hi, Mrs. Zimmerman!" she said to my mom, and my mom let her squeeze past the trick-or-treaters into the store.

"Hello, dear," my mom said, smiling big like she really was thrilled to see her. Fallon had been right—moms did love her. "It's nice to see you."

"What are you supposed to be?" I asked her. "A hippie?" She was wearing a big flowy skirt, and a dark green flowery top, with a woven leather belt at her waist. She even had bells in her hair, with braids.

"These are just my clothes," Fallon told me. But she didn't look upset about me thinking it was a costume.

I didn't understand girl fashion at all.

"Anyway," Fallon said, "I'm glad you're here." She was standing right behind where Mom and I were handing out candy in the doorway, and started digging through my plastic pumpkin for candy bars, totally interrupting my trick-or-treat flow. I slapped her hand away. "I wanted to see if you'd go to the scary movie with me," she said, unwrapping the mini Snickers she'd snagged and taking a big bite.

The movie theater showed a free scary movie every year on Halloween, except it was only scary if you were two. They were usually from about a million years ago, and almost always in black-and-white. I hadn't gone in years.

Still, getting away from the Angriest Mom on the Planet didn't sound like the worst idea. I craned my neck around the gaggle of kids currently begging me for candy, until I could see the marquee across the street.

"I Was a Teenage Werewolf," I read.

"Yeah," Fallon said. "I already watched the trailer online. It looks *terrible*!" I'd never seen anyone so excited about going to a terrible movie before. "With, like, *the* worst special effects. And wait till you hear this tagline." She shifted her shoulders back, stood up a little straighter, and put on her best movie-trailer voice. "'You'll fall flat on your face'"—she paused for dramatic effect, and her eyes went huge on either side of her scar—"'*with terror!*' Seriously, doesn't that sound amazing?"

I couldn't help it. I laughed.

"Can I go, Mom?" I asked. I wasn't super hopeful about it, but I figured if anyone could convince her, it was Fallon.

Sure enough, Fallon jumped up and down and said, "Please,

pretty *please,* Mrs. Zimmerman?" She swept the back of her hand up to her forehead like she was a swoony lady in an old-fashioned movie. "If I don't go, I just might *die.*"

"All right," Mom said at last, with only a hint of a sigh. "You can go. But only to the movie and back. I expect you back here the second it's over."

"Deal," I told her. And I didn't wait another second. I handed her my plastic pumpkin full of candy, and Fallon and I pushed our way through the mountain of kids at the door.

"You don't even know how big I owe you right now," I told Fallon as we made our way through the sea of costumes to the theater.

"I'll keep that in mind," she said with a smile.

"Hey there, Trent," Mr. Jacobson greeted me as he handed Fallon and me each a blue ticket from a giant roll like they have for raffles at carnivals. The Halloween movie was free, but there were only so many seats, so you needed a ticket. "Hi, Fallon." So I guess Mr. Jacobson knew her, too. "Your dad on duty today?"

"Yep," Fallon said.

"Well, you tell him thanks for keeping our community safe," Mr. Jacobson said.

I wondered how a perfectly pleasant person like Mr. Jacobson could have such a terrible son like Jeremiah. I wondered if Mr. Jacobson knew that his son was terrible, and if he felt bad about it, if he stayed up late at night wondering where he had gone wrong in raising his monster of a child.

"Better hurry and get a good seat," Mr. Jacobson told us. "The theater's really filling up."

"Thanks."

While Fallon went to load up on popcorn, I hurried to the bathroom.

And so obviously that's exactly where I whammed right into Jeremiah.

Wham!

He was right behind the door, standing there with one of those industrial-sized toilet paper rolls hanging off each arm. Noah Gorman was in the bathroom, too, picking his teeth or whatever he was doing in front of the mirror at the row of sinks. There were probably eight other people in there, peeing, washing their hands, doing things you do in bathrooms. So of course Jeremiah was the one I whammed into.

"Oh, sorry, didn't see you there," Jeremiah said, eyes on the ground as he shuffled away from the door. And then, one second later, he looked up and noticed that it was me who'd accidentally whammed into him, and not some super-important movie theater customer like he must've originally thought. Which I guess is also the moment he realized he'd just apologized to me. Which, as you can guess, he didn't seem too happy about.

"Look where you're going, butthole." That's what he said.

I guess I could've let it go. Not said anything. Peed and washed my hands and gone to see the movie, no problem. But I didn't exactly feel like peeing in front of Jeremiah Jacobson, even if he couldn't think of a worse thing to call me than "butthole." So instead, I decided to hold it, and I spun around on my heel, heading back toward the door. And okay, I'll admit it, I sort of not-so-accidentally *whammed* my shoulder into Jeremiah's as I went by.

"You already peed yourself?" Jeremiah called after me as I opened the door.

"Nah," I said, walking out into the lobby of the theater. "I'm just gonna whizz all over the floor later, so you'll have to clean it up."

And I really thought that would be that. I guess I thought I could get the last slam in, just this once, maybe.

I guess I thought wrong.

Thump!

Thump!

The sound of two industrial-sized toilet paper rolls hitting the floor.

A hand on my shoulder.

"What did you say to me?" That was Jeremiah, obviously.

I took a deep breath. "I said," I told him over my shoulder, and I tried to think my words through very carefully as I said them. I could feel the rage building up in my chest, the hot, angry fire, and I didn't feel like ignoring it this time.

"I said that you couldn't tell a butthole from your own face."

It was pretty obvious, from the way Jeremiah tightened his grip on my shoulder, that he wanted to punch me, and wanted to punch me hard. It was also obvious, from the way his face fell when I turned around to look at him, that there was no way he was going to do that in his parents' movie theater.

I grinned at him. "You're supposed to tell me to enjoy my movie," I said, pulling my shoulder away.

"You're right," Jeremiah called after me as I walked away. He was so mad, his voice shook a little. "I hope you and the Bride of Frankenstein have a wonderful time."

It didn't take longer than a blink for all the rage I'd been carrying around to boil over.

Before I knew it, I had Jeremiah Jacobson pressed against the wall, his back slammed into the drinking fountain, and I was giving it to him. Punching my fists into his ugly little face, and it hurt my knuckles, it burned, but I didn't care, because the burning in my knuckles was better than the burning in my chest, so I kept going, *pound pound pound*. And Jeremiah was grabbing at me, trying to get a punch in, a kick in, but he gave up, he couldn't get me anywhere, I was too fast—*pound pound pound*—so he grabbed my hair, but that wasn't going to do it. I threw my head forward—*whack!*—and slammed him farther into the drinking fountain, and I must've set it off spurting when I slammed him, because I heard the *whish!* of it, the stream of water, and that was the first sound I remembered hearing, but after that it was like I was bombarded with sound. Jeremiah groaning, shouting at me. Screams from the crowd in the lobby. Popcorn popping. Noise from the theater as the door opened and movie trailers got louder. And a holler, a real holler, as I was wrenched off Jeremiah.

"Get *off* him, Trent, jeez!"

It was Noah Gorman. He tossed me back, and I fell to the ground. Noah propped up Jeremiah, slumping over the drinking fountain. He was wet, down his front, and I didn't know if it was water from the drinking fountain or if he'd peed himself.

"Oh, my God."

I'd been in a haze, I guess, with the rage and the punching and the fire and everything. But when I heard Fallon's voice, I snapped back. Fallon was standing, not ten feet away, holding a jumbo tub of popcorn, and she was staring at me, her mouth hanging open. But only for a second. Because as soon as her eyes caught mine, she dropped the popcorn. Right on the floor, kernels everywhere.

And she ran out the door.

I wanted to run after her, tell her to wait, but I couldn't. Just at that moment I was yanked off the ground and slammed into the drinking fountain myself. At first I thought it was Jeremiah, back to really take a go at me, or maybe Noah, even, deciding to beat the crap out of me for beating the crap out of his best friend. But it wasn't.

It was Mr. Jacobson. Jeremiah's dad.

"You do *not,*" he shouted—and he didn't need to shout, seriously, because he was only one inch from my face, but I guess he felt like shouting anyway—"mess with my son. Do you hear me?"

Of course I heard him. He was shouting into my face. I looked over my shoulder at the floor, where the popcorn kernels made a yellow rug.

"Do you hear me, you little creep?" Mr. Jacobson shouted at me. He shook me as he said it, too.

I blinked and focused back on him. And when I looked at his face, it was like I could see into his brain, hear the thoughts that he was thinking.

You killed one kid already, that's what he was thinking. *I'm not going to let you do it again.*

The fire twisted in my chest. It wrenched at me, pulled all my internal organs up into my throat, until they were choking me. I couldn't swallow.

I couldn't breathe.

I broke free of Mr. Jacobson's grip, because I needed air. I needed to go outside. My face was wet. I needed air. I needed to find Fallon.

"Don't think I won't tell your mother about this!" Mr. Jacobson shouted after me as I ran out the door.

I didn't care. I was running, pushing through the zombies, the witches, the ninja turtles, trying to find her. Fallon.

Trying to breathe.

FIFTEEN

I FOUND HER, AFTER A WHILE. AFTER I GAVE up searching the crowd on the street for an angry hippie girl and finally wised up and went directly across the street into the shop. She must've gone there immediately, because by the time I stepped inside, my mom was on the phone, and I could tell just by the look on her face that I was in for it.

"Where is she?" I asked Ray, who had quit handing out candy for the moment. He was standing next to my mom on her phone, while the trick-or-treaters huddled in the doorway, confused. "Where's Fallon?"

"She's in the stockroom," he said, pointing to the back. "She locked herself in. She won't come out." He squinted at me. "What happened, Trent?"

"I'll tell you in a minute," I muttered, and I left him and Mom wondering on the saleroom floor. I headed to the back.

Sure enough, the door to the stockroom was closed.

"Fallon?" I said softly. I tried the doorknob. Locked. "Fallon?"

"Leave me alone," she said. I'm pretty sure I heard a sniffle, too.

"Can I come in?" I asked.

"No."

"But—"

"Leave me alone," she said again. "Your mom said she'd call my parents. I just want to go home."

"Fallon, can I talk to you?" I was getting angry all over again, hearing Fallon so upset. That jerk Jeremiah, he didn't know how horrible he was. "What Jeremiah said," I told her through the door, "he's just a moron. Don't listen to him. Ever. He's a moron."

"I *know* he's a moron," Fallon said. Her voice was louder then. "You think I'm . . . ?" She trailed off. Another sniffle. "Just go away, okay?"

"No," I said. And I meant it. I wasn't going away. I wasn't leaving Fallon there, to be sad or angry or whatever she was. I was going to fix it.

"I'm staying right here," I said, slouching down on the floor so my back was to the door, leaning up against it. "I'm staying right here till you come out."

And I did. I stayed there, sitting on the floor. I could see straight through to the main room, where my mom was still on the phone, glancing back at me like she didn't know whether to feel sorry for me or furious. Ray went back to the trick-or-treaters.

"Fallon?" I said again through the door.

"I don't want to talk to you."

I thought about that. There was only one thing to say.

"Why can't you ever get hungry at the beach?" I asked her.

It was quiet for a long time. But then, through the door, I thought I heard a soft padding, and then the *swift!* of a lock, and before I had a chance to stand up, the door flew back, and I thumped down on my back, lying flat, staring up at Fallon straight above me.

She blinked at me, slowly.

"Because of all the sandwiches there," she told me.

She let me in the stockroom.

"I have this dream sometimes," Fallon said softly. We were both sitting on the floor of the stockroom, backs against Ray's bookshelves, and she wasn't looking at me. She was playing with the belt on her dress, running her fingers over the woven leather. It had been silent for so long, us two just sitting there, listening to the muffled sounds on the other side of the closed stockroom door, that I'd figured she wasn't in the mood to talk. And then, suddenly, she started talking about dreams. "A lot, actually," she went on. "Ever since . . ." She dug her fingernail deep into the folds of her belt.

"What kind of dream?" I asked.

She looked up at me quickly, like she was surprised I'd said anything. Maybe she'd forgotten I was there. Maybe she'd just been talking to herself. Her eyes darted back to her lap. "It's different every time," she said. "Well, it starts out different, anyway. There's usually someone chasing me, or breaking down the door to my bedroom, something like that. Once I had a dream that someone followed me into the locker room at the public pool."

"That sounds awful," I said. Because what else was I supposed to say?

Fallon still wouldn't look at me. "I can't scream," she said.

"What?"

"In the dreams. I always open my mouth to scream, and nothing comes out." She looked up at me then, and I swear, she looked afraid. Like, really, truly scared. I'd never seen her look like that before. She always looked so confident, like nothing could ever touch her. "I just keep trying and trying and . . ." She blinked, turned her gaze back to her belt. "I have that dream all the time, about the screaming. It's horrible."

I'd never had a dream like that, but I knew what bad dreams were.

"I'm sorry," I said. Even though it wasn't my fault.

She shook her head, like she was wiping away the memory. "It's just a dream, right?" she said. And she even gave me a smile, only I could tell it wasn't a real one. She went back to playing with her belt. "Only lately I've started to wonder if maybe it's real, if maybe I actually forgot how to scream."

"What do you mean? Of course you can scream."

"Yeah, but how am I supposed to know for sure? It's not like I ever go around screaming in real life. Not like a really, really loud one. Maybe I can't anymore. If I needed to do it, it would come out all scratchy and soft, like in the dream. And the worst part is that I won't even know for sure until something terrible happens, and then tough luck for me."

I sat forward from the bookshelf. "Scream right now," I told her. "As loud as you can."

She let out a snap of a laugh. "Shut up," she said, wiping at her nose.

"I dare you," I said. "Scream right now."

"You're crazy," she said. "I'm not gonna do that."

"Why not?" I was serious. Fallon was upset, and I was going to fix it. I put my hands on my knees, rocking slightly. "Come on, it'll be great."

"Your mom and Ray will run in here and think you're murdering me or something."

I hopped to my feet. "So I'll just tell them I'm teaching you how to scream. Hold on, I'll be right back."

"Trent." She reached out and grabbed my hand before I could open the door. "Don't, okay?" She lowered her eyes again.

"Oh." I didn't know what to do after that. I shuffled my feet for a little bit, and then finally went back to sitting. But I sat across the stockroom from Fallon instead of right next to her, like before.

I wasn't sure why.

"Sorry," I said after a while.

She scrunched her mouth to the side. "It's okay," she said.

There was a thin strip of her right eyebrow, if you looked at her face carefully, that was missing, right where the scar crossed her face. Just a thin strip. And her eyelashes on her right eye, just the half dozen or so that were in the path of the scar, they weren't dark brown like the rest of them. They were white.

"I'm sorry about what Jeremiah said," I told her. "I know you know he's a jerk. But still. He shouldn't have said that about you, that you were the Bride of Frankenstein, or whatever."

She looked up at me then. Those big, round, dark eyes. One. Two. Looking directly at me, on either side of her scar.

“Is that what you think I was upset about?” she asked.

“Um,” I said. “Yes?” What else would she be upset about?

She shook her head. “You’re kind of a jerk, too, you know that, Trent?”

“What?”

She rolled her eyes at me. “I don’t need you to protect me,” she said. “You think people like Jeremiah don’t say stuff like that to me all the time? Or worse? I can take care of myself. I do it every day.”

“I know,” I said. “I know you can. But—”

“And I don’t *want* you to try to protect me.” All of a sudden, something flashed over her. She definitely wasn’t smiling anymore. “I don’t want you to get into fights, Trent. Especially not for me.”

I crossed my arms over my chest and leaned back into Ray’s filing cabinets, even though the metal drawer pulls were poking my back. “You know, it wouldn’t hurt you to get angry every once in a while,” I told Fallon. “You don’t have to just sit back and listen to everyone being mean to you without doing anything.”

“I think you’re plenty angry enough for the both of us,” she said.

And that’s when the door opened, and my mom said Fallon’s parents were on their way to pick her up. So I didn’t get a chance to say anything to that at all.

You can always tell when Mom is angry, because her mouth squinches up so small, it practically disappears. The angrier she is, the less of a mouth she seems to have.

That night, after we’d gotten home from the shop, and Doug had gone to bed (probably listening at his door to me getting in trouble), and Aaron was still out with his girlfriend, and it was just Mom and me alone in the kitchen, her mouth was so small, you'd've needed a microscope to find it.

"I'm not sure I can do this anymore, Trent," she said at last, after staring me down for a while. She'd tricked me into sitting at the kitchen table, because I thought she was going to sit, too. But it turned out she was never planning on sitting. Instead she stood at the kitchen counter with her back against the edge of the sink, her arms folded in front of her. Which made her look like she was about two feet taller than me, and way scarier than normal, with her death-ray eyes and her tiny, pinprick mouth.

Nice power play, Mom. Seriously.

"Do what?" I asked.

"This," she replied. "I love you so much, but I don't know how to . . ." She ran a hand over her face. "I think it might be best for you to stay with your dad for a while."

"What?" I shrieked. "No! Mom!"

"Just for a little while, Trent. I can't . . . I don't know how to help you anymore. A boy needs his father. Maybe it would be good for you. We've talked about it before, but now . . ."

It wasn't fire, what I felt inside then. It was cold. Icicles. The slushy black snow on the bottom of tires.

"You don't want me anymore?" My voice was a whisper.

"Oh, Trent." Both hands on her face now. She looked wrecked. What kind of horrible kid wrecks his own mother? "Of course I want you here." She sounded like she meant it. "Of *course* I do. But you're not happy here."

How could she possibly think I'd be happier at my dad's than I was here?

"I hate him," I told her.

She pulled her hands down from her face. Rested them on the edge of the sink behind her.

"Since when do you get into fistfights, Trent?"

The slush in my chest began to melt. Just like that. Turned back into fire.

"Jeremiah called Fallon 'Bride of Frankenstein'!" I told her. Maybe I was shouting.

"You're going to go around punching everyone who says something mean?" she asked me. It was not, obviously, a real question that I was supposed to answer.

"But . . ." I didn't say anything after that. There was nothing to say.

Mom looked at me for a long time, searching my face for answers. Finally she sighed a huge sigh and sat down in the chair next to me. She tugged at the legs of my chair until I was facing her, my knees pressed up against hers, and she smoothed back the hair on my forehead, like she did sometimes when I was sick. Only I didn't exactly feel sick.

"Why did you beat up Jeremiah?" she asked. "I want the real reason." Her face was calm. No squinched-up mouth at all.

So I thought about it. I really did.

"He hurt someone," I said finally. Softly. It was the only thing I could think to say that might make any sort of sense to my mom. "He hurt Fallon. And people who hurt someone deserve to get hurt themselves."

"Trent," my mom said softly. "You are not in charge of righting the world's wrongs." I looked up at her. "You are not in charge of punching Jeremiah Jacobson into being a nice person. That is not your job, do you understand me?"

I nodded at her, because I knew I was supposed to nod right then. But I wasn't sure she was right about that. If someone hurt my friend, why shouldn't I try to fix it?

"Your job," my mom went on, "your only job right now, is being in charge of yourself and your life and taking care of *you* the best you can. That includes"—she counted off on her fingers—"not failing school." She glared those death-ray eyes at me. "And not beating people up. And if something important is going on with you, you need to tell me about it. Can you do that?"

"Can *you* do that?" I asked.

All right. It wasn't the smartest thing to say, probably. But I guess the fire that was rolling around inside me just decided to come shooting out in words.

Mom blinked at me. "*Excuse* me?" she said.

Well.

Once I started, I wasn't about to stop, no matter how much trouble I knew I was digging myself into.

"When were you planning to tell me about Ray?" I asked her.

Mom's mouth wasn't a pinprick then. It was a wide-open O. I'd caught her off guard, that was for sure. I could tell she didn't know what to say.

"You are not allowed to talk to me like that, young man." That's what she finally decided to say. Which is when I knew I'd gotten her good, because that was avoiding the question if I ever heard it.

"Even when I'm right?" I said.

"Go to your room." Her words were thin, angry.

"Love to," I replied. And I marched off, just as angry.

I stood in the hall while she called my dad. Even though I knew I shouldn't have. I stood in the hall and listened. I could only hear Mom's side of the conversation, but I didn't really need to hear the rest.

"This is something we talked about, Tom," Mom said into the phone. "He needs you. I think he really needs you."

"But—"

"I understand that, but—"

"Don't you put this all on Kari. There are two of you in that house, and I know damn well that if you wanted to do something—"

"You had three sons first, Tom."

That last sentence, when Mom said it, she wasn't arguing anymore.

She'd already given up.

I was just slinking back to my room, silently, so Mom wouldn't hear, when I noticed Doug, peeking out from his own room, watching me. He'd been listening too.

He looked like he felt really sorry for me.

"Shut up," I hissed at him. And I closed myself inside my room.

It shouldn't have felt so terrible, knowing that my father didn't want me, especially since I didn't want him either.

But it did. It did feel terrible.

I curled up on my bed, still in my jeans and T-shirt. I didn't even have the strength to pull the covers over me. I just lay there, curled up in a tight little ball, trying to squeeze the fire out.

Sometimes you only get one chance. That's what Dad had told me.

But what were you supposed to do when that chance had come and gone?

SIXTEEN

THE NEXT DAY I WAS IN A ROTTEN MOOD, AND I guess you can probably figure out why.

As soon as I got to P.E., I didn't even bother to give Mr. Gorman an excuse for why I couldn't participate (it was volleyball, like I was so sad to miss *that*). I just headed straight up to the bleachers. I'd brought a book with me, one I'd snagged from Aaron's room a couple of days before. It was a Mike Lupica book he'd read when he was my age, and so far it was pretty good. Actually, I was so into the book that it took me a while to realize I wasn't alone on the bleachers.

Noah Gorman was there too. Standing just in front of me, eyeing me carefully.

"What are you doing here?" I asked him, lowering my book. "I don't want any trouble."

But Noah didn't punch me or spit on me or yell at me or any of the other things I thought he might do. Instead, he sat down on the bleachers. One level below me. "I don't want any trouble, either," he said.

Whatever.

I guess I was getting pretty into the book again. The next time I looked up, Noah was staring at me—and you could tell he'd been doing it for a while, because as soon as I noticed him, he got all embarrassed and spun around in his seat super quick.

"What?" I asked him.

"Nothing," he said. He pretended he'd been watching the volleyball game, which is definitely not what he'd been doing, since he'd been facing a totally different direction. The squeak of sneakers and shouting and balls bouncing echoed off the walls. I hadn't even noticed until right then.

I went back to reading.

"Is that a book about baseball?"

That's what Noah Gorman asked me.

I looked up at him. He was turned around again, staring at the cover of my book.

"Um," I said. There was a picture of a kid pitching a baseball on the front cover, so the answer to Noah's question seemed pretty obvious. "Yeah."

I went back to reading.

But I was only at it a few minutes when Noah interrupted me again.

"Why are you reading a book about baseball?" he asked me.

I set the book down in my lap. Squinted at him with one eye.

"Because I like baseball," I told him. He should've been able to guess that, really, since we used to be friends and everything.

"Oh," he said. I watched him awhile, to see if he'd say anything else. But he didn't, so I lifted the book to my face again.

"I figured you didn't anymore, since you didn't join intramurals."

That's what Noah said to me as soon as I had gone back to reading. Lucky for me, it wasn't a question, so I didn't have to say anything back.

I turned a page in my book, then realized I hadn't finished the one before it. I thought about turning back to it, but Noah was still staring at me, so I thought that would be weird. But pretending to read a book when someone was staring at you turned out to be pretty weird, too. I was almost glad when Noah said something else, because it saved me from having to pretend to read anymore.

"I hate baseball," he said.

I huffed as I looked up from my book, like I was super annoyed he'd interrupted my really important reading. But I asked him, "So why are *you* on the team then?" Because I guess I was curious or whatever. I'd always thought Noah hated baseball, but then he'd gone and joined the stupid team.

"My uncle's the coach," Noah told me. "I don't really have a choice, do I?"

I wasn't sure if that was true or not, but Noah seemed to think it was true, so maybe it was.

I flipped back to the previous page in my book, so I could finish reading from where I'd left off.

"You already read that page," Noah told me.

I set my book back down in my lap.

"What are you, the reading police?" I asked.

Noah blinked at me, like he was thinking about something important. "You shouldn't have beaten up Jeremiah," he said.

I went back to reading. He interrupted my book for *that*? "Jeremiah's a jerk," I muttered as I read. I had to read the same line over three times, though, because thinking about how big a jerk someone was at the same time you were reading turned out to be sort of hard to do.

"Yeah," Noah agreed. "But you still shouldn't have beaten him up."

He didn't say anything to me after that, for the whole rest of P.E. I looked up once, when I was turning a page, and he'd stopped staring at me. Turned all the way around to watch volleyball.

During lunch, I noticed that Noah wasn't sitting at the table with Jeremiah. He was all by himself at a table near the lunch line.

"What are you looking at?" Fallon asked me.

I shook my head. "Nothing," I said. And I took another bite of my beans.

Fallon wasn't particularly chatty at lunch. Which was weird, because she was always chatty. Instead of chatting, she poked at her burrito with her spork (it wasn't a particularly delicious-looking burrito).

"Are you mad at me?" I asked her finally.

She didn't look up from her burrito. "No," she said. *Poke. Poke.* "Why would I be mad at you?"

"I don't know," I said, because I didn't. "But you're sort of acting like you're mad."

"Well, I'm not," she said. *Poke. Poke.*

"Oh," I said. "Okay."

She still didn't talk to me.

"What movie do you want to watch today?" I asked. Movies always got Fallon talking.

Fallon set her spork down on her tray. "I can't do Movie Club anymore," she said. Only she wasn't exactly looking at me. "My parents are making me do drama instead. I have to be in the play. We have rehearsals every day after school. *The Wizard of Oz.* Isn't that lame?"

I squinted at her. Studied her dark brown eyes, darting all over the cafeteria, at everything but me.

She was lying.

"Yeah," I said softly. But *why* was she lying? "That's pretty lame. It sucks, actually."

"Yeah," she said. "Sorry."

Fallon went back to poking at her burrito, and I went back to eating mine, but I wasn't hungry. I wanted to ask her about her dream, about the screaming. I wanted her to talk to me the way she had in the stockroom. But somehow I knew she wouldn't talk about that.

After five minutes or so of not really talking, I pulled my Book of Thoughts out of my backpack.

"Hey, I can draw a picture for you, if you want," I told her. "Anything you want, even a scar picture."

Poke. Poke.

Not looking at me.

I tried again. "I thought maybe I could draw one of that totally tragic typewriter accident you were in when you were a kid. Remember that?"

Fallon pushed back her tray and stood up. Just like that.

"I have to go," she said.

Still not looking at me.

"What's going on?" I asked her.

She picked up her tray and climbed out from behind the bench. "See you later, Trent."

And just like that, she was gone.

During social studies, when Ms. Emerson asked me why I hadn't turned in my homework, I told her, "Bite me."

The classroom went good and silent, let me tell you.

"Excuse me?" she said.

I looked up from my oven station, toward the clock on the wall. The final bell was going to ring in forty-two minutes, and then what was I supposed to do with myself? Not go to dinner with the dad who didn't want me, that was for sure.

"I said, 'Bite me,'" I told her. "Are you hard of hearing or something?"

A couple of kids started snorting, but they hushed up quick when Ms. Emerson stood up from her stool.

She leaned forward across her stovetop, arms right on the coils, and looked at me.

Everyone in the classroom sucked in one deep breath.

Finally, after a moment that threatened to stretch on forever, Ms. Emerson smacked her lips together, like she'd made up her mind, and, still looking at me carefully, said, "You know, Trent, sometimes

I do have trouble with my hearing. Thank you for your considerate question." Then she stood up to her full height, clapped her hands together, and said, "Now, class, who can remind us where we left off yesterday with our maps?"

And that was all there was of that.

After school I really wanted to talk to Fallon. Find out why she'd been acting so weird, why she'd been lying about joining Drama Club. But I didn't know where she was. She might've gone straight home, but if I went there and she didn't want me around, her cop of a dad would probably snap my head off.

And then I thought about where she'd gone when she was upset before.

I slammed shut my locker, took a deep breath, and walked back down the hall the same way I'd just come.

"And to what do I owe this pleasure?" Ms. Emerson said as I opened the door to her room. She was sitting at her stovetop desk, glaring at me. She made the word *pleasure* sound like a nasty word.

"Uh." I shuffled my feet. "Is Fallon here?" I darted my eyes around the room, like I thought she might be hiding somewhere. "Fallon Little."

"No," Ms. Emerson told me. She went back to grading papers or whatever it was she was doing.

"Oh," I said. "I thought she might be here."

"You are free to check all the ovens," she told me without looking up from her desk.

I figured that meant Fallon really wasn't there.

I meant to close the door and leave then. I really did. But for some reason I just stood in the doorway for a second, like a moron, gripping the doorknob tight in my hand. I don't know why. Maybe I was avoiding going outside in the cold. Maybe I was just thinking.

"Trent?" Ms. Emerson asked, finally looking up from her papers. She asked it not in the way you would say someone's name if you wanted to ask them a question, but rather in the way you would say it if you wanted to know why the heck they were standing in your doorway, gripping the doorknob, staring at the wall.

"Why wouldn't you give me detention today?" I asked her.

"Why did you want it?" she replied.

Well.

"Fallon comes in here sometimes, right?" I asked her, instead of answering her stupid question that didn't have an answer anyway.

"She does," Ms. Emerson confirmed. "She is, for one thing, a student of mine."

"Well, when you see her," I said, my hand still tight around the doorknob, "can you tell her I want to talk to her? She has my phone number."

"I am perfectly capable of doing that," Ms. Emerson said. "Although perhaps such information would be more suitable coming from you."

There was something peculiar about the way wrinkled old crones talked. Like they were trying to give you an English lesson with every sentence. Anyway, I understood her fine, it just took me a second.

"I think Fallon's mad at me," I told her. I don't know why I told her that. It was none of her business. "I mean, whatever. Thanks, I guess." That time I started closing the door for real. "Bye."

"Trent?"

That time she said my name like there was a question after it. Or more of a statement, maybe.

I opened the door a little wider.

"I find that when people are angry, there's usually not much to do to alter their emotions. But there are often things you can do to cool them down a bit."

I raised an eyebrow. Cooling down Fallon's anger. Maybe that would be useful. "Like what?" I asked.

"Well." She thought for a second. "My plants could use watering."

The other eyebrow went up. "How is watering your plants going to make Fallon like me again?" I asked.

"Oh, I meant me," Ms. Emerson said. "And it won't sway me completely in your favor, of course. But, as I said, it might help me dislike you slightly less."

Well.

"Watering can's over there," she told me, pointing. Then she gestured toward the sink. "The water should be tepid."

I watered Ms. Emerson's stupid plants. I don't know why. Who cared if the wrinkled old crone liked me or not? But I guess I didn't really have anything better to do. So anyway, I watered them. The spider plant on her stovetop desk, and the fern by the door, and all the millions of pots of flowering green things along the windowsill.

Ms. Emerson had a *lot* of plants.

"Trent?" Ms. Emerson said again as I was leaving the room. She had a habit of that. She didn't say one word to me the whole time I was in the room, but as soon as I was about to leave, suddenly she got chatty.

I swiveled around. "Yeah?"

"The plants will be thirsty again tomorrow," she said. And with that, she shooed me out the door.

I could've gone home after the plant watering, probably. I bet no one would've argued too hard if I'd just not gotten in the car to go to the St. Albans Diner. No one wanted me there anyway. But I didn't want to be at home.

So I wandered. Down Maple Hill as fast as I could. Trailing circles through the park, past the screaming little kids in their puffy coats.

Down to the lake.

I hadn't been to that side of Cedar Lake since that day last February. The Jared Richards day. As I pulled my bike up into the reedy grass, where it started to get muddy at the edge of the bank, I noticed that it smelled different. Warmer. Muddier. Thicker. It sounded different too. Birds still chirping, the ones who hadn't left yet for the winter. Water lapping, just a bit. Wind blowing.

I found a log, at the edge of the water, and I sat.

November was when it started to get cold in Cedar Haven. It was coldest at the lake.

I sat there a long time, in the bitter wind, and I stared at the lake, my Book of Thoughts open on my lap in front of me. But it turned out I didn't have too many thoughts.

Instead of thinking, I tossed rocks into the water. One. *Plop.* Two. *Plop.* Ten. *Plop.* Fifty. *Plop.* After a while, the tossing turned to skipping. Rocks across the surface—*shick shick shick.* I aimed for more skips, then more and more. I got up to five, but couldn't get any higher.

I guess what I thought about, actually, was Fallon. I thought about how scared she'd looked, the night before in the stockroom, telling me about her dream. And I wondered what that would feel like, to not know if you had a scream in you or not.

I knew I had plenty of screams in me.

I'd never had a dream like Fallon's, but I knew what nightmares were. For a while back in February, and all the way into March, I'd had the same one over and over. I was out on Cedar Lake, right near this spot, and it was completely frozen, just like the day Jared died, only in the dream there was no one there but me. I was walking along the ice in my bare feet, wondering how I'd gotten onto the lake in the first place, and where I could get some shoes or socks at least, when I started to hear this pounding noise, and I couldn't figure out where it was coming from until I started to feel the ice thumping underneath me, and then I looked down. And there was Jared, underneath the ice, trapped, pounding to get my attention, and I knelt down on the cold, cold ice, and I tried to break through the ice with my fingernails, but it was too thick, I couldn't do anything, and we were pounding, both of us together, trying to break the ice, but neither of us was doing anything, and I couldn't get him out in time.

I could never get him out.

When I ran out of smooth round rocks to skip, I spied my Book of Thoughts sitting on that log by the water. And I don't know why, but I picked it up, and I threw it, as hard as I could.

It hardly even made a splash.

I stood at the edge of the lake for a long time, imagining I could see my Book of Thoughts sinking, sinking, down to the bottom of the lake.

When my fingers were numb and my brain was empty, I headed home.

SEVENTEEN

WHEN I WALKED INTO P.E. THE NEXT DAY, Thursday, and Mr. Gorman was standing at the door with his clipboard, I didn't even wait for him to ask me his stupid question—*Am I going to like the kid I meet today?* I just told him, "Nope." And made my way to the bleachers.

Noah ended up there again, too. I bet his uncle didn't like him too much either.

I didn't talk to him, because we weren't exactly friends anymore, but when he started looking really bored in the middle of the volleyball game, I lifted my book up so he could read the back cover.

Fallon was acting weird again at lunch.

She spent most of the period doing her homework. Instead of talking to me. She worked on pre-algebra, the whole lunch period, while she ate her sandwich.

Was I really more terrible than pre-algebra?

When I poked her in the side enough, she looked up and said "What?" and I told her I was bored and wanted to talk to her. Fallon sighed huge like I was seriously upsetting her homework time.

"What do you want to talk about?" she asked me.

I shrugged.

So eventually Fallon started going on and on about this girl Keisha in her art class, how she was thinking about hanging out with her, but she wasn't sure, because what if Keisha was a snob, and did I think Keisha was a snob? She didn't give me a chance to answer.

Anyway, I didn't really know Keisha.

It sort of seemed like, to someone who didn't know any better, that Fallon was still mad at me. Only, two things I couldn't figure out.

The first thing was, when I asked her if she was mad at me, she said, "No." And "Shut up." And then she told me to stop asking her if she was mad at me, because she wasn't at all, but all my asking was *making* her mad at me, and if she was mad at me, she'd tell me, wouldn't she? Only it didn't really seem like she would.

And the second thing was, if you were mad at a person, wouldn't you stop having lunch with them altogether? I would think you would. So either Fallon *wasn't* actually mad at me, and maybe I was just going crazy or something, or she *was* mad at me, and she figured having lunch with someone she was mad at was better than having lunch by herself.

I was starting to think it was probably the second one, which kind of sucked, if you asked me.

Two minutes before the bell rang, I asked her, "What's the real reason you won't watch movies with me anymore?"

She just rolled her eyes at me. "I *told* you," she said. "My parents are making me be in the school play. The director cast me as a tree. A *tree,* can you believe that?" Fallon took another bite of her sandwich while I watched her, trying to figure out what the truth was. "Just let it go, okay?" she told me. "Stop acting so weird."

I definitely wasn't the one who was acting weird.

Fallon *was* in the play. I snuck into the auditorium after the final bell rang that afternoon. Slipped through the door and stood in the back. No one noticed.

Fallon was there all right. But she wasn't on stage. She was sitting in the corner of the room, all by herself, tossing a handball at a wall. She wasn't talking to anyone. She wasn't laughing. She wasn't telling jokes or making up stories or quoting movie lines or doing any of the things I thought of when I thought of Fallon Little. She looked pretty miserable, actually.

I guess she'd been telling the truth, about her parents making her be in the play. About being a tree and everything. Only, it didn't make any sense to me why her parents would do that. I know I hadn't talked to them a whole lot, but they seemed like people who cared about what their daughter wanted.

And she very clearly didn't want to be a tree.

I don't know why, but after I went to the auditorium, I went to Ms. Emerson's room to water her plants. It's not like I really cared if the wrinkled old crone hated me or anything. And it didn't seem to be working too much anyway. She hardly looked up from her papers the entire time I was there, watering all four billion of her plants.

Until, finally, she did.

"What do you do, Trent," she asked me, with her wrinkled-old-crone voice, "after you leave school every day?"

I jumped. I couldn't help it. I'd almost forgotten she was there.

"I don't know," I said. Ms. Emerson got up from her stovetop desk and walked over to hand me a roll of paper towels, to mop up the water from the watering can I didn't realize I'd spilled. I took them. "Just stuff."

Ms. Emerson watched me mop up my puddle for a moment, and then she said, "I thought I saw you yesterday. On your bike, by the lake."

I wadded up a new paper towel and inched it into a corner by the window. "I ride my bike a lot," I said.

"It seems a little cold for bike riding," Ms. Emerson replied. "Seems like it might make more sense to do something at home."

"I have a good jacket," I told her. And I walked over to the trash can to throw away the wet paper towels. Ms. Emerson was still staring at me, though, so I felt like I had to say something else. "Anyway, sometimes it's nice not to go home right away." That's what I said. Then I got back to watering. There were still a lot of plants to go.

Ms. Emerson didn't say anything after that, the whole rest of the time I was there, until I was at the door ready to leave. That's when she said, "Trent?" I turned around, hand still on the doorknob. "The plants will be thirsty again tomorrow."

Talk about a wrinkled old crone.

When I came in to homeroom the very next morning, I noticed that Ms. Emerson had acquired about a thousand more plants. Seriously, there was hardly room for all of them on the shelves along the windowsills.

She stopped by my oven station as she was handing out flyers for class elections.

"I hope you don't mind, Trent," she said quietly, so no one else could hear. "But I'm afraid I brought in several more plants last night. I know it will require much more effort on your part to keep them hydrated, but I simply couldn't help myself. They needed a home. Do you think you can stay a little longer than normal after school?"

"That's okay," I told her. "Sure."

"I appreciate it," she said.

Ms. Emerson was right. It did take a lot longer to water all the new plants. I didn't finish till almost five o'clock.

"The plants will be thirsty again on Monday," she told me as I left.

Ms. Emerson was crazy for sure. But I guess I was starting not to mind so much.

EIGHTEEN

I'D BEEN ABSOLUTELY DREADING SATURDAY all week. The community basketball program. Spending my entire day helping some moron first-grader with a turtle-shaped lunch box learn to dribble, just so I didn't fail sixth grade. I could think of about four hundred things I'd rather be doing.

But as soon as I got to the Cedar Haven Community Center Saturday morning, I discovered that I hadn't been dreading the day nearly enough.

"I have exactly the basketball buddy for you," the lady in charge—Julie—told me. "One of the older elementary kids. Just signed up for the program."

It was not a first-grader with a turtle-shaped lunch box.

"This is Annie," Julie said, all smiles, bringing me over. "Annie, meet Trent. He's going to be your basketball buddy all month."

I seriously hated this town.

Annie went from wary smile to angry glare in one-point-two milliseconds. I tried to keep my face emotion-free, but honestly I felt sick inside. Burning fireball of rage mixed with terror mixed with icy panic. It was like an emotion-slushie in there.

The whole time Julie explained the drills she wanted us to do that afternoon, and *how much fun we were going to have* and *how we were going to be best buddies, just you wait and see,* I pretended to look at the Community Center floor. The floor was not very interesting, but it was a whole lot better to look at than Annie, who was busy glaring at the side of my head. Even without looking I could tell that's what she was doing, because all the warmed-up glary air she forced at me with her eyes was making my cheek burn.

"So there you go," Julie said, tossing us each a basketball. "Your hoop's on the far end, over there." She pointed. "Ask me if you have any questions, and I'll come check on you guys in a few."

"I have a question," Annie said, before Julie could make a break for it. "Do you have anyone else? Another buddy you can sign me up with?"

Julie paused for a moment. You could tell she'd never been asked that question before.

"I'm sorry," she said, glancing between the two of us. "All the buddies have already been paired up. But I know you two will get along like gangbusters. Don't you think so, Trent?"

"Um," I said.

"That's the spirit!" Julie squeezed my shoulder. "Don't forget to have fun, you two!"

I was pretty sure we were going to forget to have fun.

Annie and I were silent the whole way to the basketball hoop. I didn't know what Annie was thinking about—probably how to get out of this basketball program she'd signed up for. But *I* was thinking about what would be worse, spending every Saturday for the next month with Jared Richards's little sister, or repeating sixth grade.

It was a close call.

"Um," I said, when we got to the basketball hoop on the far end of the floor. Because *one* of us had to say something at some point. "So do you want to go first?" I asked her. "Julie said you're supposed to demonstrate your rebound shot. Or I could do it first, as an example, if you want."

"I don't like you."

That's what Annie said to me.

My head shot up. "Oh." Because what exactly are you supposed to say about a thing like that? "Look, I'm sorry about the soup thing the other week. I . . . I shouldn't have splashed soup at you. Or whatever." But we both knew that wasn't really what I was apologizing for.

Annie was staring at me. Just staring at me, like I was a painting on a wall. She had her basketball gripped tight in both hands. "I know you're the one who hit the hockey puck," she said.

I looked down at the basketball in my hands. Suddenly I felt like an idiot for holding a basketball while I was having this conversation. It didn't seem like the kind of conversation you should hold a basketball during. But what was I supposed to do—toss it at the wall? That would be even more awful.

"I'm sorry about that too," I told Annie. Which was the truth.

"Did you do it on purpose?" she asked me. Still staring.

"No!" My hands were starting to get sweaty on the ball. "Of course not. It was an accident."

She thought about that. "I hate you," she said at last.

I cleared my throat. "I think I'd hate me too, if I were you." That's what I told her. And it was still the truth.

I could tell from the look on her face that Annie wasn't expecting me to say that. "Is that supposed to make me hate you less?" she asked me.

I shrugged. "Nope. It's just the truth."

"Well. It doesn't matter. I still hate you."

"Join the club." I don't know why, but I started dribbling my basketball then. It still felt weird, but at least it was something to *do*. "There's a whole ton of people who hate me. You could be the president."

"Yeah?" Annie asked. She seemed honestly interested. I started dribbling down the court, and she followed me, doing her best dribble. "Like who?"

"Oh . . ." I reached the edge of the court, and then did a pivot-turn to head back the other way. I passed Annie and dribbled around her. "Like, you, my dad, my stepmom, most of my teachers, my best friend, my brothers. My mom, at the moment. Probably my mom's new boyfriend. Maybe a dog or two."

Annie was at the edge of the court, trying to turn. She lost control of the ball, though, and it rolled off toward the wall. She went to fetch it. When she retrieved it, she ran back until she was standing right beside me, and we took up dribbling again.

"That's a lot of people who hate you," she said after a minute.

"Yep," I said. "I told you."

"But I could be president?"

"Definitely. You could start charging anyone who wanted to join, and then you'd make a whole lot of money." I stopped dribbling and watched her for a second. "You're getting a bad angle on the ball when you dribble," I told her. "And don't take such big steps when you walk." I showed her. "Yeah, that's better."

It was a weird thing, but talking to the person who hated me more than anyone else in the world turned out to be not so terrible. Because I knew that no matter what I did, there was no way she could hate me more than she already did. So I could just be myself.

And in the meantime, maybe I'd teach her a thing or two about basketball.

"Hold on," I said, when she started to get the hang of dribbling and walking. "You can't do that—that's traveling."

"What's traveling?" she asked me.

We worked on dribbling until Julie came over and told us that that wasn't the drill we were supposed to be doing. So then we shot hoops for a while. Annie was pretty good at that, actually. She got three in a row right away. We started trading off, one shot after another, so I could get some hoops in, too.

I was just lining up a shot when Annie told me, "Doug doesn't hate you."

I wasn't expecting her to say anything, so when I threw the ball, it went off at a bad angle. "What?" I said, rushing to retrieve the ball before it bounced into the next court over.

Annie waited until I was back on our court. "Doug doesn't hate you," she said again. "You said before that your brothers hate you. But Doug doesn't. He likes you a lot."

That was news to me. All I'd done lately was refuse to help Doug with his pranks. If I were him, I'd hate me for sure. "Why would he like me?" I asked her.

Annie threw the ball. Didn't score, but it was close, just a little low. "Beats me," she said as I ran to grab the ball. "Sometimes I think he's kind of dumb."

I laughed at that.

"Try again," I told her, passing her the ball. "You get a do-over, since you were talking."

That time, the ball *swished* through the hoop.

At the end of the day, Julie said Annie and I were a natural team. She grinned at us. "See you both next Saturday?"

I glanced sideways at Annie, who was glancing sideways at me. "Sure," I said, just as Annie said, "Yeah, okay."

I was kicking up the kickstand on my bike outside the Community Center when I sensed somebody behind me. I turned around.

It was Annie.

"I don't need an older brother," she told me. "I had one already and—" She stopped. Blinked at me. For a second I thought she was going to say, "and you killed him," which I think might've gut-punched me so hard, I'd've fallen over. But she didn't. *Blink, blink.* "He's gone now."

"Well, good," I said. I wasn't feeling particularly great about myself, but at least I wasn't feeling gut-punched, either. Besides, I sort of liked this Annie girl. She wasn't some weepy sad-sack little priss like I thought she'd be. I could kind of tell why Doug liked hanging out with her. "I mean, not about him being gone. But . . . Anyway, I don't need another little sister. I have one of those already, and a little brother, too. And he stinks."

Annie thought about that. "Doug does stink," she agreed.

I threw my leg over my bike and placed my feet on the pedals. "See you next week?" I asked.

She nodded. "I still hate you," she told me.

I nodded back. "See you then," I said.

It wasn't until I was all the way home that I realized my arms hadn't gone clammy once the whole day.

NINETEEN

MOM TOLD ME I COULD WORK AT THE STORE on Sunday again, to make a little money. I wasn't sure I wanted to, what with her being so mad at me, but really, what else was I going to do? Doug was hanging out with Annie and Rebecca. Aaron was hanging out with his girlfriend. (He said he wasn't, but it was a lie, obviously. Doug stole his phone and saw that Aaron had called Clarisse the night before. Then Doug squealed like a girl and ran all over the house until Aaron socked him and made him give him the phone back.)

So all day Sunday, I was at Kitch'N'Thingz.

At first, I mainly ignored Ray. I made Mom hand him his doughnut, and when he waved at me and told me good morning, I just sort of grunted. But it wasn't like it was a big store. I knew I was going to have to talk to him eventually.

He came over when I was rearranging the baking shelf. November was a big month for the store, usually, because people were getting ready for Thanksgiving, and that meant lots of kitchen gadgets. Basters, fat separators, roasting pans and roasting racks, oven thermometers, fancy dishes and napkins with orange leaves all over them, and all sorts of other boring stuff I couldn't have given two hoots about. For the store it meant lots of money, but for me it mostly meant rearranging and restocking.

"Hey," Ray told me. I was moving the fancy pie plates to the front of the shelf, like Mom had told me to. You had to be careful with those because they were really fragile.

I thought about icing Ray out, but I didn't.

"Hey," I said back.

He stood there for a while, watching me rearrange pie plates, sort of leaning against the shelf. Which seemed dangerous to me, because there was a lot of breakable stuff right where he was leaning, but it was his store, so I didn't mention it.

"I think you know I like your mom, right, Trent?" he said after a minute.

I darted my eyes quick across the store. Mom was at the register, going over yesterday's numbers.

"I should hope so," I said, picking up a pie plate super carefully and swapping it for a slightly uglier one. "Otherwise it would be weird that you were kissing her."

I thought Ray was going to get mad at me for that one, or sigh a big grown-up sigh at least, but he didn't. He snorted.

"A fair point," he said.

“Look, I don’t need, like, a man-to-man talk,” I told Ray, still rearranging. Jeez, there were a lot of pie plates. “I’m twelve—I know about dating and stuff. You like my mom, my mom likes you, fine. We don’t need to *talk* about it.”

Ray rubbed the top of his bald head, thinking. “Okay,” he said slowly. “Well, that’s good, I guess.” He rubbed some more. “Sometimes I forget how old you are, Trent. I’ve known you since you were a toddler.”

I wondered if Ray had liked my mom even back then, even when she and my dad were still technically married, even if they probably shouldn’t have been.

“Do Aaron and Doug know?” I asked. I hadn’t told them yet—who wanted to talk about their mom’s love life?—but I figured they should probably find out sometime.

“Aaron might be beginning to figure it out,” Ray said. “I don’t think Doug knows.” I nodded at that. If no one told Doug, he probably wouldn’t realize it until Ray moved into our house. “Your mom wants to tell them soon, I think. It’s—” He cleared his throat. “Things are getting pretty serious, between your mom and me.”

“Between your mom and *I*,” I corrected him.

“Actually I think it’s *me*,” Ray said.

“Really?”

“We can look it up.” Ray went back to rubbing his head. “The point is, Trent, you’re probably going to see a lot more of me in the future. At your house—some nights for dinner, probably. Maybe you boys might even come over to my house sometimes . . .” He took a deep breath, and I stopped stacking to look at him. He seemed nervous. I'd never seen Ray nervous before. "Is that okay with you, Trent?"

"Sure," I said. "Whatever."

"I hope so," he told me. "Because, Trent?" I waited. "I like your mom, a lot. But part of the reason I like her so much is that she has such great kids. It means a lot to me that you'd be okay with me dating her."

I squinched my mouth to the side, debating over two pie plates, which one should be at the front of the shelf. Part of me really wanted to tell Ray where to stuff it. It seemed like the thing to do in this situation. But the other part of me . . . Well, I kind of actually *liked* Ray.

"It's okay with me," I said. "For now. I mean, I get to change my mind if I want."

"Fair enough," Ray told me. And he left me to my pie plates. When he got back to Mom at the register, I noticed that she bumped his shoulder a bit, smiling, like she was really happy.

I liked seeing Mom really happy.

"Trent!" Ray called over to me a minute or so later. I jerked my head up. He had his phone out, looking at something.

"Yeah?"

"It's *between you and me.* I looked it up." He held up his phone, to prove it. "I was right."

"Well, aren't you special?" I called back, and he just laughed.

Mom could tell I was getting bored late that afternoon, I think, because she assigned me the job of "brightening the store window," which basically meant arranging things so they looked pretty. I don't know why she ever asked me to do that, because she always changed whatever I did the next morning when I wasn't there, but I guess it was better than stacking gravy boats.

So anyway, I was on my knees in the store window, arranging the turkey stuffed animal that Mom had bought for the display case last Thanksgiving, only I'd decided to make it even better than last year and give it basters for butt feathers (which I knew Mom was going to hate, but I was doing it anyway). And that's when I happened to look up at exactly the right moment to see Fallon's parents standing outside the movie theater across the street, reading the movie times.

I jumped down from the window display, knocking over an entire pile of basters.

"Be right back!" I called to Mom. I was out the door before she had a chance to say anything about it. I didn't even think to grab my coat.

"Um, Mr. and Mrs. Little?" I said when I reached them. I was sort of out of breath, from the running, and I think they were surprised to see a kid they hardly knew darting across the street and then stopping right in front of them to talk. They'd probably just thought they were going to see a movie.

Fallon wasn't with them, which I thought was a good thing, given what I wanted to talk about.

Mr. Little looked down at me, his chin tucked into his thick blue scarf. Right this second he was looking more than a little intimidating.

"Yes?" he said.

"I'm, um, Trent," I told him. "Fallon's friend. We met before?" I gestured vaguely across the street to Mom's store, like that might help them place me.

Mr. Little frowned at me. "I know who you are, Trent," he said.

"Aren't you cold?" Mrs. Little asked me.

"I'm fine," I said. "I just saw you guys from the window, and I wanted to talk to you really quick about—"

"We were about to go in," Mr. Little told me, nodding toward the theater.

"It'll only take a second," I said. "I promise."

He raised his eyebrows at me, but didn't say anything. Mrs. Little looked like she was just worried about my body temperature.

"Um," I said slowly. Because now that they were actually listening to me, I wasn't sure exactly what I'd wanted to say. "Um," I said again. "I know this is none of my business probably, but you shouldn't make Fallon be in the school play. She really hates being a tree."

"Look," Mr. Little said. I could tell he was getting impatient. "I know you must think it's unfair, our not wanting Fallon to spend time with you anymore."

"Wait," I said. "What?"

I wasn't cold anymore. I wasn't cold at all.

"Trent, you have to understand," Mrs. Little said, leaning down a bit to talk to me, even though I was just as tall as she was. "We're sure you're a good kid. But Fallon is our only daughter. And given her past trauma . . . we just don't think that it's healthy for her, being so close to someone with a history of violent outbursts."

I blinked at her. "What are you talking about?" I blinked at

Fallon's dad, too. "You told Fallon she's not allowed to hang out with me?"

Now they were both frowning. "Oh," Mrs. Little said softly. "Oh dear. You didn't . . . ?"

I shook my head. "I just knew she didn't want to be a tree."

My chest burned. My neck, my stomach, my legs down through to my sneakers.

"Trent," Mrs. Little said. Fire. I was on fire. "Please understand. We only want the best—"

But I wasn't listening anymore. I was backing away. "I understand fine," I said. I was *not* going to shout. I was *not* going to yell.

I was not going to cry.

"Thanks for talking to me," I said. "I really appreciate it."

I may or may not have done one of the things I swore not to do on my way back to the store.

"Trent?" my mom said. She was standing in the doorway. I think she'd been watching me. "What happened? Are you okay?"

"I forgot my coat," I told her. That's all I said. No matter how many times she asked.

When we left for the night, Mom told me she loved my baster turkey. I knew she was lying, but I think it was the only thing she could think of to cheer me up.

TWENTY

I DIDN'T KNOW WHAT TO SAY TO FALLON ON Monday at lunch. What was I supposed to say? *"I know you're not allowed to hang out with me"? "Why do your parents think I'm so terrible?" "Why didn't you just* tell *me?"* None of that seemed right, and anyway, when Fallon sat down next to me, instead of whipping open her pre-algebra book and not talking to me, she actually smiled and said, "Hey, Trent, what's shaking?"

An actual smile.

I'd missed that smile.

"Ummmm . . . ," I said, peeling the wrapper off my cafeteria hamburger. "Saltshakers? Or . . ." I tried to think of a good one. "Maracas?"

She raised an eyebrow at me. "Maracas?"

"Yeah," I said. I bit the edge off a mustard packet and began to squeeze a little onto my burger. "You know, those weird gourd instruments we had to play in music class in kindergarten?" I did a fake shake in the air with both my hands, as though to demonstrate. "Maracas," I said again. "That's what's shaking."

She laughed that laugh that took over her whole face. "You're one weird dude, Trent," she said.

"Thanks," I told her, and I took a bite of my burger.

If she didn't need to talk about her parents, I figured neither did I.

On Tuesday, I brought Noah Gorman his own Mike Lupica book to read, one about football. Only because otherwise I knew he'd just go on staring at me, looking pathetic and bored.

Sitting on the bleachers not playing volleyball *was* pretty boring.

"Keep it," I told him when the bell rang. "Aaron has, like, a million."

"Thanks," Noah said.

On Wednesday while we were reading our books, I don't know why, I decided to say something. "You know," I decided to say, "apparently you can fail sixth grade just for not participating in P.E." Maybe it wasn't my business, but it had taken me a long time to figure that one out, so I thought I might as well spread the word.

Noah shrugged and turned the page. "He can't make me participate if I don't want to" was all he said.

On Thursday, I brought the flyer for the Basketball Buddies program that Ms. Emerson had given me. It had spent more than a week at the bottom of my backpack, so it was mashed and wrinkled, but Noah took it anyway.

Fallon might have been talking to me again, but she was still acting weird. She wouldn't talk about the play at all, for one thing.

"You should at least make them let you be something better than a tree," I told her. "You're way too good an actress to be a *tree.* Do you even have any lines?"

She pushed her peas around on her tray. "I get to throw an apple at Dorothy," she said.

"You should *be* Dorothy." Just the thought of a really great actress like Fallon, stuck inside a tree suit, made me seriously furious. "I'm going to tell that stupid play director what's what," I said. "I'll make him re-audition you. I bet their Dorothy *sucks.*"

"Trent."

"What?" I said, starting to really get excited about the idea of yelling at some hack middle school theater director who clearly didn't even know a star when he saw one. "So you maybe had a bad audition, so what? That doesn't mean they have to make you a *tree.* You should get to try out again."

"Trent."

"If they just knew how *amazing* you were, I'm sure they'd—"

"Trent!"

Fallon slammed her spork on the table. It didn't make a lot of noise, because it was plastic, but it did send up a tiny spray of peas.

"I asked to be a tree, all right?" she said. She said it so quietly,

I almost didn't hear her. She was staring straight into her lunch tray.

"What?" I said. "Why would you do a thing like that?"

Instead of answering, Fallon pushed her tray across the table, straight into the garbage can. It fell in with a *thunk.*

"I don't feel so good," she told me. "I think I need to go to the nurse's office."

I didn't follow her, because I could tell she didn't want me to. I stayed at the table and finished my lunch by myself, thinking about how Fallon had just added one more thing to the list of things we couldn't talk about.

It started raining that afternoon, really hard. Buckets, practically, dumping out of the sky. It got worse while I was in Ms. Emerson's room, watering plants.

"I hope I haven't kept you too late," Ms. Emerson told me as I was leaving. It was dark outside the window, and the wind was howling, rain throttling the glass.

"No," I said. "That's okay."

"You know," she said, "if you don't mind staying here another twenty minutes or so, I can give you a ride home. I usually leave school around five o'clock."

I squinted an eye at her. Getting in a car with a wrinkled old crone did not exactly sound like my idea of a good time.

Then I glanced outside the window, at the rain.

"Yeah, okay," I told her. "I'll read my book, maybe. Or do some homework."

"That sounds grand."

Ms. Emerson graded papers until 5:00 on the dot, and then the wrinkled old crone drove me home, with my bike in the back of her car. She was silent as stone the whole way, only nodded as I told her which corners to turn.

"Trent?" she said when she'd pulled up in front of my house and I was about to open the door into the rain. I turned to look at her. "The plants will be thirsty again tomorrow," she said. Then she popped open the trunk of her car. "And don't forget your bicycle."

It rained the next day, too. Not nearly as hard, but still, when Ms. Emerson asked me if I wanted a ride home again, I said sure. I wasn't a moron.

We were almost halfway to my house when I recognized something out the window, in a place I wasn't expecting.

"Wait, Ms. Emerson, can you stop for a second?"

It was Aaron's car, in the parking lot of the library. I squinted through the darkness. Aaron was there, too, peering under the hood.

There was a girl standing next to him, crossing her arms around her body and squeezing her hoodie sweatshirt closer to her for warmth.

"Everything okay?" Ms. Emerson asked me as she pulled off the road into the parking lot, on the far end from where Aaron was standing at his car. The lot was empty, apart from our two cars.

"That's my brother," I told her. "Aaron."

She shut off her car. "Huh," she said, looking at the clock on the dashboard. 5:08, that's what it said. "The library closes at four thirty on Fridays." She glanced back at me. "Let's go see what's going on, shall we?" And just like that, she hopped out into the drizzle. I followed her.

I could hear the girl's voice across the stretch of parking lot immediately. "Aaron," she said. Her hoodie was soaked. "I'm just going to call my dad. This is ridiculous."

It was Clarisse, I realized. I recognized her from her photo in the contact info on Aaron's phone. Only she didn't really look the way I'd imagined a girlfriend would look, because for one thing she was obviously furious.

When Ms. Emerson called, "Everything okay out here?" across the parking lot, both Aaron and Clarisse darted their heads up. And the looks on their faces, you would've thought we'd caught them robbing a liquor store, not standing in the parking lot of the library.

Something was up.

"Trent?" Aaron called into the rain. "What are you doing here?" He did not sound happy to see me.

"Ms. Emerson was driving me home," I said. I pointed. "She's my homeroom teacher."

"Homeroom?" Aaron said. "It's like, four thirty."

"Five-oh-eight," Ms. Emerson corrected, putting up a hand to shield her eyes from the rain.

The wind howled.

"Do you kids need help?" Ms. Emerson asked.

It was weird to hear someone call Aaron a "kid." For as far back as I could remember, he'd always seemed like such a grown-up, bossing Doug and me around and lecturing us about "responsibility." But right then, in the rain, with a broken car, and a wet and annoyed Clarisse by his side, he did seem a little like a kid.

"My car won't start," he said.

"We were at the library," Clarisse said quickly when she saw Ms. Emerson's eyes dart inside the empty car. "I was helping Aaron study for a test on Monday, and then his car wouldn't start and . . ."

"The library closed a while ago," Ms. Emerson put in.

"We've been stuck here forever," Clarisse said. "Aaron won't let me call anyone. He says he can fix it."

"I *can* fix it," Aaron grumbled.

"What's the problem?" Ms. Emerson asked. And when Aaron described what had happened, she told him, "You probably just need a jump. I have cables in my trunk." She turned to Clarisse. "Young lady, why don't you help me get them?"

While Ms. Emerson and Clarisse walked back across the parking lot to the car, I told Aaron, "No way you were studying." I had no idea what he *had* been doing, but I knew it was something awful. I could tell by his face how worried he was that I was going to figure it out.

But then in the backseat of the car, I noticed Aaron's math book, and a notebook. The notebook was covered with Aaron's scribbles. Numbers, all over. Crossed out and scribbled up the sides. I smooshed my nose harder against the window. There were tons of pages of scribbled numbers wadded up and tossed on the floor in the backseat.

"You really were studying," I said.

"Shut up," Aaron replied.

"What's so terrible about that?" I asked. "So you were studying with your girlfriend. Who cares?"

"I'm failing trig, all right?" Aaron told me. He sounded like he was angry at *me* for some reason, like if I hadn't found him in this parking lot, he wouldn't be failing at all. "And I told you, Clarisse isn't my girlfriend." He coughed, clearing his throat. "She's my tutor." Across the parking lot, Ms. Emerson had turned on her car, and she and Clarisse were making their way back over to us. "If I don't pass this test on Monday, I'm probably going to flunk the whole semester, and then I'll have to do summer school."

"So why the heck are you spending all this time trying to fix your stupid car?" I asked Aaron. "You should've called Mom. I bet she has jumper cables or whatever. Or Ray. You don't have to stand out here in the rain. You're already late to meet Dad for dinner."

"Shut up."

This was an Aaron I didn't know. The Aaron I *did* know was calm and polite and mature and always in charge. He was funny. Charming. He pulled pranks. He didn't stand in the freezing rain like an idiot staring down into the hood of a car freaking out about math tests.

Ms. Emerson parked in the spot right beside Aaron's, and then opened the hood of her car, too. Then she showed us all how to hook up the cables, and how to jump Aaron's car. "A useful skill is never learned too early," she told me as she instructed me where to clip the cable.

Aaron's car started up in seconds. Ms. Emerson had been right. It was a really easy fix.

Ms. Emerson said she'd drive Clarisse home, and I went with Aaron, after we transferred my bike. I wasn't too sad about that arrangement, because Clarisse was growling like she wanted to murder somebody.

"She's just in a bad mood," Aaron said when I told him I was glad she wasn't his girlfriend because she was awful. "It's late and she's mad at me for not calling someone. Plus, I think she was really cold."

"She should get an actual coat."

"Mm," Aaron said as we headed toward home.

"Why wouldn't you call anyone?" I asked him.

He didn't answer.

"Aaron?"

"Mom has enough to worry about, all right?" he said. "She doesn't need to know about me and stupid trig, or my car breaking down at the library."

"But—"

"She worries all the time, Trent," Aaron said. "You don't see it, because you're always so busy thinking about your own stuff, but Mom worries all the time. She worries about you. And it's my job to take care of her, and I'm not going to give her one more thing to worry about. So just shut up about it, all right? And don't you dare tell her."

"But—"

"Shut up, Trent."

I didn't see how any of this was my fault—Aaron's car breaking down, or him almost failing trig. If it weren't for me, he'd've been stuck in that parking lot until morning. I hadn't done anything wrong, and I knew it.

So why did I feel guilty anyway?

TWENTY-ONE

WHEN I GOT TO THE COMMUNITY CENTER ON Saturday morning, Julie was waiting for me, standing next to Annie.

"Hi, Trent," she greeted me. "I was just telling Annie here that we have a new volunteer today. So if the two of you are still interested in switching, I can arrange that."

"Oh," I said, because I guess I was surprised. Then I looked at Annie, who shrugged, so I shrugged, too.

"So that's a 'no,' then?" Julie asked.

"I guess not?" I said slowly. And Annie nodded to agree with me, but the nod was mostly toward her shoes and not Julie.

"We're fine," Annie said.

"Well, great then," Julie told us. "All right, when the rest of the group gets here, I'll explain our first game."

"Just so you know," Annie said, looking up to talk to me when Julie had wandered off, "I'm not done hating you."

But she didn't actually look that mad, the way you would if you truly hated someone.

"Good," I told her. "Because if you were, they might make you stop being the president of the club."

"Exactly," she said.

The new volunteer, it turned out, was Noah Gorman. Julie paired him up with another volunteer and a really little kid who looked like she could use extra help.

The first game was a relay race, where we had to dribble two balls at once while running to the far side of the gym, and then on the way back we had to cross the balls at least once before passing them off to our buddy, and then it was the second person's turn. Everyone was terrible at it. There were basketballs flying everywhere, and kids knocking into each other, and two second-graders got so confused about whose basketball was whose that for a second it looked like they were going to wrestle each other for it. Annie and I came in third. Noah's team was dead last.

He waved at me across the gym when he saw me. I waved back.

One thing was for sure. Basketball Buddies was *way* better than volleyball.

When Julie let us out for the day, after our afternoon snack (another thing this program had going for it over P.E. class), Annie and I left the Community Center together. And there was Doug, sitting on his bicycle, waiting for us.

Well. Waiting for Annie, anyway.

"Hey, Annie!" he greeted her, waving her over. "Want to help me get some stuff for a"—his eyes darted at me—"thing?"

I knew it was a prank. I'm not a moron.

Annie stuck her hands into her pockets. "I can't," she said. "Rebecca wants me to help her set up for her hamster's birthday party. She would've invited you, too, but her mom said she could only have one friend over this afternoon."

"Oh," Doug said. I could tell he was disappointed. "That's fine. Anyway, I should work on the . . . thing."

"I know it's a prank, Doug," I said from where I was kicking up my bike's kickstand.

"It's not a prank!" he said, way too loudly. Which meant that it was definitely a prank.

Annie left, and I waved good-bye to Noah, and there was Doug, looking sad and pathetic on his bicycle. I rolled my bike over to him and punched him in the shoulder, the way Aaron always did to me. "You want to go to Rosalita's?" I asked him.

He looked up at me. "Yeah?" he said, rubbing his shoulder.

"Yeah. I have some money from the store last weekend."

"All right," he said. "But I'm not going to tell you about my prank. That's a secret."

"Deal," I said.

It wasn't far to Rosalita's. We locked our bikes outside and ate indoors instead of ordering from the window, because of how cold it was. Marjorie even gave us an extra taco to split, just because she liked us.

It wasn't until we were chowing down on our meal that I realized something.

"Hey, why aren't you at Dad's?" I asked Doug. I did the math in my head, and it was a Dad weekend for sure.

He took a long slurp of his soda, then pushed it away from him and picked up his second taco. "You're not the only person who's allowed to hate going there, you know," he said. Which, okay, surprised me.

"I thought you and Dad got along fine," I said.

"You're not always there," he replied. Which I guess was true.

We went back to tacos.

After a while more of eating, Doug said, "You're being nice to Annie, right?" He took another slurp of soda. "Because she needs people to be nice to her. Because of everything that happened. You know, with her brother."

I clenched my jaw tight. "I *know* what happened with her brother, Doug," I said.

He darted his eyes up at me, his mouth still around his soda straw. "Oh," he said. "Oh, yeah, I guess so." He leaned back in his seat. Used his fork to push around a couple stray pieces of shredded lettuce on his plate. "I just feel bad," he said. "That's all. So I always try to be extra-nice to her."

"Why would *you* feel bad?" I asked him.

"Because." He sighed big, like he wasn't sure he wanted to talk about it. He popped two lettuce pieces into his mouth and talked while he was chewing. "I was the one who told you they needed an extra for hockey." He wouldn't look at me.

"Doug," I said. "That's stupid. Anyone could have told me that. That doesn't make it your fault her brother died."

"Yeah, but"—Doug went for another piece of lettuce—"they only needed another person because I convinced Brad not to play. I wanted to hang out with him, so I told him not to. And if I never would've done that, then . . ." He didn't finish his thought.

He didn't need to.

"So that's why you're always hanging out with Annie?" I asked Doug. "Because you feel guilty?"

Doug chewed some more, looked up at the ceiling. "Well, that and 'cause she's nice," he said.

I reached for my second taco, but I couldn't bring myself to eat it. I just kept staring at Doug. I couldn't believe that all this time, while I'd been feeling so guilty about Jared and that hockey puck, he'd been feeling the exact same way.

"You couldn't have known," I told him. "You didn't do anything wrong."

He slurped at his soda and didn't say anything. I slurped at my own soda and didn't say anything either.

"Thanks for the tacos," he said at last.

"Now what's this big prank of yours?" I asked him.

Doug threw a shred of lettuce at me. "Wouldn't you like to know?"

"So?" I asked Aaron on Sunday night, when Mom and I got home from Kitch'N'Thingz and Aaron had returned from his solo weekend at

Dad's. He was in the kitchen tidying, even though he'd been gone all weekend so none of the things that needed tidying were his. "Are you ready for your big test tomorrow?"

Aaron didn't say anything, just looked up from where he was standing at the sink, rinsing dishes to put in the dishwasher.

"Your trig test," I said. "Did you study some more? Are you going to pass it?"

"Maybe instead of being nosy," he replied, his eyes darting past me to the door. No one was there to hear us, so I guess that's why he went on. "You could help me with the dishes."

Well.

I started gathering Doug's cereal bowl from the table—what else did I have to do?—and pushed past Aaron to rinse the empty milk carton for recycling.

He still didn't answer my question, though.

"I'm sure it wouldn't be so bad," I said after a little while of tidying, with Aaron not talking to me. I didn't like when he wasn't talking to me. "If you had to take summer school, I mean." I'd had to take summer school once, for extra reading help back in fourth, and it wasn't as terrible as I'd worried it would be.

"What do you know?" Aaron snapped.

"It's just one class," I said. "And in summer school they make everything easier anyway, so—"

"If I have to go to summer school," Aaron said, "I have to cut back at Swim Beach." He held a plate over the sink, right in front of the stream of water from the faucet, but not under it, so it didn't get rinsed. He was staring at me, not the water. "If I work fewer hours, I get less money. And if I get less money, how am I supposed to pay for college, huh, genius? You tell me that. If I ever get *into* college in the first place." He went back to rinsing the plate. He scrubbed it with a sponge, kept scrubbing even after all the food was off.

"Hey, Aaron?" I said softly. "Aaron?" He didn't answer, just kept rinsing.

"I don't need you to tell me that it's okay, all right?" he said. "It's not okay."

"Uh." I blinked. "I was going to tell you that I think that plate is super clean now."

Aaron closed his eyes and took a deep breath, then slowly set the plate down on the counter and turned off the faucet. He flicked driplets of water off his hands, and turned around to face me.

"I'm sorry I exploded," he told me.

"It's okay," I said.

"It's not your fault I'm failing trig."

"Duh," I replied.

Aaron laughed.

I picked up the plate and started drying it with a dish towel. "So?" I asked him again. "Are you ready?"

Another deep breath. For a while I thought he might blow up at me again, but when he did answer, he sounded much calmer than before. "I think so. Maybe. I guess we'll find out on Monday."

"I'll keep my fingers crossed for you," I told him.

TWENTY-TWO

ON MONDAY, FALLON SAT WITH ME AT LUNCH, LIKE usual.

"How's the play going?" I asked her.

"Fine," she said.

"How's art class?"

"Fine."

I was starting to figure out why my mom got so annoyed when she asked us about school.

I tried another tactic.

"Why can't you ever get hungry at the beach?" I asked her.

She rolled her eyes at me. "I'm not really in the mood, Trent," she said.

"Well, what *are* you in the mood for?" I grumbled.

We didn't talk much after that.

I was getting pretty sick of this Fallon—the moody, grumpy one who never talked to me anymore. I was beginning to wonder if it was even worth it, trying to be her friend.

"Hey, here's a joke I bet your uncle never told you," I said after a while of not talking. I don't know why. Because not talking at the lunch table was worse than not playing volleyball, probably. "I read it in one of Doug's joke books a million years ago. It's terrible. You ready?"

She plopped a stewed carrot into her mouth and didn't say anything.

"What will a pirate pay to cut off your ears?" I said.

She chewed. "What?" she asked. She didn't really seem that interested.

I put on my best pirate voice anyway. "A buccaneer," I told her, squinting one eye like I was wearing an eye patch or something. "Get it? A *buck-an-ear*."

"That's *awful*," she told me.

But her eyes were lit up, on either side of her scar. And she was smiling at me.

"Right?" I said.

She was worth it, I decided. Fallon Little was definitely worth it.

I went to Ms. Emerson's room that day after school, just like I always did. I filled up the watering can at the sink just like always, too.

But then I set it down.

Ms. Emerson was at sitting at her stovetop desk, as usual, grading papers. She sure had a lot of papers to grade all the time. I wondered if she'd had nearly so many when she was a home ec teacher. Probably not. I wondered if she'd liked teaching home ec a lot better.

"Ms. Emerson?" I said.

She didn't look up from her papers. "Yes, Trent?"

"Would it be okay if I didn't water the plants today?"

At that, she did look up. "You don't want to anymore?"

I thought about that. It wasn't, actually, that I didn't want to water Ms. Emerson's plants. I didn't hate going there after school as much as I had at first. Not at all, really.

"I do," I said. "It's just . . ." The reason I'd started watering the plants to begin with was so Ms. Emerson wouldn't hate me so much. And it seemed like it had worked okay. I was pretty sure she didn't hate me anymore. There was even a tiny chance that she sort of liked me.

That didn't mean that the plants didn't need to be watered anymore, of course. Plants needed to be watered nearly every day, or they would die.

"I was just wondering if it might be okay if I took a day off," I said.

If watering Ms. Emerson's plants had made her not hate me anymore, I wondered if it might work on someone else.

"There's something I sort of need to do," I told her.

She raised an eyebrow at me. "Everything okay?"

I nodded. Then I stopped. I shook my head. "I think Fallon's still mad at me. She won't talk about it, and I don't know what to do. I mean, I don't really want to talk about it either. But . . . ," I trailed off. I didn't know what came after the *but*. Instead I stared at the watering can, like there might be some answers in there.

"Talking can be hard sometimes," Ms. Emerson said. I was sort of surprised she said anything, because she didn't say too much too often. "I can understand about not wanting to talk."

I nodded at that, still staring at the watering can.

"But Trent?" She paused. "Here's something I think is very important." I waited. She took her sweet time to tell me, that was for sure. She must've thought that what she was about to say was *extremely* important, that it deserved my absolute full and undivided attention.

I looked over at her. "Yeah?" I said.

"When you do choose to speak," she told me, "speak truths." And with that, she went back to her grading.

I stood there, staring at her as she graded papers, feeling like a bit of a moron for a while, because I didn't know exactly what to say. What I finally said was "So it's okay if I take the day off?"

She nodded.

"Thanks," I told her.

"And Trent?" she called after me on my way out.

I spun around. "The plants will be thirsty again tomorrow?" I asked. But I guess maybe I was sort of smiling when I said it.

Ms. Emerson was maybe sort of smiling, too. "Yes indeed," she replied.

Pedaling my bike was practically the hardest thing in the world that afternoon. Right foot up, left foot down. Steer around the corner, but not too hard. Don't forget to balance. It hadn't rained since Friday, the street was dry as a bone, but still, you would've thought I was pedaling through quicksand, what with how difficult it was to just ride in a straight line. But I got there, eventually.

To the Littles' front door, I mean.

Knocking was hard that afternoon, too. Form a fist, bend your right elbow, reach out with your upper arm, bend your wrist, and rap on the door. Once, twice, three times. Arm down at your side.

Half of me was sort of hoping he wouldn't be there. But he was.

"Oh," Mr. Little said when he opened the door. That's what he said. *Oh.* Like he was hoping to find the mailman with an early Christmas present, and instead he got me. "It's you."

"Hi," I said. "Um—"

But Fallon's dad cut me off.

"You shouldn't be here, Trent," he said. And he didn't sound entirely mean when he said it, even though it was sort of a mean thing to say. He said it more like he felt sorry for me. "Anyway, Fallon's not home right now."

"I know," I said. "She's at play rehearsal. That's why I came now. I wanted to talk to you."

Mr. Little was on his way to closing the door on me when I said that last part, but as soon as he heard it, he opened the door again.

"Me?" he asked.

I scuffled my feet against the doormat. "Yeah," I said, even though I was starting to think that this had been a really terrible idea.

"I have an early shift today," Mr. Little said, super annoyed. He looked at his watch. "I leave in an hour." His eyes darted back to me. "What was it you had to say?" He didn't invite me in.

"I . . . um . . ." I was starting to realize that I hadn't thought through this part of it very well. "I wanted to water your plants."

Well. *That* went over about as well as you'd expect.

Mr. Little sighed. It was the sigh of a man who was about to slam the door in a twelve-year-old's face and felt kind of bad about it but not bad enough not to do it. "Good-bye, Trent," he said.

"Wait!" I said. And for whatever reason, Mr. Little didn't slam the door closed. "It doesn't have to be plants. It can be anything. I just . . . I know you and Mrs. Little don't like me, that's why you don't want me hanging out with Fallon. But I thought if you *did* like me . . ." I went back to scuffling the doormat with my feet, then realized that kicking around the doormat of the person I was trying to impress was maybe not the best idea I'd ever had. I straightened it out against the edge of the doorframe with my toe and went back to talking. "Fallon's really important to me," I said. I was trying to speak truths, like Ms. Emerson had said. "She's my friend. And I want to hang out with her. But only if it's okay with you and Mrs. Little. So I guess I just thought . . ." Mr. Little was giving me a look like I had three heads. "If you have anything that needs dusting?" I said. "I'm good at dusting. I do it at my mom's shop all the time. Or vacuuming? Or . . . I can come every day. As many times as you want. As long as it takes."

Mr. Little looked at me. Up and down. Very slowly. And in case you didn't know, being looked up and down very slowly by an enormous police officer is not the most fun thing that could ever happen to a person. But I didn't squirm. Not even a little.

"Fallon is very important to me, too," he said at last.

I nodded. I got the feeling I wasn't supposed to say anything right then.

"Did she tell you to come here?" he asked me. He was squinting at my face, like he was using his special police officer skills to decide if I was telling the truth.

He didn't really need to do that, though, because the truth was exactly what I planned on telling. "No," I told him. "She doesn't know I came. I thought she might be . . ." I was going to say *mad,* but Fallon didn't exactly get mad. "I didn't tell her."

Mr. Little straightened up to his full height and looked down his nose at me for a long time. That wasn't entirely comfortable either, but I still didn't squirm.

"Well, I'm not going to force a sixth-grader to do manual labor just to get in my good graces," he said.

My shoulders might have slumped just the tiniest bit when he said that, but quick as I could, I straightened them again.

"But . . ." My shoulders got even straighter when I heard that *but.* Mr. Little looked behind him, into the house, like he was deciding something. "I was just about to eat dinner before I left for my shift. Why don't you come join me?"

He definitely said that last bit the way you'd ask a skunk to spray in your soup, but I didn't care. He was asking. My heart leaped up in my chest, but I did my best not to leap in real life. "Thank you, sir," I said. "I'd love to."

For dinner, Mr. Little made baked chicken and a pasta dish from scratch, with tomatoes and basil and mozzarella cheese, and there were green beans, too, which he boiled in a pot and then at the last minute doused in a bowl of ice water. Most of the food was already prepared when he let me into the kitchen, except for the green beans. I swear, he really did that, dumped fresh-cooked green beans into a bowl of ice water. It was the craziest thing I'd ever seen.

"It makes them crispy," he muttered at me when he saw me looking at him funny. That was the first thing he said to me after we came inside the house, and the last thing he said for about ten minutes after that. I was starting to figure out where Fallon got her knack for not talking when she didn't want to.

Mr. Little got down two plates from the cupboard, and spooned some pasta and green beans onto each one. On one of the plates he added a chicken breast. Then he spent a long time packing up the other two chicken breasts he'd baked, and putting the rest of the pasta and the green beans into plastic containers, and setting it all carefully in the fridge. I figured that was for Fallon and her mom, for their dinner, but I didn't want to ask. I knew Mr. Little probably only had a few answers left in him, so I wanted to save them up.

When he was finished packing up leftovers, Mr. Little handed me the plate without chicken on it, and a fork, and said, "Here." Then he walked past me into the living room with his own plate, where he sat himself down on the couch. "Sit," he told me, glancing down at the couch next to him.

I found the farthest bit of couch I could, and I sat.

As soon as I did, Mr. Little looked at his plate of food on the coffee table and said, "I forgot the pepper."

"I'll get it!" I said, shooting out of my seat. I figured that was the least I could do, since Mr. Little was feeding me afternoon dinner, not to mention talking to me at all. But Mr. Little scowled at me.

"Sit down, Trent." He said it like an order. "You're not going to make me like you just by getting me pepper."

Well.

When he sat back down with the pepper, Mr. Little glanced sideways at me. I took an enormous forkful of pasta and shoved it into my mouth, then smiled at him like it was the most delicious thing I'd ever eaten. It *was* really good, actually, but I was having trouble eating, because, one, it was like three forty in the afternoon, so I wasn't exactly starving, and two, Mr. Little was making me pretty nervous.

"So," he said. And he said it in the sort of way that I imagined he'd say "So" to a criminal he was about to grill in his interrogation room down at the station. "Tell me about yourself, Trent."

"Um." That was the sort of question that sounded easy enough to answer, but wasn't at all. "What do you want to know?" I asked.

Mr. Little sawed at his chicken with his knife. "Whatever you think I should."

"Um," I said again. "Well, I'm twelve. I, uh, go to school with Fallon. I'm in sixth, too." Mr. Little nodded. He already knew all that, obviously.

"Parents?" he asked me.

"Sorry?" I said.

"Do you live with both your parents?" He took another bite of chicken. "What do they do?"

"I live with my mom and my brothers," I said. "She works at

Kitch'N'Thingz, across from the movie theater." He nodded. "My dad and my stepmom live in Timber Trace. He does investing, or something, I don't really know. She makes jewelry. They just had a baby."

Mr. Little was looking at his plate, not at me, but somehow I still felt like I was being drilled down to my soul. "Do you get along with your family?" he asked.

When you choose to speak, speak truths. "Most of them," I said. "My mom and brothers, yes. Most of the time. Not my dad so much, or Kari. The baby's fine, I guess."

"I see." I couldn't really tell what that *I see* meant, so I didn't say anything. I ate some green beans instead.

They were pretty crisp. I ate some more.

"How do you do in school?" he asked me.

I swallowed my mouthful of green beans as quickly as I could. "Okay," I answered. "Some classes better than others."

"Grades?"

"B-minuses mostly. I'm not doing so well in P.E., but I'm making it up right now." This truth thing wasn't easy.

He set down his fork and knife, crossed like a long X on his plate, and turned to look at me full-on. "Why do you want to be friends with my daughter?"

Now *here,* I thought, was the big question.

"I don't know," I said. That was the truth. "I don't think I *want* to be friends with Fallon, I think we just *are* friends. Fallon's . . . well, she's funny. She's weird." I looked up at Mr. Little, because I didn't want him to think I was being rude. "In a good way, I mean. Most people try really hard not to be weird, but Fallon's different. And she's nice. And . . ." Had I been talking too long? I wished I had some water. "She doesn't feel sorry for me."

Mr. Little nodded again, taking it all in.

"Can I tell you something else?" I said. I mean, as long as I was being honest . . . "I don't want to get Fallon in trouble or anything, so I really hope this doesn't, but I think I should tell you that Fallon and I have been having lunch together. I didn't know at first you said we couldn't hang out, but even after I found out last week, we've still been having lunch. I only wanted to tell you that because I didn't want you to find out later and think I was lying about it." I was talking fast now, trying to get it all out. "And I know you don't like me, and I know sometimes in life you only get one chance, but Mr. Little, I sure hope you'll give me another one anyway, because Fallon . . . She's . . . she's my friend, and . . . well, I guess that's all. I'm sorry for talking so much."

When I started telling the truth, I really got going, I guess.

Mr. Little chewed in silence for a long time. I chewed in silence too.

Finally, he said, "You know, Trent, I appreciate your coming here. That was brave of you, and I have to give you credit for that. I know I'm not always the easiest person to approach."

"No, sir," I said. Which was exactly when I probably should've kept my mouth shut, judging by the sideways glance Mr. Little gave me then, but he kept going anyway.

"Unfortunately," he said, and for a splash of a second I felt that heated ball of rage inside me, but it was extinguished almost immediately by my heart, which sank right on top of it. I guess I didn't even have room for rage in my body, that's how hurt I was. I gulped a dry scratch of a gulp. "I'm afraid I'm not the one you have to convince to trust you," Mr. Little finished.

I swallowed over the scratching again. "I'll talk to Mrs. Little too," I said. "I'd be happy to. I'll answer any questions she wants. I can come every day. I can come to her work. I can—"

Mr. Little stopped me with a raised hand.

I waited for him to talk.

"I'll need to talk to my wife, of course," he told me after a minute or two of just chewing, "but I think she might be turned in your favor. It's Fallon you'll really need to work on."

I paused with a forkful of pasta halfway to my mouth. "Fallon?" I said.

"Look. I know my daughter likes you. She likes you a lot. And you're clearly a good friend. But she's also pretty fragile sometimes." I scrunched my eyebrows together at that. Fallon? Fragile? "And you scared her pretty badly that day at the movies."

My heart, which had only recently started beating again, whimpered once more.

"She's the one you need to talk to, Trent," Mr. Little told me. "Worry about Fallon trusting you, all right? Then you and I can talk again."

Here's something I needed to figure out.

With some people, when they didn't like you, you could do something silly and unimportant, say, water their plants. If you showed up every day, showed you actually cared, they might start to like you. Just a little bit.

With other people, if they didn't like you, you could talk to them. Tell them the truth. And maybe they wouldn't like you, but if they listened, really truly, maybe they'd learn to trust you just a little. Maybe they'd start to.

And with other people, you only got one chance. If you screwed up, that was it. It was over. And you knew that it was over.

And all those sorts of people made sense to me. Like it or not, I could work with all those kinds of people.

But what were you supposed to do with the sorts of people who didn't have plants to water? Who didn't seem to dislike you, but didn't totally trust you, either? What were you supposed to do with the sorts of people who would talk about everything under the sun except the things you knew they really wanted to talk about? What did you do with people who never ever got mad, but who were somehow mad at you?

That was the thing I needed to figure out.

TWENTY-THREE

I TRIED AND TRIED TO THINK OF A WAY TO make Fallon trust me again, but I had nothing. If I got her to crack a smile at lunch, I felt like a winner.

But I knew I hadn't won yet, not really. It was going to take something a lot better than a bad joke to get Fallon back.

On Tuesday I bought a new sketchbook at Lippy's corner store, and slowly I began to think things through on paper.

Wednesday afternoon Mom picked me up early, right after lunch, for an eye doctor's appointment. I'd told Ms. Emerson ahead of time that I wouldn't be able to water her plants that day, and she told me, "That's okay. They can be a little thirsty now and again. It builds character."

I had to admit I was starting to like her a little bit.

After the eye appointment ("Twenty-twenty, Mr. Zimmerman!" the optometrist declared), Mom took me to the store to work with her.

It was a slow afternoon. Mom and I were sitting at the counter, not doing much of anything, when Mom said, "How about a movie tonight? Just you and me?"

I followed her gaze across the street to the theater marquee.

"Which one?" I asked her warily. There was a 5:30 showing of *Hawk & Dove,* a superhero movie I'd been bugging her to see for a while, and a 6:15 of *Lucky in Love.* I didn't need to know what that one was about to know that I didn't want to see it.

"Your pick," she said.

I was surprised, I guess. Not about her letting me pick the movie, but about suggesting we go at all.

"Aren't I supposed to have dinner with Dad tonight?" I asked her.

"Were you actually going to show up?" she asked back.

I guess that was a fair point.

Mr. Jacobson wasn't at the window selling tickets, which I was pretty glad about. It was one of the other workers, one whose kid I hadn't beaten up on Halloween.

While Mom went for a last-minute bathroom run before the movie started, I went to get the popcorn. That's when I noticed Jeremiah behind the counter. There were two other kids back there with him—older kids, high schoolers—and I prayed and prayed that I would get one of them instead of Jeremiah when my turn came. But no such luck.

Actually, at first Jeremiah pretended to ignore *me,* asking the guy behind me what he wanted. Which was kind of funny, really, because

I was busy ducking down to study the candy counter, like I really didn't know which was better, Milk Duds or Junior Mints, and here was Jeremiah not wanting to help me either. Unfortunately, the guy behind me, who had obviously forgotten how much it sucked to be in middle school, said, "I think this kid is next."

"I'm still thinking," I told the guy, barely glancing up from the candy.

He ordered a soda.

By the time he was finished, Jeremiah was still the only person free behind the counter, so finally I straightened up. I did my best impression of someone who had never met Jeremiah Jacobson before and said, "Two small popcorns, please. Thanks so much."

Jeremiah did his best impression of someone who hated my guts. "Next!" he shouted over my shoulder.

"Dude, Jeremiah," one of the high school kids, who was filling up three sodas at once, told him, "help that kid, all right?"

Jeremiah glared at me. I'd done a pretty great job of dodging him the last two weeks at school, and it was starting to occur to me that maybe it'd been so easy because Jeremiah didn't want to see me either.

"What do you want?" he asked me. He did not say it very nicely.

I could feel the ball of fire starting in my chest, but I thought happy things—Movie Club with Fallon, the Dodgers winning the World Series—and pushed it down. "Two small popcorns," I said. I even managed to smile a little bit.

Jeremiah didn't nod or anything. He didn't ask if I wanted butter. He turned around and filled up one small popcorn bag barely to the top. Usually the high schoolers packed it till it was overflowing.

"Eight fifty," he said, slapping the bag on the counter so hard that one of the corners crumpled and at least ten pieces spilled out. He rang me up, and the price clanged on the front of the register.

I stared at him. I didn't want to start anything, I really didn't, but I wasn't sure what to do. Eight fifty was technically what I owed him, but that was for two bags of popcorn. He'd only given me one.

"Eight fifty," he said again, like he was bored or something.

Over my shoulder I heard someone growl, "Hey, kid, you gonna pay or what? It's a long line."

Luckily, the high schooler with the sodas seemed to notice that something was up. "Everything okay?" he asked me. The way he said it, I could kind of tell he was aware what a major jerk Jeremiah was. Which made me realize that working beside Jeremiah at the concessions stand might be almost as terrible as going to school with him.

"I, uh," I said, doing my best not to look at Jeremiah as I said it, "I was just waiting for my second popcorn." Pushing down the fire.

The high schooler darted his eyes toward Jeremiah. "Ah," he said. "Small?" he asked me.

I nodded. "Thanks."

As Jeremiah took my money, he told me, "Enjoy your movie, dill hole." Only he didn't say "dill hole."

There was the fire again. But instead of letting it radiate out to my arms, my legs, my everything, I clenched my fists tight and did my best to stop it.

"I'm sorry about Halloween," I told him. Speaking truths.

And I didn't wait to see what he said to that, or what his face looked like when he heard my apology, because none of that mattered, I decided. What mattered was that I'd said what I felt. I unclenched my fists and grabbed the two bags of popcorn.

Mom was standing right beside the line. I hadn't even seen her. She was smiling at me, a proud motherly smile.

"Ready for the movie?" she asked me.

"I think so," I said.

After the movie, Mom insisted we get dinner at the Mad Batter, and I didn't argue, because the Mad Batter was delicious.

But I did ask, "You think Ray's all right at the store by himself?"

Mom waved a hand in front of her face. "He's got fifteen minutes till close," she said. "He'll be fine. I want to talk to my boy."

I got my usual, grilled cheese with bacon and a side of fries. Mom got a western omelet with extra onions. You weren't technically allowed to have breakfast after 11:00 a.m., but Mom said that was one of the benefits of being friends with the owner.

"So," Mom said, sipping her coffee while we waited for our food. I just had water. "I had a good talk with Aaron the other day."

I concentrated on Mom's coffee mug, which had a giant picture of the Cheshire Cat from *Alice in Wonderland* on it. I didn't want to say anything that would give away Aaron's secret, in case he hadn't told her everything. He was my brother, after all. "What about?" I asked, rearranging my utensils on top of my napkin.

"Trig, mostly," she said. She took another sip of coffee.

She knew. Aaron had told her everything. I could see it in her face.

"How did his test go?" I asked her. I really wanted to know. Aaron hadn't told me yet.

Mom frowned. "Not so well. He works so hard and he's such a smart kid, but math's never been his strong suit. He still has time to get back on track, but there's a chance he'll have to do summer school."

"Oh," I said. "That sucks."

"Yeah." I was playing with my fork on my napkin again, flipping it over and over, and Mom reached out her own fork and jabbed the tines together. "We'll figure it out, though. It'll be okay." We had a mini fork-joust. I let Mom win.

"Aaron said you were the one who told him to talk to me," Mom said after a while. Our waitress, Giulia, brought our food then, so Mom paused while Giulia set it down. "Anyway, thanks for that." She dug into her omelet. "Anything *you* wanted to tell me about?"

I picked up my grilled cheese. Studied it. Thought about what I wanted to say to Mom. If I'd learned anything from lunches with Fallon the past couple of weeks, it was that it was a lot more fun to eat with someone who talked back to you.

"Things are okay," I said. "I mean, mostly." She nodded, looking for more. "Basketball Buddies is pretty fun, actually. They paired me with Annie."

"Annie Richards?" Mom seemed surprised. "How's that going?"

"Not bad. She's nice. Well, she says she hates me, but I don't think she does."

"I guess that's good then."

"Yeah."

"And I've been watering plants for Ms. Emerson. Every day after school."

Mom raised an eyebrow. "Oh?" she said. "I thought you hated Ms. Emerson."

I thought about that. I think lately I hated Ms. Emerson the way Annie Richards hated me.

"It turns out she's not so bad."

"I'm glad to hear it." Mom took another big bite of her omelet. "Anything else going on?"

Speak truths.

"I think I might have ruined things with Fallon," I said.

Mom set down her fork, all concern. Listening, waiting.

"That night, at Halloween," I went on. "She was really upset. And I don't know how to fix it. I've been trying, but . . . I think maybe I ruined it."

"I can't imagine your friendship would be over," Mom said, thinking things through. "Not just like that. I don't believe you only ever get one chance."

I was starting to understand why it hadn't worked out so well between her and Dad.

"But Fallon doesn't talk to me," I said. "Not really, anymore."

Mom picked up her mug. Took a long sip. Stirred in a little more cream.

"I've heard Fallon talk to you plenty," she said. "Maybe you're just not listening to the right parts."

That Cheshire Cat was grinning big at me, like he knew something I didn't. I stuck a few fries in ketchup and chewed them. "Maybe," I said slowly. But I wasn't so sure.

"Keep me updated?" Mom asked. I nodded.

When Mom had finished her entire giant mug of coffee and was on a second cup, she told me, "I like you when you're chatty, you know, Trent. I like knowing what's going on with you."

"Yeah?" I said.

She smiled. "Yeah."

"Okay," I told her, and I set my grilled cheese down on my plate. Folded my hands together. "Now it's your turn. Tell me all about you and Ray."

In the car on the way home, Mom told me, "I had a good time hanging out tonight, Trent."

"Me too," I said. Because that was the truth.

"It wasn't really fair, though, was it?" she said. I glanced sideways at her. "I mean, it was your dad's night with you."

I didn't say anything to that.

"He misses you," she said.

"He doesn't," I told her.

"He's bad at showing it," Mom said slowly. And I could tell it was hard, saying anything even remotely nice about Dad, because she probably hated him more than I did. "But he loves you, a lot. And I think it would be nice if you went easy on him sometimes."

I wanted to say that he was the one who should go easy on me. I wanted to say that if he loved me so much, then why did he have to be such a jerk all the time.

But I looked at Mom's face, and she was so *hopeful.* She was trying so hard to raise a good kid, not a screw-up. So instead I just said, "I'll try."

When I opened the door to my bedroom, I saw them right away. Fake black plastic spiders. Hundreds of them. Doug must've gone to four different stores to find so many. They were everywhere—taped to my light switch, crawling up the walls, crunching under my feet as I walked. Sprinkled on top of my pillow.

Not for one second did I think they were real. Not for one second was I even mildly close to having a heart attack. This prank might've been even worse than the soup one, which was saying something.

But I didn't tell Doug that. What I did instead was let out an incredible fake scream, as loud and shrill and girly as I could. And when I heard Mom holler, *"What? What happened?"* really worried, from down the hall, I called back, "Uh . . . Nothing! Sorry, I just thought I saw a . . . mouse." But I kept a tiny hint of fear in my voice.

From outside my door, I heard a muffled giggle.

After Doug went to bed, I slipped a note under his door. It said:

I'll get you back for this, Doug. Just you wait.

It was the least I could do, really.

TWENTY-FOUR

I WENT TO THE STORE THURSDAY AFTER school, too, because it wasn't the worst place to be. Mostly I spent the afternoon drawing in my Book of Thoughts, thinking over what Mom had said at dinner, about me listening to the right parts of what Fallon was saying.

I drew a lot of different pictures. I'd always thought Fallon had a good face for drawing, and it turned out I was right. Every picture I drew of her turned out to be better than the last, and it wasn't because of my incredible artistic skills.

The more I drew, the more I figured out.

Fallon leaping up to pause a movie, startling Squillo so badly, he tumbled off the couch.

(Fallon might talk nonstop sometimes, I figured out as I drew, but she kept some words tucked away deep inside.)

Fallon on a roller coaster, hanging upside down, laughing.

(Fallon might seem like she was the bravest person in the world, but she was afraid of some things, too.)

Fallon sitting on the floor of the stockroom, her back against Ray's bookshelves, playing with her hippie leather belt, describing her dreams.

(Fallon might not trust me completely, not yet, but she trusted me enough to tell me something really important.)

Fallon with her mouth open wide, screaming her guts out.

(Fallon had a scream inside her somewhere. I just knew it.)

"How's everything going over here?" Ray asked me, pulling up a stool beside me at the counter.

"Just thinking," I said, looking up from my sketches.

"A noble pastime."

I closed my Book of Thoughts. "Hey, Ray?" I said.

"Yeah?"

"Mom told me you used to coach high school baseball."

He smiled at that. "Years ago," he said. "Before I moved to Cedar Haven. In my previous life." But you could tell he had good memories of it.

I sniffed, thinking very carefully about what I wanted to say next. "Mom said . . . I have a question."

"Shoot."

"Would you be able to help me sometime?" I asked. "With, like, my hitting and pitching and stuff? I haven't played in a while, and I'm sort of rusty."

The look on Ray's face, you would've thought I'd asked him to split my winning lotto ticket. "I'd love to, Trent," he said.

"There's . . . something else, too," I told him. He waited for me to go on. "Sometimes when I'm playing ball, I get, like . . . my arms, I mean. They get sweaty, sort of? Not normal. And I can't breathe and it's . . ." I shifted my Book of Thoughts this way and that on top of the counter. "I don't know if that's something you could help with."

Ray rubbed his bald head for a moment, thinking.

"How's this weekend work for you?" he asked.

As soon as I sat down at the lunch table next to Fallon on Friday, I pulled my Book of Thoughts out of my backpack and set it between our two trays. "Here," I said. "I wanted to show you." She was squinting at me. "Go ahead. Open it."

"But you never let me look."

"This time's different," I told her.

Fallon opened the book, then immediately sucked in her breath and poked her nose down close to the page. "Is this us?" she asked.

"Mm-hmm." I took a bite of tuna casserole while she examined the picture.

"This is really good, Trent."

It was the two of us at her birthday party, that's the picture she was looking at. Fallon and me, sitting in the bumper car, with Fallon pretending to steer. I even remembered to add the foil wrappers tossed near the trash can.

Fallon turned the page.

The next picture was the one of us at Movie Club, where Fallon was jumping up to pause the TV. I was pretty proud of that one, because

I'd captured the way Fallon's face lit up, those big brown eyes on either side of her scar, when she got so excited about a continuity error.

Fallon turned the page again. And again, examining each picture closely. She seemed to like them all. I closed the book before she got to the last one, though, with the scream. I wasn't quite ready to show her that one yet.

"You have to do more," she told me as I returned the notebook to my backpack. "Those were really awesome."

"Thanks," I told her. "Hey, Fallon?" I said, spitting it all out at once so I couldn't chicken out. "Can you ask your parents if you can hang out with me this Sunday? I wanted to show you something. It's a surprise."

Fallon frowned. "Oh," she said. "I mean, I don't know if . . ."

"Tell your dad I'm watering plants," I said.

Fallon looked at me like I was insane. Which I was thinking for a moment I might be.

"He'll know what I mean," I told her. "I mean, I hope he will."

Fallon took a deep breath, like she wasn't sure what she wanted to say. But finally what she did say was "Okay. I'll ask."

"Aaron and I will pick you up at ten sharp. Dress warm."

Fallon was ready at ten on the dot on Sunday, just like she'd promised.

"Where are we going?" she asked as she piled into the backseat of Aaron's car next to me. Aaron said he felt like a tool driving around with me in the backseat and no one in the front, like he was some sort of chauffeur, but I'd promised to do his chores for two weeks so he'd have more time to study, and he hadn't mentioned it after that.

"Trent didn't tell you?" Aaron asked as he carefully pulled out of the driveway onto the street.

"He said it was a surprise," Fallon replied.

"Well, aren't you full of mystery?" Aaron said, glancing at me in his rearview mirror. "He won't tell me much about his master plan either."

"We're going to Swim Beach," I told Fallon. "Aaron's work."

"Aaron's work unless he gets fired for going there during the off-season," Aaron said, turning right on Woodbine.

"Two weeks of chores," I reminded him. "Anyway, I thought you said you cleared it with your boss."

"I did," Aaron told us. "But she doesn't make good decisions."

"Aaron's boss, Zoey, is in love with him," I told Fallon, leaning over so I couldn't see Aaron's eyes in the rearview.

"Oooooh-oooooh!" Fallon said. I think that was the bit of information she needed to loosen up a little, because suddenly she seemed much more relaxed. Much more like herself. "Is she cute?"

"She's very cute," I said.

"Hey, back there, settle down now!" Aaron called. "I'll have none of this nonsense."

"Carry on, driver," I said, in my best fake snooty British voice. "You do the driving, and we'll do the talking."

Fallon joined in too. "Oh, Edward," she said in her own accent. I assumed I was supposed to be Edward. "Isn't there some sort of screen you can put up so the driver can't *hear* us? I do hate when the help tries to *talk* to you."

"You two are seriously bizarre," Aaron told us. But Fallon and I were too busy laughing to care.

It took a while to unlock the rowboat from the boathouse. The whole thing was closed up for the season, the boats all piled up on their metal racks with a giant chain wrapped around them—so some nutter wouldn't break in and steal one to take out on the freezing cold lake, I guess.

All right, so maybe my plan was sort of crazy.

Anyway, with the three of us helping, we managed eventually. The boathouse was dark, and the light was burned out, and I was sort of afraid of spiders (since these were actual creeping, nasty spiders, and not the stupid fake plastic ones Doug had plastered all over my room), but I pretended not to be. When Fallon found a spider crawling all the way up her arm to her shoulder and simply said, "Oh, hello there" in the calmest voice I'd ever heard, and let it walk onto her hand, and then set it carefully on the windowsill, I pretended that's exactly what I would've done too. Not scream like a little girl.

"So what are we doing?" Fallon asked. "We're not actually going to go out on the lake, are we?"

"Apparently," Aaron said, tossing us each a neon-orange life vest. He grabbed one for himself, too. "We are."

Fallon looked at me for confirmation, and I nodded. "Why, exactly?" she asked.

"You'll see," I promised.

Fifteen minutes later we were out in the boat rowing. We'd even managed to get inside and push off from the shore without any of us getting our feet wet. Aaron was in charge of most of the rowing, although Fallon and I helped a little.

"All right, little brother," Aaron said. "Where to?"

I pointed straight ahead, to the little spit of island with the clump of pine trees.

Sitting there, waiting for us.

Aaron was sitting behind me in the rowboat, so I couldn't see his face. But when he answered, "Sure thing," he didn't sound a bit surprised. He picked up speed with his oars.

The shore of the island was rockier than I'd expected. Full of tiny round pebbles, all of them smooth, perfect gray ovals. Fallon hopped out of the boat first, since she was in front, and did her best to scramble up the slopey shore. "Careful!" she warned us. "It's slippery!"

I hopped out next.

"Um, actually," I said to Aaron as he moved to get out too. "Would you, um, mind leaving us here for a little bit? Just, like, an hour maybe?"

At *that* he looked surprised. "Leave you here?"

"Yeah," I said, shrugging like it was no big deal, even though I'd known all along this was going to be the trickiest part of the plan to get Aaron to agree to. "Just, you know, row back to shore and then stay there a while and then come back to get us?"

"You want me to leave you all alone on a deserted island for an *hour*?" Aaron said. He'd never sounded more like an old man.

"Forty-five minutes, then," I said. *"Please?"*

"What are we going to do on the island?" Fallon said.

Aaron was looking back and forth between us. "You two aren't going to make out or anything, are you?"

Well. I didn't see *that* coming.

"Um, *no,*" I said. Fallon's face had turned bright red.

"Because if I leave you two here, and you start making out and stuff, you are seriously going to be in for it. You guys are *twelve.*"

"Sheesh, Aaron, I know we're twelve," I told him. He *did* think he was an old man.

"I don't want to make out with Trent," Fallon said.

"See?" I told Aaron. And I wasn't even offended, either. This wasn't about making out. This was about friends. "It's nothing like that," I said. "I promise. I just . . . We need some time. And it has to be just us." I stretched out my navy-blue glove then and reached for Fallon's hand. I wasn't entirely sure she was going to offer it.

But she did.

She looked down at our hands—my navy-blue glove and her red-and-purple knitted mitten—and squeezed just a little tighter. "Please, Aaron?" she said. "We'll be okay."

Aaron puffed his cheeks and let out a giant breath. I saw it, a cloud of white smoke in the crisp, cold air.

"Thirty minutes?" Fallon bargained.

"I'll give you twenty-five," he said at last. Fallon let out a tiny squeal and I did a happy dance, but Aaron—old man that he was—just grouched at us. "I'm going to row straight back to shore, then turn around and immediately come back here. You better be waiting *exactly on this spot* when I get back."

That was good enough for me. Perfect, even.

"Thank you," I told him.

We waited there, standing on the rocky shore, Fallon's mittened hand in my gloved one, until Aaron and his boat were hardly the size of a dime.

"So," Fallon said, turning to me. She had that look she got on her face when she was excited about something, really, truly. The look she got when she found a terrible mistake in a movie. "What are we doing? What's this great plan of yours?"

"We," I said, raising her hand and squeezing it just a little tighter in mine (this was the moment of truth), "are going to scream."

Okay, so I thought she was going to be confused. I expected that.

She looked very, *very* confused.

"Scream?" she said.

I nodded. "You said you were worried you couldn't. So"—I shrugged—"we're going to find out."

"Here?" she asked.

"Why not?" I swept my non-mitten-holding hand across the expanse of the lake. "There's no one around to hear us."

Fallon bit her lip. She was thinking, I could tell. "We're going to *scream*?" she repeated, thinking it over.

"As loud as we can."

Fallon stretched her neck out as though she was examining the lake. There were a few stray birds who either hadn't left for warmer temperatures yet or were never going, sitting on top of the cold water. There was Aaron, a quarter of the way to the shore. There was the wind, with a bit of a howl to it. Other than that, empty. Still. Quiet.

She cleared her throat. "You'll scream too?" she asked, examining the water.

"If you want me to."

"All right," she said.

I wasn't sure exactly how I thought it would go, with the screaming. I guess I hadn't thought things through too hard, after convincing everyone it was a good idea and getting to the island. If anything, I thought maybe Fallon would have a little trouble with the screaming at first. Maybe she'd start out quiet, like a whisper of a scream; maybe she wouldn't want to be truly loud at first. Maybe she'd have trouble with it, because it was something she'd been worried about for so long.

But I should've known that whatever I expected was going to be wrong. Fallon never failed to surprise me.

As big as the ocean. As steep as a roller coaster. As sharp as a cannon. As loud as a runaway train. As sweet as a swim in a deep, deep pool.

It was sudden, Fallon's scream. And it was loud, and it was long.

It was wonderful.

I joined in, as loud and as long and as wonderful as I could scream, too. We screamed, the two of us together, alone on that island. Because we could. Because no one could hear us. Because it was perfect, to be alone on an island, with your best friend, screaming at the top of your lungs. We held hands and hollered at the nearly frozen lake. And the screaming turned to laughter, and back into screaming, and I don't know how Fallon felt about it—that was a thing you could never know for sure—but as I watched her, she tilted her head far back on her neck so her whole body got in on the act, and I thought that maybe, just maybe, she was feeling brave.

I hoped so.

We screamed until our voices went hoarse, until our throats scratched and burned. And this probably wasn't true at all, but I could've sworn that some of the ice that had settled along the edges of the lake began to crack and break apart, just a little, with the screaming.

When we didn't have any screams left inside us, we collapsed back onto the cold, pebbly shore and sat there, not saying anything at all, just watching the lake lap icy waves near our toes. And we were still sitting there, not too long, in silence, when we heard a sharp *splash!* behind us, and the sound of boots on rocks. And we turned, both of us I'm sure expecting it to be Aaron, sneaking up on us around the side of the island where we wouldn't see. But it wasn't. It was an old man in a gray wool cap, with a thick beard. He had some sort of rubbery overalls on, and giant boots. Out fishing, probably.

"You kids okay?" he asked us. He was all a-huff. Out of breath. "I heard you screaming, from way out there." He pointed. "Never heard screaming like that in my life. You were *loud*."

And Fallon—she didn't even answer. She rolled over on her side, right in the pebbles, laughing. Sucking in air with the giggles like she couldn't get enough.

The fisherman looked at us like he thought we might be lunatics. "Is she okay?" he asked me.

It was Fallon who answered. Although I don't think her answer would've made much sense to anyone but me. "I can scream," she said, still laughing into the rocks. "I can scream."

"She's fine," I told the fisherman. "We both are."

TWENTY-FIVE

MONDAY MORNING, AARON AND I WERE sitting at the breakfast table, waiting. He was trying to get me to try his coffee, which he said was good, but I'd tried coffee before, and I already knew it tasted like boiled garbage.

"You want eggs or something?" Aaron said. He was bored, I could tell. He kept looking at his watch. "I could make you eggs."

It seemed to me that Aaron had changed a lot, the past year. Doug, he was always the same—even when you looked at photos of him when he was two, it was the same old goofy Doug, trying to make everybody laugh. But Aaron, he had gotten way bigger. Taller. I was pretty sure he was shaving at least three times a week already. He told me he'd teach me how, but I had nothing there to shave.

"Since when do you know how to make eggs?" I asked him.

"Dad taught me," he said. "It's easy. I make them for dinner sometimes when I visit on weekends." He took a gulp of his coffee and wiped his chin with his hand. Then suddenly he sat up straight in his chair. "That's him," he whispered. "You ready?"

"Yup," I said.

It had been my idea, after all.

As Doug came stumbling out of his room with his hair slabbed down on one side of his head, Aaron and I shot up from our seats and began frantically stuffing papers into our backpacks.

"Oh man, Doug!" Aaron called to the doorway. "Did you just get up?"

Doug rubbed his eyes. "Yeah," he said. "My alarm just went off."

"Wait, seriously?" I said. "We thought you'd been up for a while."

Doug yawned, still standing in the doorway. "Nah, I just got up." He scratched at the sliver of skin between his pajama bottoms and his sleep T-shirt. "So what time is it?"

Aaron, still busy flipping through his chemistry folder to make sure he'd brought his homework, waved over his shoulder at the clock on the wall. "It's *late,*" he said.

The clock on the wall read 7:48. The clock on the stove did, too. The one on the microwave said 7:50.

Doug's eyes went huge. "Mom's gonna be so mad!" he said.

"Mom already left for work," I told him. "You're gonna have to walk to school."

"No, wait," Aaron said. And I did my best not to smile, because this part had been my idea, too. "I can drive you. But only if you're ready in like"—he darted an eye at the clock on the stove—"one minute. I've already been late once this week, and Mr. Vallera's gonna kill me."

"Yeah, no problem," Doug said. And I was kind of surprised, actually, that he hadn't started to catch on to anything yet, because even though Doug was usually pretty easy to prank, this one had been going on a while. "Here, let me just . . ." And he raced down the hallway to his room and came back not three seconds later wearing a pair of jeans that had clearly been crumpled in a ball on his floor. He had on the same T-shirt he'd been sleeping in, and as he walked, he was trying to cram his bare feet into already-laced-up sneakers. "I'm ready!" he called, doing his best to hoist his backpack onto his shoulders.

Aaron and I shot each other a quick glance. We hadn't really figured that things would go this well. But we did what any seasoned pranksters would do in such a situation—we improvised.

"Can you drive me too?" I asked Aaron. No way was I missing any of this. "I'm right on the way."

Aaron pretended to think about it. "Okay," he said, and he tilted his head back to slam down the rest of his coffee. "Everyone get in the car."

We raced to Aaron's beat-up car in the driveway, and I thought Doug would catch on then—the pitch-black sky, the silent neighborhood, no Mr. Normore walking his wiener dog across the street, or the mailman in his tiny white truck.

But no. We piled into the car.

And I *swear* it wasn't until we'd pulled onto the boulevard and were halfway to Cedar Middle that Doug, his face still marked with pillowcase wrinkles, leaned forward from the backseat and poked his head between me and Aaron and said, "Aaron, your clock's wrong. It says four thirty-five."

And I kept it together, I totally did. But Aaron, he cracked. He let out one wicked *garumph!* of a snort. And, okay, then I lost it too.

"Wait . . . ," Doug said slowly, looking outside the window at the dark world around him as in the front seat Aaron and I dissolved into total bellyaching laughter. "Oh, man," he said, finally realizing. "Oh, *man*."

"It was Trent's idea," Aaron said, making a U-turn on the empty boulevard and heading back toward home.

Doug sat back in his seat. "It was pretty good," he admitted.

I smiled to myself as I stared out the window, watching us near our street in the black predawn. "Thanks," I said.

"No way I'm getting back to sleep," Aaron said. "I never should've downed that coffee. But I was so *committed to the moment*."

I laughed. The way Aaron was with pranks, you'd think he was going for an Oscar.

"It was good," Doug said again. And I could tell, without even looking at him, that the wheels in his brain were spinning.

"Uh oh," Aaron told me. "Looks like someone's planning his revenge. I'd be on the lookout, little brother."

I settled into my seat as the tip of our roof appeared around the corner. "Bring it on," I said.

That morning, when I walked into the gym for P.E. first period, I'd made up my mind. I passed Mr. Gorman, holding his clipboard in the doorway, and without him even asking, I told him, "You're going to like the kid you meet today." That's what I'd worked out I was going to say when Ray was helping me with my swing over the weekend. Then I went to the locker room with the other guys and dressed for P.E. That's what I'd worked out I was going to do, too. Ray said visualizing what you wanted to achieve was an important part of any sport.

I bet most athletes didn't have to visualize lacing up their sneakers without their arms getting all clammy, but anyway, it worked, so I guess I couldn't complain.

I even served twice in volleyball. (I'd only visualized that happening once, so it was a nice surprise.)

Noah looked a little lonely up there on the bleachers, but I figured he'd be okay. After all, he had a good book.

"You want to come over and watch a movie this afternoon?" Fallon asked me at lunch. She was flipping through my new drawings in my Book of Thoughts. I had lots from the lake, and not to brag, but they were pretty good. I was getting better. "It's been a while. Have you ever seen *Rikki-Tikki-Tavi*? It's *weird.*"

I was pretty stoked Fallon wanted to watch a movie with me again, but I guess I was surprised, too. "Don't you have play practice?" I asked her.

She shrugged. "I'm thinking of quitting. It turns out I kind of hate being a tree."

"You shouldn't be a tree," I told her. "Anyway, I do want to see another movie, but I probably can't do it till the weekend. Is that okay?"

She looked up from the notebook. "You got plans or something, Zimmerman?" she asked.

I knew I should speak truths, but I wasn't totally ready yet, so I decided not to say anything. "Maybe," I said. "I'm not totally sure." And that wasn't really a lie.

"Well, this weekend should be fine, anyway. My dad said next time you come over, you have to stay for dinner and he'll make you his famous Bolognese."

"It's a deal."

Fallon came to the last picture in the Book of Thoughts then, my favorite so far. It was a close-up of Fallon's face, the way she was when she didn't know anyone was looking at her. I thought I'd done a really good job on that one. Her frizzy hair. Her big brown eyes. The way her lip curled into her scar just the tiniest bit. She studied it a long time, and then she shut the book.

"Sometimes I get jealous of you, you know," she said. She stared at the cover of the Book of Thoughts when she said it.

"Of me?" Fallon must be crazy. "Why would you be jealous of *me*? Everyone in this town hates me."

Fallon rolled her eyes. "First of all, pretty much no one hates you," she said in that matter-of-fact way she had. "You might *wish* everyone hates you, but pretty much no one does. And secondly, yeah, I get jealous of you." She ran a finger over the wired spine of the Book of Thoughts. "When you leave this stupid town one day, you can be anyone you want. You can make up a new life for yourself, a new story, and everyone will believe you. But me . . ." Her voice got really quiet. "I'll always just be the girl with the scar."

I felt a ball of fire in my chest then, but it wasn't rage. It was something else.

"Fallon . . . ," I started, but she waved her hand at me. Pushed the book my way.

"Never mind," she told me. "Forget I said anything. I was just feeling sorry for myself. It's no big deal. Hey, actually, Mrs. Hillard said they're doing understudy auditions for the play in a few weeks. I could audition to be understudy for the head tree, what do you think? I'd have, like, two lines, even."

I looked at her then. Really looked at her. Scar and all. That slice that cut through her face. The end of the story that everyone always wondered about.

Except that the story wasn't nearly over yet.

"You don't have to be a tree," I told her.

When the bell rang after social studies, I walked right up to Ms. Emerson's stovetop.

"Yes?" she said, looking up slowly.

"I just wanted to let you know that I won't be able to water the plants for a while," I told her.

Ms. Emerson's mouth twitched, but I couldn't tell if it was forming into a frown or a smile.

"But it's not because I'm a screw-up," I said. "I have to . . . I'm going to try something else." I cleared my throat. "But I know the plants will still be thirsty, so I found someone to take my place. He should be here in a second."

The twitch turned into a definite smile.

"Well," Ms. Emerson said. Slowly. Thoughtfully. "That's just fine."

"It is?" I guess I was surprised it was that easy.

She nodded.

"Have a good afternoon," she told me.

I walked to the door.

"And Trent?" I should have known. I turned, my hand on the doorknob.

"Yeah?"

"The plants and I will be here if you need us."

I thought I'd have that walking-through-quicksand feeling, heading out to the field. But I didn't. Walking there was easier than I thought.

Opening my mouth, that was the hard part.

"Mr. Gorman?" I said.

He turned to look at me. He looked half surprised to see me, half not.

"Trent," he said. "What brings you here?"

I looked around at all the guys on the ball field, stomping their feet to keep out the cold. Jeremiah Jacobson. Stig Cooper. All sorts of kids. Right away my arms got clammy. My chest tightened so it was hard to swallow. Hard to breathe. But I did my best not to freak out. Instead, I practiced what Ray had taught me that weekend, when he was helping me with my swing. I focused my thoughts on what I wanted to have happen. I steadied my breathing, until it was back to normal.

It was hard, what Ray had taught me. But it wasn't impossible.

"I, um, I know it's probably too late," I told Mr. Gorman when I was feeling almost normal again. I focused on him, no one else. He wasn't so scary, really. "But I wanted to see if I could join intramural baseball for the rest of the season." I stuck my hands into my pockets. "If that's okay."

Mr. Gorman tapped his fingers on the back of his clipboard. At last he said, "Normally I'd tell you it's far too late," he replied. "But today must be your lucky day. We're down one man, since my nephew quit this morning. Something about watering plants."

I bit my lip.

"So it's fine with me," Mr. Gorman said, "if it's fine with the team. What do you say, gang? All in favor of letting Trent here join us?"

A couple of people didn't raise their hands. Jeremiah Jacobson and Stig Cooper, for two. But almost everyone did.

"Looks like you've got yourself a team," Mr. Gorman told me, and he handed me a bat.

I had to admit, it felt good in my hands.

It didn't happen the first time the ball cracked against the bat. Not the second time either. But at some point, during that practice, just as I connected with the ball and the vibrations of it surged all through my body, it occurred to me. It was obvious, really, but I guess it took a long time for me to figure it out.

My story wasn't over either.

Dad was shocked, for sure, when I showed up at the St. Albans Diner that evening after baseball with Doug and Aaron. Heck, *I* was shocked.

But I tried not to let it show on my face as I walked through the door. I nodded at him and Kari and even Jewel as I slid into the booth across from them. “Hey,” I said.

“Hey,” Dad said back. He paused while Aaron and Doug settled in beside me, and then he said, “It’s really good to see you, Trent.”

Maybe he meant it. Maybe he didn’t. But I decided that either way, it was time to give my dad more than one chance.

So I spoke the truth.

“It’s good to see you too,” I said.

TWENTY-SIX

THE SECOND DAY OF DECEMBER WAS MY FIRST Saturday back at Kitch'N'Thingz, now that Basketball Buddies was over. I told Annie I'd still help her with her dribbling, though, and she agreed to come over sometime soon, which was good, because she needed plenty of practice.

I was setting up a display of Santa Claus cookie jars when Fallon came into the store. My mom spotted her before I did, probably because I was on my knees surrounded by cookie jars.

"Hey, Fallon!" she greeted her. "What's going on?"

Fallon was flushed from the cold. Her scar was a little purpler than normal, so you could tell she was really chilly. But she was grinning all over.

"I had to come over to tell Trent—where's Trent?"

"Here!" I pulled myself out from the cookie jars. "I'm here. What's up?"

"Trent!" She came squealing over. I really thought she might break nine Santa noses off their faces the way she was barreling toward me, but she stopped just in time. "Mrs. Hillard called!"

"Who's Mrs. Hillard?" my mom asked.

"The director of the play," Fallon said, whipping around to tell her. I guess she didn't care that Mom was being super snoopy. "*The Wizard of Oz*."

"And?" I held my breath. I knew it was going to be good news, from the way Fallon was squealing, but I wanted to hear her say it anyway.

"They want me to understudy the Wicked Witch. Isn't that awesome?"

"Oh, you'll be so good!" my mom said. She was squealing now, too.

"'*I'll get you, my pretty!*'" Fallon cackled in her best Wicked Witch voice.

I laughed. "Congratulations," I told her. "That's what you wanted, right?"

She nodded at me, suddenly looking shy. "Yeah," she said. "Thanks for making me try out. I mean, I'll probably never get to actually *be* the Wicked Witch, but if Sarah gets sick, I get to wear green makeup all over my face, and these killer red nails, and . . ."

"You'll be awesome," I told her.

"'*And your little dog, too!*'" she cackled.

I let out another laugh. "Want to help me with cookie jars?" I asked her.

She stuck her hands into her coat pockets. "Actually, um . . ." She'd gone shy again.

"What's up?"

"Do you have your Book of Thoughts?" she asked.

"Sure. Want me to draw you as the Wicked Witch?"

"Something else," Fallon said. And the way she said it, it made me super curious. "Is it okay if I borrow Trent for a while?" she asked my mom.

"As long as you return him in one piece," Mom replied.

"Grab your coat," Fallon told me. And she raised her eyebrows at me, like she knew she was being mysterious.

We left the Santas in the middle of the floor.

"Where are we going?" I asked Fallon. She tugged me along through Main Street, past the shops, farther, faster, toward the edge of the lake. "Where are you taking me?"

She didn't answer until we reached the water. It was a spot usually only old people and kids came, where there were a couple of scattered benches and the water was shallow, so it was a good place to toss bread to the ducks. There was no one there today. The benches were covered with a thin layer of frost. All around us, nobody.

"Are we screaming again?" I asked her. Fallon nodded for me to sit on one of the benches, so I did. She sat beside me.

"Nah," she said. "I already know I can scream." She held out her hand, and I took it. I was beginning to grow very fond of that red-and-purple mitten. "Now I want to talk."

I looked up at her. She was staring straight ahead, at the lake, which was just beginning to freeze in larger patches. Icy. Windy. Cold.

She squeezed my gloved hand, and I squeezed back, my Book of Thoughts clutched tight against my other side. I looked out at the lake, too.

"It was seven years ago," she said softly. "When I got my scar. I was five years old." And maybe it was my imagination, but I couldn't help thinking that the wind around us stilled, that the ice spread itself out just a little bit more across the lake, that the clouds froze in place as she spoke.

As she told me the beginning of her story.

QUESTIONS FOR DISCUSSION

1. Why do you think Lisa Graff chose to write this book from Trent's point of view? How do you think this book would be different if it were written from Fallon's point of view? Or from the point of view of a narrator who knew what everyone was thinking all the time?

2. Throughout the novel, we see that Trent turns down opportunities to meet with friends and family. He's even reluctant to befriend Fallon. Why do you think that is? What lesson is revealed by the end of the novel?

3. Lisa Graff writes about fire throughout the novel. What feeling does fire represent in the story? Do you think it was an effective metaphor? Why or why not?

4. Trent went to intramurals with the intention to play on the team but quickly changed his mind after hearing the crack of a bat. Why do you think the author included this event in the novel? How does it give readers a better understanding of Trent's character?

5. There was a pivotal moment in the book that changed the course of the story and enabled Trent's character to grow. What event do you think was the turning point toward positive change for Trent?

6. Why do you think the author chose to end the novel before Fallon reveals the story about her scar?

7. How does Lisa Graff enforce the theme of friendship in the novel?

8. What do Fallon and Trent have in common?

9. Toward the end of the novel, Trent overcomes his anger. What technique does he use to suppress his anger?

Turn the page for a sample of
Lisa Graff's magical novel

A Clatter of Jars

Companion to the NATONAL BOOK AWARD nominee

A Tangle of Knots

1

Lily

LILY STOOD OUTSIDE THE DOOR TO THE INFIRMARY, winding the length of swampy green yarn around her right thumb. In every corner of the woods, campers were squealing, laughing, making friends, and generally kicking up a lot of dust. But Lily was focused on that length of yarn.

"Liliana Vera?"

In front of Lily stood a lanky counselor wearing a pine green Camp Atropos T-shirt, the name *Del* printed below the neckline.

"Are you Liliana?" Del asked. "I'm gathering Cabin Eight campers."

Lily glanced past Del to the flag circle, where four campers stood amid their luggage. "I'm Lily," she said.

"Great!" Del jerked his chin toward her duffel bag. "Need help with that?"

Lily shook her head, her wavy brown hair grazing her shoulders. "I got it," she said. Del looked skeptical, probably because Lily was hardly taller than the duffel was long. But Lily focused her thoughts at the bridge of her nose and, darting her eyes to the duffel, the bag rose—one inch, then five—off the ground. Lily took a step forward in the dirt, and the bag took a step with her.

"No need to ask what *your* Talent is," Del said, watching the bag drift forward. "Been a while since we had a Pinnacle here." Lily swelled with the smallest inkling of pride. "Welcome to Camp Atropos for Singular Talents, Liliana Vera. A haven for the most remarkable children in the world." As they neared the flag circle, Del pointed to each of the four campers, rattling off names. "Miles, Renny, Chuck, and Ellie." Lily did a double take when Del named the last two. Chuck and Ellie were identical twin girls. "Your bunkmates for the next two weeks. Let's get you all to Cabin Eight, shall we?"

"Hi!" Ellie greeted Lily as they began their trek through the woods. Lily could tell the twins apart because, despite having identical faces and identical dark brown skin, Ellie had a headful of teeny braids pulled into a ponytail and was wearing pale blue sneakers, while Chuck's hair was styled into wavy cornrows, and she wore Kelly-green high-tops. "Do you like frogs?" Ellie asked. "Chuck and I can identify any species."

"Uh," Lily replied. "Cool."

That's when one of the boys, Miles, piped up. "Singular Talents are understood as feats beyond standard human abilities and/or the laws of physics," he said. His voice was flat, his gaze fixed on the dirt in front of him as he walked.

"Huh?" Ellie asked.

"I think what he means," said the other boy, Renny, "is that identifying frogs isn't a Singular Talent. Either that or he just likes showing off how much of that textbook he memorized."

Beside her sister, Chuck snorted. "Oh, man," she said. "They're on to us now, Ellie. I guess we'll have to leave and go to regular person camp."

Ellie poked her twin in the side. "Chuck, *please*," she said.

They were deep in the shadows of the trees when Renny joined step beside Lily. He was tall and skinny, with pasty white legs. "Is this your brother?" Renny asked, his nose buried in a small photo book. He flipped a page. "Cute kid."

"Hey!" Lily cried, realizing what Renny was holding. "Give me that!" Focusing her thoughts at the bridge of her nose, she tugged the photo book toward her through the air. With her concentration no longer upon it, her duffel thunked to the dirt. The front pocket had been zipped open.

Lily inspected the album for damage, wiping away a smudge from the photo of Max's fifth birthday party three years earlier. It was one of Lily's favorites. Her little brother was balancing a plate of chocolate cake on his pinkie, his other arm wrapped around Lily. Lily, meanwhile, was using her own Talent to push the cake toward Max's nose. It was the last birthday she and Max had celebrated before their mother remarried and their stepsister, Hannah, buzzed into their lives like a housefly. Hannah had to go and be born the same day as Max—same year and everything—so in every birthday photo after that, it was Hannah that Max had his arm around.

At least Hannah had been assigned to a different cabin for the two weeks of camp, Lily reminded herself, zipping the photo book back in its pocket. She hoisted the duffel to her shoulder, which immediately ached in protest.

"You should keep a better eye on your stuff," Renny said. And when Lily scowled, he didn't even have the decency to look sorry. Instead, he stretched out his arm, like he wanted to shake hands. "Renwick Fennelbridge," he told her. "You might have heard of me."

Despite herself, Lily was impressed. She'd studied the Fennelbridges last year in her Singular Education elective, and she found them fascinating. Every family member was Singular, with some of the most fantastical Talents ever recorded.

"Can you really read minds?" she asked.

That's when the other boy, Miles, piped up again. "Renwick Chester Ulysses Fennelbridge," he said, his eyes still fixed on the dirt. "Eleven years old as of his last birthday. The only living

Scanner, according to A *Singular History.* Fun fact: Renwick Fennelbridge was once flown to Rome, Italy, to read the mind of the pope, but got food poisoning on the plane and had to go home."

"*Please* find a new fun fact, Miles," Renny grumbled.

"You really know your Talent history, huh?" Lily said to Miles. Singular Education had been Lily's favorite class last year. Her teacher had been so impressed with her report on Ekers and Coaxes that she'd had Lily read it during the opening ceremony of the Talent festival. "Do you know about Evrim Boz?"

Miles responded without hesitation. "Evrim Biber Boz. Born 1576, died 1602. Talent: Coax. Able to wheedle Talents from one person to another and back again, even transferring Talents into inanimate objects to create Artifacts. Fun fact: The Talent Library in Munich, Germany, has eight of Evrim Boz's Artifacts on display, including a cooking pot that makes anything boiled inside taste like lentil stew."

"Did you know that later in her life, Evrim Boz said she wished she'd never created any Artifacts at all?" Lily asked, scurrying to keep up with him. Unlike Ekers, who could only steal Talents, Coaxes could pass Talents on—either to other people or to objects. "Because once you make an Artifact, you can't get the Talent back out. Evrim Boz tried once, with a pair of scissors that she'd Coaxed a beard-trimming Talent into, and instead she accidentally replaced the beard-trimming with her brother's

Talent for cartography." Lily had always had a particular interest in Artifacts and the people who used them. "Evrim Boz's brother never spoke to her after that."

Miles didn't even glance at Lily before continuing his recitation. "Maevis Marion Marvallous. Sixty-seven years old as of her last birthday. Talent: Mimic. Able to duplicate the Talent of any person she comes in contact with for approximately one year."

"Now you've set him off," Renny muttered. "When Miles gets started on Talent history, good luck getting him to stop."

"Fun fact," Miles went on. "Maevis Marvallous alleges that she lost her Talent over three decades ago, although scholars debate the claim."

Suddenly Lily noticed that Miles and Renny had the same sharp nose. Same auburn hair. Same pasty knees. Miles was a bit broader, but they were brothers, no question.

"I didn't know there were two Fennelbridge kids," Lily said. She was sure *A Singular History* had mentioned only one. "What's his Talent?"

Renny halted midstride to tug at the top of his right sock. "Make enough Fennelbridges, and one of them's bound to be Fair." He let out a sour laugh. "That's what our dad likes to say."

"If you ask me," Chuck chimed in, "there are two Fair kids in the Fennelbridge family."

"What do you mean by that?" Renny snapped.

"You obviously stink at reading minds," Chuck informed him.

"I've been mentally threatening to pop you in the jaw for the past ten minutes, and you haven't flinched once."

Lily couldn't help it. She laughed.

Oblivious to the awkwardness behind him, Del pointed to a sturdy building hewn from logs. "There's the lodge," he called back. "Meals are served on the mess deck. All-camp slumber party's the second Friday of camp, and the Talent show's that Sunday, before your parents take you home."

At the mention of the Talent show, Lily's heart snagged her chest. Maybe there was still time to come up with a new act to perform with Max.

A lot could happen in two weeks.

"The lodge also houses the office of our camp director, Jo," Del continued. "She plays a mean harmonica."

Miles broke from his Talent history just long enough to tell the dirt, "I play a nice harmonica. I learned last year in music. Cassandra Colby Donovan. Born 1851, died 1900. Talent: Quest. Fun fact: Cassandra Donovan was the Needle-in-a-Haystack champion of Baxley, Georgia, for forty years running, until they retired the competition."

"Up ahead is the archery ring," Del went on. "There's the fire pit, where we hold our campfire each Friday. And if you squint, you can make out the lake through the trees."

At that, Miles stopped walking. "No water!" he squeaked.

Del offered Miles a friendly smile. "What's wrong with a

little"—he spit into one hand and pressed his palms together before sprinkling miniature icicles in the dirt—"*water*?" He took in Miles's alarmed expression. "Not a fan of a classic Numbing Talent, huh?" Del cleared his throat. The ice-spit at his feet was already melting in the sun. "Uh . . . canoes are available every day after breakfast, and if you feel like swimming, Jo encourages you to grab your towel any time of day and hop right in the water."

"*No water!*"

Miles shrieked it that time. And he began flicking his fingers, too—*flick-flick-flick-flick-flick*!

Quick as lightning, Renny grabbed his brother's hand. "You guys sell Caramel Crème bars at the camp store, right?" Renny asked Del. Miles's fingers slowly ceased their flicking. "Miles loves Caramel Crème bars."

"I want a Caramel Crème bar," Miles said, pulling his hand free. If Lily hadn't witnessed the scene herself, she'd never have believed that Miles had been in a near panic thirty seconds earlier.

"Uh . . ." Del scratched a spot below his ear. "What was the question again?"

"Caramel Crème bars," Renny reminded him.

"Oh. Right."

As Del went over the store's hours, Lily wound the length of yarn around her thumb, watching Renny with his brother. Lily had tied the yarn around her thumb three weeks ago. Since then, the lime green strands had turned swampy, thinning and separating, and the skin underneath had grown raw from constant rubbing. It had stung for some time, like a blister—insistent, sharp, painful. But Lily hadn't untied it.

She tugged her duffel farther up her aching shoulder, her attention stolen by the music drifting through one of the lodge's windows. It was a song Lily was quite familiar with. This was an instrumental version, without lyrics, but Lily knew the words by heart.

> *Los golpes en la vida*
> *preparan nuestros corazones*
> *como el fuego forja al acero.*

Lily and Max's father had sung them the melancholy lullaby countless times, on nights when he wasn't traveling for work. When he sang the tune, the notes swept you up and cradled you, made you feel safe.

("Why do you always have to travel?" Lily had asked him last year, when he'd been in Prague instead of her school auditorium for the opening ceremony of the Talent festival. He'd responded as he always did. Not that it was his job—not that he *had* to be away so often, that he had no choice—but rather: "Oh, Liria. Traveling helps ease my heartache." Which didn't explain why her father had begun his travels long before he and Lily's mother had been married.)

Lily let the words of the song sink in. Her father had translated the lyrics for her once, but she never felt she truly understood them in any language.

The blows of life
prepare our hearts
like fire forges iron.

Summer camp, Lily thought, pulling herself from the music to rejoin the tour, didn't seem like a place for melancholy songs.

When they reached Cabin Eight, Del creaked open the door and let them inside.

"Cordelia Fabius Sibson," Miles said as he entered the cabin. "Eighty-two years old as of her last birthday. Talent: Scribe."

Lily wound the length of yarn around her right thumb, staring at the three bunks that lined the cabin walls.

Three bunks.

Six beds.

"Are we waiting for another camper?" Chuck asked Del. "There are six beds, and only five of us."

"The assignments for this cabin were a little odd," Del admitted. "I don't know what Jo was thinking, but you don't question Jo. Anyway, you were supposed to have one more cabinmate, but at the last minute, he—"

Lily dropped her duffel with a heavy *thunk*. "I need to go to the infirmary," she said.

"You okay?" Del asked, stitching his eyebrows together.

"I have to go," Lily repeated. And she squeezed past him out the door, racing down the path. Kicking up dirt.

It should have been Max in that sixth bed. It should have been their summer together, while Hannah the housefly was far off in a different cabin, buzzing at someone else. But they weren't together, because three weeks ago, Max had gotten hurt.

Around and around went the length of yarn.

Lily was the one who'd hurt him.

Albie has always been an almost.
He's almost good at tetherball.
He's almost smart enough
to pass his spelling test.
He almost makes his parents proud.

And now that Albie is starting a brand-new school for fifth grade, he's never felt more certain that almost simply isn't good enough. With everyone around him expecting him to be one thing or another, how is an almost like Albie ever supposed to figure out who he really wants to be?

How far would you go to get something you really wanted?
Would you lick a lizard?
Wear a tutu to school?
Dye your hair green?

New kid Kansas Bloom (self-proclaimed King of Dares) and Media Club maven Francine Halata face off in a crazy Dare War to determine the future news anchor for the fourth-grade media club (a gig Francine has been dying to get forever). In a battle of wits and willpower, Francine and Kansas become fast enemies . . . until they discover that they have something surprising in common. And somehow, that one little fact changes everything.

Bernetta's summer couldn't be going any worse.

First her ex-best friend frames her for starting a cheating ring in their private school that causes Bernetta to lose her scholarship for seventh grade. Even worse, Bernetta's parents don't believe she's innocent and forbid her from performing at her father's magic club. Now Bernetta must take immediate action if she hopes to raise $9,000 for tuition. But that's a near impossible task with only three months until school. Enter Gabe, a boy con artist who's willing to team up with Bernetta to raise the money. But only if she's willing to use her talent for magic to scheme her way to success.